SUNKEN WORLD

By
STANTON A. COBLENTZ

ARMCHAIR FICTION
PO Box 4369, Medford, Oregon   97501-0168

*For more information about Armchair Books and products, visit our
website at…*

www.armchairfiction.com

Or email us at…

armchairfiction@yahoo.com

WELCOME TO THE CITY OF ATLANTIS...

It was the launching of a new, futuristic submarine, the mighty X-111. But the country was shocked when its Captain and crew were reported lost at sea shortly after launch. It was an abrupt ending to a maiden voyage that had started so promisingly.

However, it was only the beginning, the beginning of an underwater adventure never before heard of or imagined by the land-dwelling peoples of Earth. Keep company with the men and women of a truly remarkable underwater city, whose existence in our history has only been noted as rumor—or myth.

This is Stanton A. Coblentz's epic tale of Atlantis…the lost continent of old, described as no other author before him…

CAST OF CHARACTERS

ANSON HARKNESS
Mourned as dead, this soul survivor of the ill-fated X-111 returned one day to tell a tale of unbelievable adventure!

CAPTAIN GAVISON
His unsinkable ship was…sinking… Now he was a stranger in a strange land in charge of a very nervous crew.

PHIL RAWSON
He had no qualms about entering the gates of an unknown city. But he hadn't given much thought about how to get out.

JIM STRANAHAN
He was quite excitable and definitely superstitious, but this common seaman would always obey his Captain's orders.

AELIOS
She was a staunch believer in the Submergence, aka "The Good Destruction." What would it take to change her mind?

XANOCLES
Member of the unpopular Emergence Party. His goal: convince his fellow Atlanteans that going topside was a good idea.

PELIADES
His wisdom was ridiculed, referred to as nonsense. He was ignored as a doomsayer…but was he right?

CONTENTS

INTRODUCTION

It was in the summer of 1942 that the United States submarine X-111 was commissioned as a reply to the German commerce raiders that were threatening our lease-lend shipments to England. The first of a fleet of unique undersea craft, this vessel was constructed upon lines never before attempted. Not only was it exceedingly long (being about three hundred feet from stem to stern), but it was excessively narrow, and a man had to be short indeed to stand upright on its single deck without touching the arched ceiling. The ship, in fact, was nothing more nor less than a long pipe of reinforced steel, able to cleave the water at tremendous speed and ram and destroy any enemy with its beak-like prow.

But this was only its slightest point of novelty. At both ends and at several points along the sides it was equipped with water-piercing searchlights of a power never known before; and it was provided with a series of airtight and waterproof compartments; any one of which might be pierced without disabling the vessel. Hence the X-111 was generally known as unsinkable

The sinking of this "unsinkable" ship is now, of course, a matter of history. Observers of naval events will recall how, in August, 1942, newspapers reported the disappearance of a United States submarine. All that was known was that the craft had been ordered to the danger zone; that it had not returned to its base; and that two months had passed before the only clue as to its fate was found. Then a British destroyer, on scout duty in the North Sea, picked up a drifting life preserver bearing the imprint "X-111." For strategic reasons this fact was not divulged; and, for strategic reasons, it was not made known that the missing submarine was of a new and previously untried type. But the mystery of the X-111's disappearance weighed upon the minds of naval officials, and secretly they resolved upon exhaustive investigations. All in vain! Not a trace could be found of the lost ship, or of the thirty-nine members of its crew!

Five years went by. Amid the preoccupation of the global war and its sequel, the X-111 had been all but forgotten. Then suddenly the mystery was fanned to life again. A bearded man, with a strange greenish complexion and eyes that blinked oddly beneath wide, colored glasses, appeared at the offices of the naval department at Washington, and claimed to be one of the company of the X-111. At first he was taken for a madman; but he was so persistent, and so anxious to prove his identity, that at length a half-hearted investigation was undertaken. The results were such as to leave the world gaping in amazement! The testimony of a dozen witnesses, as well as the evidence of fingerprints and handwriting, proved that the wild-looking stranger was none other than Anson Harkness, mourned as dead as Ensign on the ill-starred X-111. Now for the first time the truth as to the vessel's disappearance was known; and the public was treated to a story so extraordinary that only the most irrefutable evidence could make it seem credible.

But while numerous accounts of the discovery are extant and the furor of discussion shows no sign of waning, the public has yet to read the tale in Harkness' own words. For this reason, the accompanying history possesses a peculiar and timely interest. The author has unaffectedly described the most perilous exploits which any man has ever survived; hence his pages should prove of interest, not only to the student of world events, but to that larger public which values a rare and stirring bit of autobiography.

S. A. C., 1948

HARKNESS EXPLAINS HIS DISAPPEARANCE

THE MAIDEN VOYAGE OF THE *X-111* was ill omened from the first. Perhaps the new inventions had not yet been perfected, or perhaps, in the haste of the emergency, adequate tests had not been made, for the vessel developed mechanical trouble after her first half-day at sea. To begin with, the rudder and steering apparatus proved unmanageable; then, after hours spent in making repairs, the overworked engines showed a tendency to baulk; and finally, when we had about solved the engine problem, we had the misfortune to collide with a half-submerged derelict, and one of our water-tight compartments sprang a leak.

Immediately following the accident, we had risen to the surface, for the break was about on a level with our waterline, and the compartment could not be completely flooded so long as we did not submerge. Yet Captain Gavison warned us not to waste time, and the men worked with desperate speed to repair the damage, for we knew that we were in the zone of relentless U-boat warfare, where any delay might prove fatal. Unfortunately, the sea was unusually calm, and the day blue and clear, so that even our low-lying hulk could be sighted miles across the waters.

I do not know at what precise position we were then stationed but it was at some point in the Eastern Atlantic, where, according to the warnings of our Secret Service, the German submarines were on the prowl for American vessels. At any other time, we would have leapt at the opportunity to strike; but in our disabled condition, we kept a lookout with black misgivings, and silently prayed to be able to repair the damage before the enemy slank into view. Yet it was slow work to man the pumps and at the same time to solder a strip of metal across the jagged gap in our side; and hours passed while we stood there working thigh-deep in water, our heads bent low, only two or three feet beneath the iron ceiling, and suppressed growls and curses coming from our lips each time a surge of the waters quenched the soldering flame. Meanwhile, all was in confusion; the men working with the inefficiency of terror, the chief contents of the compartment floating about almost

8

unnoticed. I distinctly remember that several articles, including a life preserver that one of the recruits had unfastened in his fright, were washed overboard.

Still, we did make some progress, and after four or five hours, just as the blood-red sun was setting, our task was approaching completion. A few minutes more, and the soldering would be accomplished; a few minutes more, and darkness would be upon us, and for eight or ten hours we need not fear attack.

It was just when we felt surest of deliverance that the real danger flared into view. A trail of white shot across the waters to westward, and, advancing at tremendous speed, vanished in a long frothy furrow just in our wake. "U-boat! U-boat two points—off port bow!" frantically cried the watch; and we scrambled from the flooded compartment as the Captain ordered, "Submerge!" Now we heard the rapid churning of our engines as we went plunging into the blackness beneath the sea; now we made ready to launch a torpedo of our own as our periscope showed us the disappearing tip of an enemy submarine; now we were hurled into an exciting chase as our prodigiously powerful searchlights illuminated whole leagues of the ocean, even revealing the dark, cigar-shaped hulk of the foe. Had we not been impeded by the dead weight of a compartment full of water, we would have overtaken and rammed the enemy; even as it was, we seemed to be gaining upon it, and had hopes of shooting up bullet-like, and with tremendous impact smiting it in two. Not even the unexpected appearance of a second submarine altered our plans!

But at this point mechanical troubles again betrayed us. Overworked by our excessive speed, our engines gave signs of sputtering out; so dangerously overheated had they become that we had to halt, almost within striking distance of the foe. Our position now was precarious; at any moment the German searchlights might spy us out and a few depth charges might send us to the bottom.

Compelled to seek the surface in order to attack, we but increased the peril; both enemy vessels were now in a position to answer us blow for blow. But trusting to the gathering darkness and our aggressive tactics, we unhesitatingly rose to the level, and, with as little delay as possible, discharged a torpedo towards the dim, low-lying form of the foe.

Whether the missile reached its goal none of us will ever be able to say. Judging by the furious eruption of spray in the enemy's direction, I am inclined to believe that this was among the U-boats later reported missing; but, again, the projectile may merely have struck some floating object. Unhappily, none of us were in a position to observe, for at the same moment a gleaming streak shot towards us across the dark waters, and we went sprawling about the deck as a fierce thudding crash came to our ears and the vessel shook as though in an earthquake's grip.

Half-dazed, we gathered ourselves together and rose uncertainly to our feet, staring at one another in blank consternation. And at the same moment, one of the seamen burst into the cabin, despair and terror in his eyes. "Central compartment!" he cried. "Fix central compartment! It's flood—flooded!"

As if in proof of his words, we felt ourselves sinking, slowly sinking though no one had ordered us submerge; and the darkness of the twilight skies gave way to the darkness beneath the ocean.

It was minutes before we quite realized what was happening. Accustomed as we were to undersea travel, we did not at first understand that this adventure was quite out of the ordinary. Even when the waters had lost their first pale translucency and had become utterly black, we did not grasp how terrible was our predicament; and only after our vessel was listing violently, the deck sloping at an angle of forty-five degrees, did we recognize the horror of our position. Although we could not see one inch beyond the thick glass portholes, I had an indefinable sense that we were sinking through vague and unknown abysses; and the stark helpless terror on the assembled faces showed that the others shared my feelings. Not a word did we speak, and, indeed, speaking would not have been easy, for a low, continuous roaring was in our ears, a hoarse, muffled roaring reminding me of the murmuring in a seashell. At the same time, a strange depression overwhelmed my senses, as though the atmosphere had suddenly become thick and heavy, too heavy for breathing; or as though an unnatural weight had been piled upon me. Yet I did notice that the vessel would quiver violently and lunge upwards every few seconds, as if struggling to right itself. I did fancy that at times I heard the intermittent buzzing of the engines; and I found myself, like all the others, hanging to the brass rails to steady myself when the ship heaved and shuddered, or merely to remain on my feet when we again slanted downwards.

After perhaps five minutes, the forward door was thrust open, and Captain Gavison climbed precariously into the cabin. All eyes bent upon him in silent inquiry; but his grim, stoically firm countenance was not reassuring.

Apparently he had something to say, and did not care to say it; several anxious minutes passed while he stood glowering upon us, undecided whether to speak.

Yet even at this crisis he could not forget discipline. His first words brought us no information; his first action was to station us about the room, assigning each to some specific duty.

"I will not keep the facts from you," he declared, with slow deliberate accentuation, when we were all in position. "Three compartments are flooded. The others seem to be holding, but the mass of water in our hold is plunging us downwards, and the engines are unable to neutralize the effect. At the last reading, we were nine hundred and twenty-seven feet below."

"Great God, sir!" gasped one of the seamen, his eyes bulging. "What can we do about it?"

"Suggestions are in order," stated the Captain, laconically.

But no suggestion was forthcoming.

"Of course, we are in no immediate danger…" he resumed. But he might have spared his words. We all knew that the danger was real enough!

Although we could no longer guide our course, our searchlights were brought into play, piercing the water with brilliant yellow streamers. Yet they were as searchlights in a tomb; they showed us nothing except the minute wavy dark shapes that occasionally drifted in and out of our line of vision. There was something ghastly, I thought, about that light, that intense unearthly light which glided in long curves and spirals about the darkness; its very penetrating power served only to accentuate the horror. For the illumination ended in nothingness; nothingness seemed to stretch above us, beneath us, and to all sides of us; we were enveloped in it as in a black mantle; it seemed to reach out long arms to fetter us, to enfold us, to strangle us.

11

Slowly the moments moved by. Slowly we continued sinking, down, down, down, ever down and down, while our instruments recorded first twelve hundred feet, then fourteen hundred, then sixteen hundred, then eighteen hundred below sea level.

As we descended, we were aware that we were not the only living creatures in those depths. Our searchlights were the center of attraction for myriads of scaly things; whole squadrons of fishes were gathering moth-like in the vivid illumination. Some were long snaky monsters, with thin heads set with rows of spike-like teeth; some were lithe sea-dragons, with wolfish mouths and sabre-like bony appendages projecting from low foreheads; some were multi-colored, rainbow-hued or streaked with black and scarlet; some had chameleon eyes that flashed first green and then blue according to the play of the light...

But, as our depth increased, our finny visitors began to desert us—or, rather, gave way to others stranger still. When we were twenty-two hundred feet below, our searchlights were no longer necessary to reveal the denizens of the deep; the inhabitants of those unthinkable regions carried their own lamps. Suddenly, out of the deathly blackness, a spurt of green light would appear, widening until it seemed an unearthly searchlight; and from a narrow focus of flame two huge burning emerald eyes would shoot forth, darting cold malice at us through the glass partition. Or a tiny flattened disc, softly phosphorescent and marked at one end by two bright beady eyes, would come floating in our direction, like a pale apparition. Or we would be surprised by nameless monsters with invisible bodies and lidless fiery eyes of the size of baseballs— eyes that stared, and stared, as though all the concentrated horror of the universe were glaring upon us.

And still we were sinking, till the last hope had died in the heart of the most sanguine. When we were twenty-five hundred feet below, the fury of expectation had given place to numb despondency; when the distance was twenty-eight hundred feet, each was striving in his own way to prepare himself for the fate that all felt to be but a question of hours. In our terror, we had, long ago forgotten the positions assigned us by the Captain; and the Captain himself did not appear to notice the displacement. Young Rawson, the newest of the recruits, had gone down on his knees, and with tears in his eyes was murmuring half-audible prayers. Matt Stangale, one of the most weather-beaten of the seamen, was pacing back and forth, listlessly back and forth in the narrow compartment. Dan Howlett, a veteran of many campaigns, contented himself with a suppressed growling profanity. Frank Rippley, a one-time college gridiron hero, buried himself in a corner, his face covered by his hands, though every once in a while, wistfully and half-furtively, he would let his gaze travel to a little photograph he guarded close to his bosom. And as for Captain Gavison—he merely stood near the porthole with arms clenched behind his back and thin lips tightly compressed, peering out into the dark waters as though he read there some secret hidden from his followers.

We were below the three thousand-foot level when fresh cause for anxiety appeared.

"The holy saints have mercy on us!" exclaimed Jim Stranahan, one of the common seamen, as he crossed himself piously and pointed through one of the glass spy-holes. "Look at that!"

Excitedly we crowded about him, almost tumbling over one another in our eagerness. But for a moment we could see nothing. Then, as we stood straining our eyes to fathom the blackness, we gradually became aware of a vague filmy sheet of light beneath us, widespread and twinkling faintly, like an inverted Milky Way.

A sheet of light beneath us, at the bottom of the sea! Incredulously we turned to one another, our horror all too plain in our bulging eyes. And in silence, and with fear-blanched faces, half of the company made the sign of the cross.

"Sure it's a ghost, a deep-sea ghost," ventured the superstitious Stranahan.

"It's where the sea serpents live," put in Stangale, with an abortive attempt to be jocular. "There's ten million of them down there, with devil's eyes of fire!"

"Maybe it's the Evil One himself," suggested Stranahan, not content with a single guess. "Yes, by glory! The very throne room of Hell, and them are the flames of Old Nick…"

These words did not seem to reassure the rest of the crew. Several continued to cross themselves in silence.

Meanwhile, the Captain had ordered the searchlights turned downwards. In long loops and curves, the cutting light swept the darkness.

But nothing was visible except a few flapping, fishy forms; our lanterns served only to conceal the mysterious luminance.

Yet when our searchlights were again flashed off, that luminance was somewhat more distinct than before, and seemed to stretch to infinite distances on all sides. But it was still incalculably remote.

Now, as we drifted downwards, I began to doubt whether any of us would live to solve the mystery. The air in our overcrowded compartments was becoming nauseatingly heavy; we were like men in a sealed vault. Already I was drowsy from lack of oxygen; my head ached, and I had almost ceased to care what happened. Today, when I look back on those terrible hours, I feel sure that I was not far from delirium; and when I remember how some of my comrades lay drunkenly on the floor, with half-hysterical mumblings and wailings, I am certain that few of us remained quite in our right minds.

There is indeed a blank space in my memory as to what occurred at about this time. For all I know, I may have fallen off into a doze or sodden slumber lasting for minutes or even hours. All that I can recall is that I came abruptly to myself, as from a state of coma; with a sudden jolt of understanding, I realized where I was, and observed half a dozen of my comrades gathered together in a group, pointing downwards with excited exclamations.

Staggering to my feet, I joined them—and, in a moment, shared in their agitation. The lights beneath us were now far brighter; they no longer formed a vague shimmering sheen, but were focused brilliantly in a score of golden globes, each of the apparent size of the sun. Could it be that the ocean, too, has suns? I asked myself, as when one asks dazed questions in a dream. And looking at those spectral lights that wavered and gleamed through the pale waters, I felt that this was but a nightmare from which I should awaken...

Then, as I stared transfixed, it became apparent that the great central globes were not the only source of the radiance. Smaller points of light gradually became visible, some of them moving, actually moving as though borne by living hands—and even the spaces between the lights wore an increasing, golden luster. Yet with the golden was mingled a tinge of green, a green that seemed scarcely of the waters and the mysterious depths were no longer black but olive-hued, as though the light came to us through some solid, dark-green medium.

But a more imminent peril distracted our attention. For some minutes I had been vaguely aware of something peculiar about our compartment, yet in my stupefied condition I had not known just what was wrong. But realization came to me when Stranahan, pointing upwards, wide-eyed with horror, exclaimed, "Heaven preserve us, look at the ceiling!"

We all looked—and noticed that the ceiling was bulging inches downwards, as though the terrific pressure of the waters were bursting the tough steel envelope of the *X-111*. At the same time, the deck was bulging upwards, and the bulkheads were being twisted and distorted like rails warped by an earthquake.

But now came the greatest surprise of all. "By all the saints and little devils!" burst forth the irrepressible Stranahan, pointing downwards and forgetting the state of the bulkheads and deck. "There's a city under the sea!"

"City under the sea!" we echoed. And from one corner of the room there rose a burst of laughter, which wavered and broke and then died out, uncannily like a fiend's derision.

"But I tell you, there *is* a city under the sea!" insisted Stranahan, noting our incredulous stares. "The Lord strike me dead if I didn't see its streets and houses."

Though none of us had a doubt that the Lord would indeed do as Stranahan suggested, we interpreted his remarks as mere delirious ravings:

"See, there she is!" persisted the seaman, still pointing downwards in defiance of our disbelief. And, crossing himself, he continued, in awed tones, "May the Virgin have pity on us if that don't look like a church…"

These words had such a tone of conviction that, though our doubts were still strong, we could not help looking. But after one glance, our skepticism vanished. For was this not, indeed, a city staring up at us from the green-golden depths? In outlines wavy because of the dense waters, and yet as definite of form as reflections in a still pool, half a dozen great yellow-white temples seemed to glimmer beneath the brilliant lights, with massive columns, wide-reaching porticoes and colonnades, and gracefully curving arches and domes.

Was this but a mirage? Or were these the remnants of some submerged, ancient town? But, if so, why these vivid lights?

Even as we wondered, we detected a gradual change in our movement. We were no longer sinking; we were drifting with a slow motion horizontally, or almost horizontally; and just beneath us there appeared to be an impenetrable, but transparent dense greenish wall, a wall that had the idea not been too preposterous we might have imagined to be of glass. Beneath this wall gleamed no lantern-bearing, fishy eyes, but the dazzling golden orbs and the smaller scattered lights burnt steadily with piercing radiance; and below us, at a distance of five hundred or a thousand feet, the vaults and domes and columns of innumerable stone edifices shone with a pale yellow luster...

Gradually, for some reason that we could not explain, our horizontal motion was increasing; as if caught by some rapid deep-sea current, we drifted above those dim realms of green and gold. Palace after magnificent palace, seemingly modeled by architects of old Greece, went gliding past beneath us; countless statues, tall as the buildings, pointed up at us with hands that were uncannily lifelike; avenue after avenue flashed by, and one or two colossal amphitheaters of Grecian design. But no living thing was to be seen, or at least, we thought that no living thing was to be seen, for though we strained our eyes, we could only discern shadows moving in those uncertain depths, only shadows and an occasional zigzagging fire-fly light.

Then suddenly fresh terror seized us. Our motion, after increasing slowly for many minutes, was accelerated as though by some gigantic prod. We seemed caught in some mighty movement of the waters, some maelstrom that whirled and buffeted us like a feather; a hoarse, continuous thunder dinned in our ears, and we went shooting forward with prodigious speed. Then came a violent jerk, and we found ourselves tossed to all corners of the room; then another jerk, and we were flung back again like dice shaken in a box; then still another jerk, more vehement yet, and our terrorized minds lost track of events as our vessel lunged and heaved, veered and stood almost on end, and began to spin round and round, round and round, like a gyrating top. And in that whirling confusion our senses reeled, and darkness came clouding back, darkness and sleep and nothingness.

UNTRAVELED DEPTHS

HOW ANY OF US SURVIVED IS more than I can say. In the turbulence and vertigo of that last blind roaring moment, I had vaguely felt that we had reached the end of all things. Hence it was with surprise that I found myself hazily regaining consciousness, and discovered that I could still move my limbs and open my eyes. At first, indeed, I had the dim sense that I was dead and embarking upon the Afterlife; and only the definite sensation of my comrades tumbled about in ungainly attitudes, convinced me that I was still on the better-known side of the grave.

"Sure, and I thought we went through the black gates of Hell!" came a familiar voice. And Stranahan rose unsteadily to his feet, lugubriously nursing a sprained wrist. "By all the saints in heaven, we're a devilish lot. The devil himself wasn't able to get us."

Cheered by sound of a human voice, I followed Stranahan's example, and painfully rose. I was thankful to learn that, while rumpled and battered, I had suffered no broken bones; and as my comrades one by one staggered up from the deck, I was relieved to observe that none was gravely injured.

Our vessel had re-assumed a horizontal position, but our surroundings were strangely altered. While a pale radiance transfused the waters on both sides and above us, below us the golden lights were no longer visible, and everything was impenetrably black.

Of course, the Captain again ordered the searchlights turned on—and with extraordinary results. Just beneath us, actually in contact with the bottom of the *X-111*, a flat sandy reach of ground was visible—certainly, the bottom of the sea! But this was the least remarkable fact of all. On both sides of us, at a distance of possibly two hundred yards, a high and geometrically regular embankment arose, ending in a yellow illuminated patch of water whose nature we could not surmise. The one thing apparent was that we were in a sort of submarine channel, a riverbed in the bed of the sea. This was proved by a current that sent us skimming along the soft sands, although our engines had ceased to supply us with power.

"I—can't understand it," sighed Captain Gavison, shaking his head dolefully. "Can't understand it at all. For twenty-five years I've studied the ocean currents, but I've never heard of anything like this…"

Just at this point, our searchlights showed us a long, lithe form gliding by, perhaps fifty feet above. It was as large as the largest known shark, but was shaped like no fish I had ever seen, tapering at each end to a slender, canoe-like point; and, as it passed, the water foamed and bubbled in its wake.

"Perdition take me, if it ain't a sea dragon!" ventured Stranahan, who had to have his say.

"Stranahan, be silent!" snapped the Captain, in high irritation. "You're always saying the wrong thing at the wrong time."

"Yes, sir," admitted the culprit meekly, a grave expression in his pale blue eyes.

"If you want to make yourself useful, Stranahan," continued the Captain, severely, although with less asperity than before, "go forward, and find out how far we're beneath sea level."

"Aye, aye, sir," agreed Stranahan, remembering to salute.

"How far below at the last reading, sir?" I inquired of the Captain, after Stranahan had vanished through the compartment door.

"Thirty-seven hundred feet," returned my superior, abruptly. "But we've sunk considerably since then."

Just at this juncture Stranahan reappeared, a stare of incredulous astonishment on his lean, hardened face.

"Well?" the Captain demanded. "How far below now?"

Stranahan mopped his brow as though to wipe off an invisible perspiration.

"Stranahan," growled the exasperated officer, "do you hear? I'm asking to know how far below we are now."

"Well, sir," drawled Stranahan, saluting mechanically, "wouldn't I be telling you if I knew? But, saints in heaven, sir, that machine must be bewitched... Or else I'm seeing things. I'm sure seeing things bad!"

"Did you notice the reading?"

"Yes, sir. That's what the trouble is, sir."

"Then how far below are we?"

Stranahan hesitated, as though dreading to commit himself. "Forty-four feet," he muttered at length.

A murmur of excitement passed from end to end of the room.

"Forty-four?" yelled the Captain. "You mean forty-four hundred!"

"No, sir. I mean forty-four."

The Captain's anger was a thing terrible to see. "Stranahan, you must take me for a fool!" he shouted. "This is not the moment for practical jokes! At any other time I'd have you thrown in the brig!"

"But, sir—"

"That's enough!" roared the officer, fairly shaking with fury. And, turning to one of the younger men, he commanded, "Ripley...see how far below water level we are!"

"Aye, aye, sir!" assented Ripley, and left the room. A moment later he returned with a sheepish grin.

"Well, how far below?" demanded the Captain.

But Ripley, like Stranahan, was reluctant to speak. He coughed, gasped, and stammered out an unintelligible syllable or two; then cleared his throat, stood gaping at us dully, and finally blurted out, "Forty—forty-three feet, sir!"

"Forty-three?" bellowed the Captain. "Has the whole crew gone crazy?"

Thereupon, Gavison himself went lunging towards the door, and disappeared in the forward compartment

It was several minutes before he returned. But when he rejoined us, he wore a look of undisguised amazement. Furtively, almost shame-facedly, he peered at us, like one who fancies he is losing his wits.

"Well, sir, how far below now?" I questioned.

The Captain cleared his throat, and hesitated before replying. "I—I really don't know. I can't understand—can't understand at all. If the instruments aren't out of order, we're exactly forty-two feet below."

I gaped stupidly; then suggested, "No doubt, sir, the instruments are out of order."

"They are not. I've tested them."

Again he hesitated; then abruptly resumed, "Besides, as you know, there are two instruments. They both record forty-two feet."

There ensued a moment of silence, during which we stared blankly at one another.

"But how do you explain—"

"I don't explain... According to all estimates, we should be nearly a mile deep."

For a few seconds, the Captain stood stroking his chin in grave perplexity. Then, turning suddenly to us all, he remarked, "I can't see how it can be, boys, but if we're only forty-two feet deep, maybe the engines have life enough in them to pull us out. At least, it's a chance worth taking."

Half an hour later, after the assignment of the crew to duty, we had the relief of hearing once more the churning and throbbing of the engines. At first it promised to be but a barren pleasure, for the abused machinery gasped and sputtered as though determined upon a sit-down strike; and only after many efforts were we greeted by the motors' continuous buzzing. Then we found ourselves slowly moving, at first scarcely more swiftly than the current; and by degrees we felt the deck taking on an upward slope as the nose of the vessel was pointed towards the surface of the waters. It was not an easy pull, for our three flooded compartments were a deadening drag, but eventually the engines, waxing to their full power; began to cleave the water at gratifying speed, and we moved slowly upwards.

Of course, hope came to us then in a powerful wave. Impatiently we fastened our eyes on the pressure gauges; impatiently we watched the registered distance dwindle from forty feet to thirty-five, from thirty-five to thirty, from thirty to twenty-five, and from twenty-five to twenty! Now, in sudden wild joy, we realized that probably we were saved. A pale, but unmistakable radiance was seeping in through the windows, far more distinct and reassuring than the eerie illumination we had noticed before. Certainly, this was the sunlight!

And as we rose from twenty feet to fifteen, and from fifteen to ten, the light filtering in through the portholes grew stronger. Through the clear waters, even without the searchlights, we could distinguish a steep embankment fifty or a hundred feet away. And just above us, almost within grasping distance, we thought we could detect the line dividing the water from the air.

Today, as I look back, it seems incredible that we could have expected to escape at once to the upper world. But hope had blinded our eyes and suffering blunted our perceptions, so that we could not understand that we were at the mere beginning of our adventures.

Suddenly, with a startling lunge, we were launched upwards towards the wavy, light-shot level. Suddenly a blinding brilliance was upon us, forcing us to shield our eyes. Then, when by degrees we were able to glance about us again, we found ourselves on the surface of the waters—actually on the surface! But where had we come up? In what strange and unmapped continent?

There was scarcely one of us that could suppress a cry of astonishment. We were afloat not upon the ocean, as we had expected, but on a wide, rapidly flowing river—a river that washed no shores ever pictured by human tongue.

Altogether, we beheld one of the weirdest lands imaginable. On both sides of the stream there spread a flat plain dotted with great seashells and greenish boulders, which in turn were interspersed with mossy brown vegetation and pale graceful flowers like water lilies on solitary stalks. At measured intervals, as far as the eye could fathom, were colossal stone columns, enriched with pastel tintings of pink and blue; and these shot upwards hundreds of feet, as though supporting some titanic dome. Most unaccountable of all, they ended in a dark-green sky from which glared several sun-like golden orbs, suffusing the scene in a mellow, unearthly luster that was beautiful and at the same time terrifying and ghostly.

Rubbing our eyes like children still but half-awake, we gazed at this fantastic, lovely spectacle. We spoke not a word; we had no language to voice our amazement. Only the Captain, out of the whole thirty-nine of us, retained some measure of self-possession; and though, as he afterwards confessed, he was so dazzled that he spoke and acted mechanically, he did have the presence of mind to order our vessel steered to shore and anchored.

It is still a marvel to me that we had the energy to carry out these commands. But somehow we brought the *X-111* to land; somehow, after several false starts, we managed to moor the ship to a large boulder in a sort of miniature bay.

A few minutes later, we were taking deep refreshing draughts of the pure, clean air, which came to us like a mercy from heaven after the suffocating atmosphere of the submarine.

But before we had had half the time needed to revive our starving lungs, an astounding event was to plunge us into fresh terror. All at once the golden lights above us flickered, gave out a fugitive spark or two, and, with meteor swiftness, flashed out—and we found ourselves buried in blackness, a starless, impenetrable blackness more mysterious than the loneliest abysses from which we had thought to escape.

ON UNKNOWN SHORES

NO SOONER HAD DARKNESS fallen than it seemed populated with things weird and terrible. A chorus of hoarse, unearthly voices, loud as the bellowing of a bull, resounded about us in a deep, continuous bass; and throaty gruntings and savage snorts and howls droned and echoed as though from ten thousand pairs of giant lungs. Dazed, we stared into the gloom like doomed men, with visions of enormous eyes smoldering from the blackness, jaws that struck and tore, and teeth that rent and shattered.

Then all at once, in pell-mell haste, we flung ourselves towards the submarine, almost failing to find it in the darkness, and tumbling over one another in our haste to crowd through the narrow door. Several of us were shoved accidentally into the water, and came in dripping; while the Captain walked with a slight limp dealt him when two of the crew, not recognizing him in their panic, had literally fallen over him.

But at length we were all safely on deck, with the doors barred, against the unknown peril. Several of the men were eager to get under way directly; but this idea the Captain vetoed, declaring that the *X-111* was not seaworthy. All that we could do was to try to locate the danger with our searchlights; and, accordingly, we wasted no time about switching on our powerful lanterns and revolving them in slow circles that illuminated by turns every inch of the boulder-strewn, weedy plain. Yet although the unearthly chorus could be heard even through the closed doors, our searchlights revealed nothing.

For some time we watched and waited—without results. And at last, turning to us all with a smile, the Captain advised, "Well, boys, we've had a pretty tough time of it. Suppose we just forget that racket out there and try for a little rest."

Everyone was glad enough to follow this suggestion. Several of the men were commissioned to take turns standing watch; and the rest of us were not long in seeking needed sleep. Within a few minutes, I could hear a deep, regular breathing from the nearby bunks.

For my own part, exhausted as I was, I could not so easily find relief. The events not only of the past few hours, but of many months, kept trooping through my mind. I was obsessed by my own imaginings, and from a dim half-consciousness I would awaken time after time to a vivid re-experiencing of some almost forgotten episode. And, strangely enough, my reveries were concerned mainly with a single phase of my life. My youth and early manhood might almost not have existed, for all that I remembered of them now; but I did sharply recall how, not long after Congress passed the Selective Service Act in 1940, I had decided upon the action that led to my present plight. Resigning my position at Northwestern University, where I had served as instructor in Greek, I had enlisted in the navy, had promptly been sent to an officers' training school, and had emerged as Ensign. Friends had commended my patriotism, yet not patriotism so much as the greed for adventure had governed me, and now—as I looked back—it seemed ironic that my previous uneventful days had been so much more pleasant than any of my adventures.

There was, however, one incentive that had made many of those days enjoyable. As I tossed and struggled on my narrow bunk, there flashed before me the blue eyes and laughing face of one whom I could not recall without a pang; and I lived again with Alma Huntley—those sparkling days in the Vermont hills when I had won her promise of devotion among the scented pines and to the music of rippling waters. That time was long past, yet how acutely it came back to mind! And how acutely memory restored a later day, when her cheeks were moist and she begged my forgiveness that her path lay not with me, but with my old rival Don Alders—Don Alders, the bullock-shouldered football hero. How deeply I had grieved at her defection she would never know—though perhaps the desire to forget her, to forget the old life entirely, had been mostly responsible for my enlistment in the navy.

At last, after hours of brooding, I lost my memories in unconsciousness. And after a sleep disturbed by gloomy dreams and vague images of disaster, I opened my eyes to find a bright light pouring in through the portholes.

Surprised, I leapt to my feet, and discovered that the great mysterious golden orbs were shining as before from far above, the boulder-strewn plain glimmered as clearly as at first, the massive columns were still fairylike in their tints of pale pink and blue, while the hideous noises had all ceased.

Hastily I dressed and rejoined my companions. I found them gathered about in a little circle, earnestly engaged in a discussion, whose subject I at once surmised.

None of us as yet had more than the faintest inkling of where we were or what had befallen us. That we were in some sort of a cavern beneath the sea was the belief of the Captain and several of the men, but this region seemed so oddly unlike a cavern that the explanation was not generally accepted; the more superstitious among us were inclined to hold that we had been bewitched into some supernatural, goblin realm. For my own part, I could not understand how we could be in a submarine cavern without being flooded; and even less could I understand how we could be in any known land above seas.

Obviously, the only way to solve the mystery was through exploration. And since it was not possible to do any exploring by means of the disabled *X-111* the Captain took the one available course—which was to order some of the men to set forth on foot.

Stangale and Howlett, being the most experienced veterans, were selected for the first attempt. After a few minutes' delay, they started off cheerfully together, equipped with firearms and a day's supply of food and drink, and instructed to make notes of everything they saw and return within twenty-four hours.

Twelve or fifteen hours went by while we waited impatiently. The great golden orbs flashed out as mysteriously as before, and for eight or ten hours we slept; then, upon awakening, we found the lights shining brightly again, and remarked that it was time for the return of the two scouts. But not a moving thing greeted us from the bouldery plain. The hours wore on while we strained our eyes in vain; excited speculation gave place to excited speculation, and wild rumor to wilder rumor; the suspense became tantalizing, and yet there was nothing to do—nothing but wait. Had the men lost their way? Or had they met with disaster? To these questions we could have no answer; but when the darkness had fallen again, and again we had slept and awakened to find the golden light restored, we knew that it was time to search for the missing ones.

To our surprise, the Captain called for volunteers; and after half the crew had offered themselves, the choice fell upon Ripley and Stranahan.

With what regret did I watch those gallant seamen set forth amid the reeds by the river's brink, to disappear among the boulders and behind the great stone columns. Somehow, I had a sense that we might not see them soon again.

Nor were my misgivings unjustified. Twelve hours, and the explorers had not returned; twenty-four hours, and still no word, though they had explicit orders to be back. With grim, set eyes the Captain strode alone by the river bank, gazing sternly into that wilderness which had engulfed four of his men; and the rest of the crew stood muttering among themselves, declaring that this land was "haunted" and "thick with spooks."

It was curious to note how, in these weird, unheard-of regions, outworn superstitions were springing up as from the childhood of the race; how ready the men were to believe in goblins, dragons, sea serpents, werewolves and all manner of fantastic monsters. Even the more enlightened of us, in the failure of every prop we had been accustomed to cling to, were clutching at a savage, terrorizing faith in incredible and ghostly things.

By the time that Stranahan and Ripley had been absent forty-eight hours, the crew was in a state of impatience verging upon madness—so paralyzed by alarm that, when the Captain called for volunteers to hunt for the missing men, only two of us offered our names: young Phil Rawson and myself. I do not know what strange courage had emboldened this timorous recruit while less callow men held back; and as for myself, I must admit that I volunteered not out of courage, but from the desire to escape from ennui and the half-frenzied rabble of my comrades.

Whatever our motives, we were to be launched into adventures that were not only to test our hardihood, but to prove interesting beyond anything we could have imagined.

A TOUR OF EXPLORATION

RAWSON AND I HAD BEEN gone half an hour when the aspect of the country began to change. It was as though we had passed some indistinguishable boundary, for the boulders were growing less numerous, and at length disappeared, while the odd mossy vegetation became astonishingly rich and profuse. Or, to be precise, it gave place to a different and still more unearthly growth. At the risk of being disbelieved, I must describe those incredible plants: the creepers with long leaves of lace-like brown, which twined in dainty wreaths and veils about the olive-green boles of limbless trees; the bushes shaped like starfishes, and of the hue of dried grass, with diaphanous flowers that a breath might have blown away; the cinnamon brown reeds that rose to double a man's height, ending in a profusion of cucumber-shaped fruits; the peculiar, abundant sprouts that looked at a distance like great earthen jars, but proved upon closer examination to be the hollow containers of a species of milk-white down that grew in long silken strands like untended hair.

So dense was the foliage that we would not have been able to force our way through had it not been for the little path that wound in leisurely curves close to the river's edge. It was not like a chance-created trail or one made by the tracks of wild beasts, for it had a regularity of design and an evenness of width that bespoke the work of man.

Yet what man could have preceded us into these uncanny depths?

At this mere question we shuddered, and kept a constant, half-terrified lookout for sign of human presence. And before long our vigilance was rewarded. Abruptly, the path widened to a broad highway; and above the dense vegetation we saw in astonishment the marble pillars of a Grecian colonnade. Towards this the road gracefully meandered; and within a few minutes we found ourselves at the entrance of a covered walk or "stoa" that startled me with memories of "the glory that was Greece." On both sides of us the palely tinted Ionic columns rose to a majestic height, daintily ornamented at the base with a seaweed design, and curving in symmetrical proportions that brought to mind the beauty of the Parthenon; while the marble floor on which we walked and the marble ceiling above us were frescoed with figures that seemed drawn bodily from the romance of the ancient world. They were not wholly Greek, I know, these pictures of sportive mermaids and lightning-hurling gods and dragon-slaying heroes and, misty-twilight caves; but there was something suggestively Greek about them all; and steeped as I was in Hellenic lore, I had the feeling that the hand of time had turned backwards two thousand years.

Having followed the covered walk for several hundred yards, I observed that it led to a magnificent, many-columned edifice like a temple of the ancient gods. It was a structure of solid, white marble, artistically varied with veinings of black; its pillars were massive as the trunks of the giant redwoods I had seen in the Californian forests, and, like those redwoods, produced an effect of solemnity and awe. Yet all was so perfectly designed and proportioned that, while the building occupied an area as large as a city block, it gave the effect less of magnitude than of artistic completeness and beauty. No living thing was visible about this amazing temple, nor would I have expected any living thing in

27

what I had come to regard as a realm of the dead; but I was overawed at the thought of this abandoned loveliness; and paused to regard it reflectively, asking myself whether it was some still-undiscovered survival from classical times or whether I was but seeing a vision.

A suppressed exclamation from Rawson shocked me back to reality. In the middle of the swift-rolling river, the banks of which paralleled the colonnade at a distance of a dozen paces, I observed a low-lying, gliding form, queerly elevated at both extremes. At the first startled glimpse I took it to be some fabulous monster, but soon I recognized it as some sort of boat or canoe. In its fast-moving frame, as it slid out of view, I could distinguish half a dozen dusky bobbing shapes, and half a dozen pairs of oars that rhythmically clove the waters. Later, when I had had time to think, I was to recognize this strange craft as similar to the shadowy apparition, the unknown sea monster which had terrified us in the submarine; but for the present I was overwhelmed to know that this weird place was actually peopled.

We had scarcely recovered from this surprise when an even greater flashed upon us. Out of the windows of the temple which we had believed long closed to human sound, a quaint thin music began to float, serenely beautiful, and of elfin remoteness and charm... And while entranced, we listened. There soon came the fluttering of a butterfly gown, and from the temple doors there issued a shimmering, dancing form, followed by a score of dancing, shimmering forms—scarcely human, we believed—so ethereal did they seem in the flashing and waving of arms, the swift rhythm of feet, and the play and interplay of pale blue and gold and pink and lavender and white from their multi-colored flowing robes.

Now they started down the long colonnade, tripping towards us with bird-like gestures and the airy unreality of perfect time and movement; while, fearful to disturb the vision, we hid behind the great stone columns, peeping out furtively as though they might vanish, bubble-like, at our gaze. But, absorbed in their dance, they continued gracefully towards us, not glancing to right or left—until, as the procession drew more near, I peered out too incautiously from behind my marble bulwark, and found myself staring full into the face of the most ravishingly beautiful woman I had ever seen.

There was a quality about that face which seemed to mark it not of the earth. The Madonna's of old paintings have a little of the same look, and the most perfect womanly bust that sculptor has ever conceived; but there was also a vividness, an animation that no mere work of art has ever shared. Her eyes were large, and blue with an ethereal blueness, as of a deep mountain lake; her hair was tumbled in great golden masses above her broad, pale brow; her features had sharp-cut, flawless outlines, and her thin lips quivered sensitively above a delicately rounded chin; while her whole air bespoke such innocence, such candor and kindness of spirit that she seemed a fairy, a genial child and a woman in one.

But all this I beheld in the space between two heartbeats. Even as the vision greeted me it vanished. The beautiful clear eyes were distended with terror; there came a scream of fright, followed by a chorus of screams; then a scurrying of fast-retreating feet, and the elf-like shapes had vanished, and the empty river flowed as before past the empty colonnade and temple.

THE MYSTERIOUS CITY

THE NEXT FEW HOURS showed us a continuous amazing panorama. The marble temple proved to be but one of a series connected by long colonnades; and in the central structure the Ionic and Doric architecture were mingled with a type that seemed scarcely Grecian at all, since it admitted of all variety of arches and curves unknown to classical Hellas. Most remarkable of all, perhaps, were the gorgeously ornamented vases—some of them six or eight feet in height—which were of the style of those excavated from the ruins of old Ilium. But what most caught my eye were the statues mounted in niches along the marble galleries or in alcoves of the temples—statues surely not unworthy of a Praxiteles, since even Praxiteles could not have surpassed the symmetry of form and the unstrained reality of pose and expression with which the artists had depicted their wrestling heroes and dancing fauns and stern-browed old men and queenly maidens and gracious youths.

For one nurtured on modern art, these busts and marbles were as oil paintings would be after sketches in black and white. There was none of that snowy coldness or bronzen severity of hue so common in sculpture today, but all the statues had been skillfully tinted with the complexion of life. Such was the verisimilitude that several times I gave a start of surprise when what I took to be a man proved to be only a stone image. I was interested, also, to note that none of the sculptured features had that peculiar hardness and selfish keenness so common among men I had known. All seemed suffused with a clear and tranquil spirituality; while every lyric impulse within me awakened when I observed on many feminine faces that same unearthly Madonna look which had graced the butterfly-gowned dancing maiden.

But, of course, Rawson and I did not allow our pleasure in the statuary to occupy us too much. We still kept a constant lookout for living inhabitants; indeed, we could no longer suppress the suspicion that unseen, furtive eyes were peeping out at us from behind every pillar and wall. Nevertheless, not seeing anyone, we continued to observe the wayside architecture. For two or three hours we were busy inspecting the connecting galleries of five or six temples; and having passed the last of the group, we were dazzled by a long marble colonnade, which extended for miles in a straight line amid the gray and brown fantastic vegetation.

Now it was that I made the most startling discovery of the day. At intervals along the floor of the colonnade, which was of a red and yellow mosaic of baked clay, there were deeply-graven inscriptions that I paused eagerly to survey. At first I thought them to be in no known language, but before long I had detected a resemblance between the characters and those of ancient Greek. Profiting from my study of that tongue, I puzzled over the words while Rawson stood by impatiently urging me to be off; and one by one I succeeded in identifying the letters with those of the Greek alphabet! True, I could not recognize every one of the characters with assurance; but enough of them were unmistakably Greek to offer me a clue to the whole, and to promise a translation that would solve the mystery of this extraordinary land.

But the process was a slow and plodding one. Even though the letters were clear enough, I could at first decipher but an occasional word. Evidently this was not the Greek of Plato or Thucydides, in which I had been thoroughly schooled; rather, it was to classical

Greek what Chaucer is to modern English. All in all, considering our limited time, my efforts seemed futile; and I was about to give in to Rawson's importunities and abandon this diverting study in favor of further exploration, when suddenly I came upon a simpler passage. Unexpectedly a sentence flashed upon me with clear-cut meaning—a meaning so striking and enigmatical that I drew back with a little cry of surprise.

"Placed here in the year Three Thousand of the Submergence," ran the words, which occurred in large lettering at the base of a statue of a strong man trampling down the ruins of what looked like a steel building. "Placed here…" At this point there were several words that I could not make out, "…in celebration of the Good Destruction."

"Good Destruction," I repeated, after translating the words aloud. "Sounds like a madman's ravings!"

"Maybe, you didn't read it right," commented Rawson.

"Of course, I read it right! Wonder what the Submergence can mean," I continued, meditatively. "That doesn't seem to make sense, either."

"No, it doesn't," Rawson admitted, with a thoughtful drawl.

"Everything down here seems sort of topsy-turvy. Suppose we go on and see what else we can find."

I nodded a hesitating assent, and we pushed on our way in silence. But our thoughts continued active; more than ever I was convinced that somehow, unaccountably, we were amid the remains of a Grecian or pre-Grecian countryside. Had Socrates himself stepped out from behind a column to greet me, I would hardly have been surprised; and I more than half expected to catch a glimpse of Athena's robe from amid the dark shrubbery, or to see the winged feet of Hermes or hear the clear notes of Pan!

But neither Pan nor Hermes, or any of their famed kindred presented themselves. What did present itself, after we had walked for an hour along the marble colonnade, was a scene that struck us with greater astonishment than if we had invaded a council of the Olympian gods. For some distance a series of huge templed domes and pillars, dimly visible through the rifts in the vegetation, had attracted my attention and aroused Rawson's misgivings. Then, suddenly, we saw a clay road sloping down beneath us and found ourselves gazing out over a valley more dazzling than we had ever before known or imagined.

Through its center flowed the great river; above us, as before, reached the dark-green sky illuminated with the golden suns; and an innumerable multitude of palely-tinted columns, like the tree trunks of some colossal forest, shot upwards to the sky as though to support it. But most remarkable of all were the buildings that spread across the plain. On both sides of the river they stretched. Palaces of white marble and of black, of jade and of alabaster some with an elegant symmetry of Greek columns, some with a solidity of masonry that seemed half Egyptian, some with an Oriental profusion of spires and turrets, of porticoes, balconies, arches and domes. But all alike were reared in perfect taste, and with perfect regard to the style of their neighbors; all alike faced on wide avenues, flowery lanes or lawny and statue-dotted parks; all appeared but parts of a single design, which seen from above, was like some consummate tapestry patterned by a master.

As Rawson and I stood staring at this matchless scene, I recalled the steeples and towers of that city we had observed beneath us in the submarine. A strange similarity in the outlines of the buildings impressed itself upon me—then, in a flash, it came to me that the two cities were one! It was as the Captain had suggested, we were indeed beneath the ocean, thousands of feet beneath the ocean, in some cavern inexplicably spared from the, waters and haunted by the ghosts and relics of some ancient race...

THE TEMPLE OF THE STARS

FAR FROM ECHOING my agitation, Rawson seemed actually pleased at our weird discovery. It piqued his imagination to think that we should be so far beneath the sea; he conjured up all manner of alluring possibilities that testified more to his youth than to his commonsense, and urged me to go down with him at once into the many templed city. But I pointed out that it would be wiser to hasten back to the submarine, inform Captain Gavison what we had seen, and return in greater numbers. Besides, the Captain had ordered us back within twenty-four hours; and if we dallied, some mischance might delay us until too late.

Had Rawson had any prevision of the black hours ahead, he would certainly have accepted my suggestion. But, perversely, he seemed almost without fear just when some healthy misgivings might have been useful. And since I could not let a mere boy outdo me in bravery, I assented grudgingly to his proposal. It may be however, that my motives were not unmixed, for pictures of the iridescent dancing girl kept flitting before my mind and would give me no peace; and I may have had hopes (I will not say that I did) of meeting her again in this city of fountains and palaces.

But not a living creature could be seen in the avenues of that strange town as Rawson and I began our slow descent. Once or twice we thought we saw a glimmer in the far distance, but could not be sure; the silence and the immobility gave the effect of a city of the dead. There was something ghostly about that calm, still atmosphere, something that might have turned me back in alarm had it not been for the presence of Rawson; but there was also something soothingly peaceful, a charmed quiet that brought to mind the fairy tales I had heard in childhood, and in particular that enchanted palace where the Sleeping Beauty had slumbered for a hundred years. Here, I thought, one might dream away a hundred years, or a thousand, and never know that time had passed at all; here the ancient world might lapse into the modern, and the modern into the far future, and yet there be no apparent change.

My reveries were interrupted by our arrival at the city gates. We passed beneath a high arch almost Roman in style, with marble base and facade ornamented with curious blue sea shells; then, proceeding along a winding cement walk inlaid with mother-of-pearl, we approached the most stately palace of all. In architecture it was dissimilar to anything we had ever observed before; although five hundred feet in length, it was as much like a great statue as like a building. Its form was that of a woman, who reclined at full length, her breast to the ground, her elevated head propped meditatively upon one palm; and it had been planned with subtlety and skill, such consummate attention to the details of the woman's position and form and to the beatific and yet life-like expression of the face, that Rawson and I could only pause and stare as though this work had been created through no human agency, but by some super-human master hand.

In that first spellbound moment, it did not occur to us to look for an entrance to the palace. But at length, where a lock of the woman's dark sculptured hair fell across her breast, we noted an artfully concealed little doorway. Since the gate swung wide upon the hinges, curiosity prompted us to glance within—and with results that proved a further spur to curiosity. All that we could see was a pale golden glitter against a black background; but imagination supplied visions of gorgeous halls and corridors beyond.

Had our courage sufficed, we would have entered at once. There was something mysteriously, irresistibly attractive about that twinkling darkness, something that held us fascinated; and for several minutes we stood hesitating, straining our eyes and wishing to go in, and yet lacking the boldness.

Then, when the suspense had become absurdly protracted, Rawson surprised me by exclaiming, suddenly, "I'm not afraid!" Energetically he slapped his sides, as though to prove to himself that he had no fears. "Forward, march!" he cried, with what I considered unnecessary loudness. And, feeling for his revolver, he strode resolutely in.

There was nothing for me to do but follow. But, somehow, I could not help wishing that my friend had been less rash.

Yet, once within, we lost our misgivings in contemplation of the magnificence around us. I had been in luxurious galleries before, but never had I viewed or imagined so sublime a hall. Here was a new art of the interior decorator—an art that, strange as it may seem, was akin to and yet superior to that of the modern builders of planetariums. I was scarcely conscious that I was indoors, but felt myself to be in the open, in the open at night, under the wide and glittering heavens, with the light of innumerable stars above me, and the dim cloudy arch of the Milky Way. Somehow, in his limited space, the artist had given the impression of vastness and distance, of the mystery and infinite silence of the starlight; and, as I stood there fascinated, I could imagine that I was back again on earth, gazing out into the night skies as I had gazed so often from the Vermont hills with Alma Huntley.

Nevertheless, skillfully patterned as they were, these were not the skies I had known. As I stood there watching, I became aware that certain constellations were slightly, almost indistinguishably out of position, the stars not quite in their proper relations to one another. But more striking was another alteration that had been wrought with subtle artistry: above the stars, and about the thin girdle of the Milky Way, were filmy formations of light, which gradually, very gradually, resolved themselves into human figures. One, an exquisitely graceful woman, was playing upon some lyre-like instrument; another, a youth with head uplifted in contemplation, impressed me as the spirit of all aspirations; and still others, no less consummately outlined, appeared to represent the hopes and loves and immortal yearnings of man.

But while I remained rooted there in ecstatic wonder, marveling at the paradox of beholding the stars thousands of feet beneath the sea, there occurred one of those changes by which occasionally a beautiful dream is distorted into a nightmare. Imagine the consternation of one who, gazing at the cloudless night skies, finds blackness suddenly all about him—a blackness that quenches the stars as a storm might quench a candle flame. Such consternation was ours, for without so much as a flicker of warning the lights of the seeming heavens flashed out, and darkness stretched above us and all about us, and we knew that the only exit was closed.

For a moment we were like men trapped in a torpedoed ship. Every trace of reason left us; blindly we fumbled about the darkness, in a panic-stricken frenzy to escape. Where we were scurrying we did not know, nor whether we might not plunge into still greater peril; we collided with the walls, stumbled over invisible objects on the floor, and went groping about in long loops and circles. The marvel is not that we accomplished nothing, but that we did not break our necks.

If I can judge from my confused memories of those terrible moments, it was the sound of a heavy body falling that shocked me back to my senses. The fall, which was thudding and resonant, was accompanied by a suppressed oath that seemed to come from far to my rear.

"Rawson!" I cried, stopping short in my alarm. "Are you hurt?"

"No, not much," came the drawled reply, as from a tremendous distance. And then, after a groan, "No, guess—I'm all right."

"Where are you?" I yelled back. "How can I get to you?" Rawson shouted directions, and I went falteringly towards him.

This was by no means easy, for I was guided wholly by touch and hearing, and more than once came into painful contact with some unforeseen obstacle. But, after some minutes, I found myself grasping a solid, yielding mass—the arm of my friend!

Rawson was as glad as I of our reunion. Somehow, now that we were together again, we both felt much stronger.

Yet the unknown foe still seemed terrible enough as we sat there on the floor, conferring in whispers. Although we had regained some slight composure, the falling of a pin might have sent us off into convulsions.

"What can it mean?" muttered Rawson, as he sat with one hand on my knee, as though to reassure himself by the physical fact of my presence. "What do you think it can mean?"

I did not reply, although suggestions sufficiently dreadful were piling up in my brain.

"Remember how Stranahan and all the others were lost," Rawson continued, solemnly.

"Don't see what that has to do with us," I argued. And then, with a forced attempt at bravado, "Don't you worry, Rawson. You'll see, everything will turn out all right."

"I hope so, I sure hope so. But I don't like the looks of things."

"Wish we could only *see* the looks of things," I returned, with an abortive attempt at facetiousness.

Rawson grunted dully. It was minutes before either of us spoke again. Meantime, the darkness was so intense, the silence so absolute that I was persecuted with all manner of fantastic fears. What unthinkable horrors were brewing in these serene depths? In my anxiety, I peopled the gloom with monsters of a thousand varieties, with slimy crawling serpents, with huge flapping vampire bats, with apes whose brawny arms could strangle a man, and— worst of all—with barbarous humans that crept up to seize us and stab us in the back.

By degrees my imaginings were becoming so gruesome that I could no longer endure them. Merely to find relief from myself, I whispered, "Come, Rawson, we're two jackasses to sit here doing nothing. Most likely we can find a way out. What do you say?"

"I'm all for it," assented Rawson, rising cautiously.

Without a word I followed his example, and for half an hour we groped laboriously along the walls, which were of an ice-cold stone as smooth as polished marble, absolutely perpendicular and without a flaw or break. Our movements were agonizingly slow, for the blackness was still unbroken, and in that hushed, mysterious place the slightest sound would send sharp tremors running down our spines. Even the grating of our own shoes against the floor would seem to take on a sinister, uncanny meaning; the whispered tones of our own voices would be as something unhallowed and ghostly; the occasional rapping of our fists against the walls or our clattering contact with some unseen obstruction would start the echoes reverberating with unearthly, hollow notes.

Possibly two or three times we circled that great hall, but could find no indication of any passageway or door. At length, exhausted, we crouched on the floor near the wall, miserably waiting for something to happen. Almost anything that could have happened even anything grim and terrible—would have been a relief; but it was our misfortune that the quiet was undisturbed, while we sat tense and alert, with fast-throbbing hearts, and eyes that searched the gloom in vain. How long a period passed thus I cannot say; my watch recorded hours, but certainly my thoughts recorded years...

When at last relief did come, it arrived with disconcerting suddenness. As though by the turning of a switch, a dazzlingly brilliant light flashing into view above us, shining blindingly in a pale blue field like the sun in the cloudless heavens. Then, just opposite us, while we stood shading our eyes from the glare, we observed the gate through which we had entered. It was moving inwards upon its hinges! Slowly, as if self-propelled, it made clear the way of escape!

"God help us, the place is enchanted..." muttered Rawson, in dazed fascination. "Quick, let's get out!"

Overjoyed at our rescue, we started towards the gate—only to confront a new obstacle. Half a dozen of the queerest beings we had ever seen came crowding into our path—tall, butterfly-like creatures with faces almost waxen pale and long capes and robes of pink and blue, lavender and yellow pastel tints. All had flowing light red or golden hair that reached to their shoulders. One, apparently the oldest, wore an ample beard, but the majority were smooth-shaven; none had headgear of any type, and all were shod with sandals covered with green moss, above which the unclothed legs were visible for several inches.

From the amazed stares with which they greeted us, it was evident that our appearance was as much of a surprise to them as theirs to us. But from a certain sternness and resolution which invested their faces following the first speechless astonishment, we concluded that, they had seen others of our kind, and were not too leniently disposed.

We noted also that, though quivering with dread, they kept the exit blocked. During the long staring silence that ensued, we felt in dismay that at last we had met the masters of the land, and that our chances of escape had vanished.

SAPPHIRE AND AMBER

IT MAY HAVE BEEN NO MORE than thirty seconds before the silence was broken, though it felt like many minutes. At last one of the newcomers, turning to his companions while his eyes remained fastened upon us, began to speak in low rhythmic tones that were singularly musical. I could not catch even one syllable, though I strained my ears; and could understand nothing of what his fellows said in reply, though their voices too were so soft and sweet-sounding that they might have been intoning poetry. Yet beneath the gentleness of their accent, I could detect the excitement in their manner; and their nods and gestures in our direction made me only too certain of the theme of their discussion.

After several minutes, one of the strangers approached, raised his voice as if addressing us, and motioned us to follow him.

Glad to step once more into the street, we obeyed, while the natives grouped themselves on all sides of us as a sort of bodyguard. Yet, whether out of consideration for our feelings or because they were afraid of us, they did not attempt to lay hands on us or to coerce us in anyway. But when they indicated by gestures the direction in which we were to walk, we had no thought of opposing them.

For two or three miles they led us through the streets; while we, despite our predicament, keenly observed the sights of the city. Dozens of the inhabitants had come out to peer at us; and, though they kept at a cautious distance, we could see them clearly enough: their slender, graceful forms and blond features, their amiable blue eyes and rippling unbound hair, their loose-hanging, light-tinted robes, variously colored from buff and lilac to azure and pale rose.

"Say, they don't look human at all," commented Rawson. "They're more like walking butterflies or flowers."

"Beats any Easter parade I ever saw."

"By Jove, what do you think of this architecture? Wouldn't it make a World's Fair look cheap?" continued my companion, pointing eagerly to the palaces all about us.

Truly, we were fascinated by the buildings, which proved to be even more artistically designed than we had imagined, for exquisite little statues abounded in niches between the columns or among the domes and spires, and superb frescoes decorated the ceilings of the colonnades and the outside walls of temples, and curving walks wound invitingly between terraces adorned with a lovely waxen flower, or around the brink of the rainbowed fountains. I particularly noted the width of the avenues, in whose spacious reaches the bright-robed children laughed and played; and I was delighted to observe that the buildings were separated by broad paved ways or patches of vegetation, so that the whole gave an uncrowded and leisurely effect.

But by far the most extraordinary edifice was that to which our guides eventually led us. It was not the size of the structure that distinguished it; it was that the walls and the interior circles of columns were not of any recognizable material, not of steel or stone, brick or clay, gold or ebony; they were of a translucent yellow, the hue of amber, and seemed composed, if not actually of amber, at least of glass tinted amber color.

This, however, was scarcely the most remarkable fact. The floor was likewise translucent, and shone with an entrancing blue, the blue of sapphire; and sapphire seemed also the substance of the fretted and vaulted ceiling, from which hung images of great birds with widespread wings, giving a startling illusion of flight. Three successive circles of columns, each more massive than the last and all adorned at the base with bas-reliefs of strange fishes and stranger sea plants, supported the great arching expanse of the roof; and completely enclosed by the columns, on a steep and curving incline of the sapphire floor, were rows of amber seats grouped in a half circle about a flat open space, to form an amphitheater of unique design. As Rawson and I accompanied our guides into the building, we were not more captivated by the architecture than by the weird half-light of sapphire and amber. It was long, indeed, before we could recover from the sense of entering some matchless cathedral; long before, turning our eyes upon the amphitheater, we observed that not all the chairs were vacant as we had assumed, but that the front tiers were occupied by about a hundred light-gowned individuals.

Our arrival was greeted by a sudden murmuring of low musical voices; while our attendants spoke a few words to the assembled group, then took seats at one side and motioned us to do likewise. Automatically we obeyed, but as I crossed the room I received a shock, an electrical shock of pleasure such as one experiences upon meeting a friend unexpectedly in a strange city. In the foremost row, staring up at me with a curious and kindly air, sat that enchanting lady whom I had seen dancing along the colonnades. No doubt, as a sober and practical man, and one who had sworn to avoid all womankind after my betrayal by Alma Huntley, I should not even have looked at the fair stranger; but I was sadly impressionable, and felt a delicious tremor of joy at sight of those shining Madonna features and clear, magnetic great blue eyes.

I am afraid that, during the next hour, my thoughts were more on the girl dancer than on proceedings in the amphitheater. I was aware, indeed, that some sort of a debate was in progress, a discussion in which many of the spectators took part, and during which Rawson and I were more than once pointed out with expressive gestures. But, since I understood no word that was spoken, I let my imagination travel to the beautiful unknown. So pleasantly was I occupied in contemplating this fascinating being and her scarcely less fascinating fellows, that it seemed but a moment before the debate was over and the debaters rose and began to leave.

With a start, I sprang to my feet, realizing that they had probably reached some critical decision as to Rawson and myself. And when four or five of the men approached and motioned us away, I had the feeling of a captive being led back into imprisonment. The loveliest of all women had been lost to view amid the crowd, and I was more concerned at her disappearance than at the thought of my personal sufferings. But as I walked slowly out of that sapphire and amber palace, gentle strains of music began to play on unseen instruments; and gradually and insensibly I was comforted, and somehow was convinced that I should see that glorious womanly apparition again.

Once more we were escorted through the streets, but this time only for a few hundred yards; after which we ascended the steps of it columned marble mansion, and passed into a long hall whose stained glass windows cast a subdued illumination. We were wondering what to do, when our guides motioned us to cushioned seats of woven seaweed; and after we had settled ourselves at ease in the great sofa-like chairs, two of the men left us momentarily and returned with a feast of some substance reminding me of mushrooms flavored with honey.

At first we were suspicious, and hesitated to eat; but the honest, frankly puzzled faces of our hosts persuaded us of our folly; and we found the dish, while strange to our palates, not only appetizing but also invigorating after our long fast.

When we had eaten and the remains of the meal had been borne away a man came in laden with five or six variously colored cloths, which I recognized as the native costumes; and having spread these out before us, he motioned us to discard our clothing and take our choice of the new apparel. Our attendants then politely withdrew, leaving us more perplexed than ever.

It was long before we could make up our minds to try the native garb. And while we stood casting doubtful glances at the colored garments our gaze traveled to a score of paintings on the walls, most of which arrested our attention by their startling subject matter. More than half were of a marine type, and depicted ocean caves where the giant squid or octopus wavered through the gray depths, or sea-gardens where the many branching coral was the playground for shimmering blue and yellow fishes; while the other and more remarkable half-portrayed scenes of ruin and destruction on a scale to stagger the imagination.

One, for example, pictured a city with slender skyscrapers not unlike those of New York, but all of them were crumpled and toppling as from some titanic blast. Another, which likewise represented a many-spired city, showed the ocean rolling up in one colossal wave and battering and washing away the buildings; and a third, the most ghastly of the group, depicted a sea bottom strewn with the wreckage of great stone edifices, among whose vacant towers and windows the sword-fish and the eel sported and the fanged shark pursued its prey.

"What a morbid people," I remarked, "that its artists should delight in scenes of flood and ruin. Or have they striven to represent some actual disaster?"

"Maybe we'll soon know," Rawson suggested—when suddenly I heard something that made me stop short and forget all about tidal waves and sunken cities.

"Saints in heaven, that's a good one! Yes, that's sure the time I put it over you, boys!" came to me in indistinct tones, accompanied by a loud guffaw. And Rawson and I, our mouths falling wide open, gaped at one another in joyous surprise.

"Stranahan!" we cried.

A moment later, having made our way through a columned hallway into an adjoining room, we were met by the strangest sight we had yet seen in this land of many wonders.

Sprawled on the floor, absorbed in the distribution of a pack of cards, were the four lost seamen, all of them looking grotesque beyond words in their colored native garments, and Stranahan appearing particularly outlandish in his gown of pale green, his trouser legs showing from beneath, his blue sailor's blouse conspicuous through the open neck in front.

THE WILL OF THE MASTERS

"LORD HAVE MERCY on me, if it ain't Harkness! And Rawson, too!" exclaimed Stranahan, leaping to his feet, and seizing our hands in a crushing grip. "By all things holy, I thought I'd never see you again!"

For a moment we were unable to reply, so great was the confusion of shouts, greetings, and questionings. Delighted as we were, our first words came in gasps.

"Well, and what're you doing in this part of the country?" Stranahan finally asked, with a smile, "I thought you were safe in the old *X-111*."

"Nothing is safe in the *X-111*," I replied. "Captain Gavison sent us out for you when you didn't come back."

"I'm sorry to hear that," declared Stranahan, ruefully. "You know I hate to disobey orders, but I'm afraid I'll have to. We won't be coming back just yet."

"What makes you think not?"

"I don't think it—I know it," he maintained. And, leaning on one foot against a marble column while one brawny hand stroked his chin, he continued, ruminatingly, "suffering sea snakes, take me for a fool? Suppose I'd be here if I could find a way out?"

"But can't you?"

"No, by the devil! Neither can you... We're all prisoners here."

"You mean, prisoners in this building?"

"No. God blast you, not in this building! In this town!"

"Well," I laughed, "this town makes a fair-sized jail."

"You won't think so for long," warned Stranahan. "Lord strike my heart from my breast if I ever saw a deader place, except maybe my own home town on a Sunday afternoon!"

Recovering from this outburst, he recounted his experiences. Like us, he and Ripley had reached the city after ambling among the outlying colonnades and temples; but, unlike us, they had not been so unfortunate as to be trapped in one of the buildings. Upon entering the city, they had been met by several natives; and, suspecting that these strangers were hostile-minded, Stranahan had whipped out his revolver and fired a warning shot towards the crowd. So far as was known, no one had been injured, but all had been badly frightened; and for a while the two seamen had had the freedom of the town.

They were ultimately stopped, however, by a band of determined looking natives. Though they were apparently unarmed and used no violence, these men overpowered the intruders in some inexplicable way. Not only were Stranahan and Ripley deprived of their pistols, but they were rendered docile as children and were escorted, as we had been, to the palace of amber and sapphire where a hundred pale-robed individuals debated their fate. Next they were brought to their present dwelling, where they were clothed, fed, and reunited with Stangale and Howlett, who had preceded them to the city. They had now been living here for several days, during which they had been treated with unexpected civility and even allowed to roam at will through the streets; but whenever they had approached the boundaries of the town they had encountered a band of citizens who, by shouts and gestures and a mysterious but irresistible power of suggestion, had convinced them that they must not leave.

Drawing towards the end of his recital, Stranahan was telling how he had been compelled to wear the local costume when he was interrupted by the entrance of several natives, who had been looking for us in the adjoining room and seemed annoyed at our disappearance.

Unceremoniously they led us back to the other apartment, where the half-dozen robes lay in wait; and, realizing from their gestures that we must don the native garb, I promptly slipped into an orchid gown, while Rawson exchanged his sailor's suit for an outfit of daintiest lemon. Both of us had difficulty in adjusting the garments, which were fastened at the shoulders by fish-bone devices resembling safety-pins; and we had our doubts about the sandals, which were drawn on at a stroke, and yet were held firmly in place by inconspicuous cords. But though we puzzled over our new apparel for many minutes, Rawson found in the end that his was on inside out, while the front of mine was where the rear should have been. Of course, we did not discover these mistakes for ourselves; but our attendants, on returning indicated the errors with smiles and laughter, before assisting us to dress like self-respecting natives.

As soon as this perplexing business was over, one of the men motioned me to a sofa in a corner of the room, where he seated himself beside me; and a second led Rawson to an opposite corner, while the others unceremoniously took their leave. My attendant, who was a tall man, neither young nor old, with classic features and keen gray eyes beneath a wide forehead, now began to go through a series of apparently meaningless gestures, accompanied by no less meaningless words. First he would tap his head and emit a peculiar sound; then he would touch his arm, his knee, his foot, always slowly and carefully pronouncing one or two unintelligible syllables. In the beginning, I might have thought him mad, had Rawson's attendant not been conducting a similar performance. But when at length he drew a small pad of paper from his pocket and began to write upon it with an instrument resembling a fountain pen, I understood clearly enough that he was trying to teach me his language; and now I gave him my undivided attention, noting carefully each object he touched and the corresponding sounds as well as the characters he jotted down upon the paper.

Then suddenly I saw light amid the darkness! At the first glance, I had observed the resemblance between the letters my instructor was writing and those of the old Greek, even as I had noticed the resemblance on the clay inscriptions; and it was not many minutes before I had discovered that some of the words, although not recognizable when pronounced, were written in a style closely similar to the Greek, and obviously built upon Greek roots. This was not true of all the words, but was the case with so large a percentage that I had hopes of being able soon to speak the language.

After about two hours, my instructor arose, shoved the pad of paper back into his pocket, and indicated that the day's lessons were over. But he smiled as though to imply that I was not an unpromising pupil, and spoke a word that I thought I recognized as "Tomorrow." Then, saluting me with a courteous wave of the hand, he joined Rawson's instructor, and went ambling out of view.

It was with a wry smile that Rawson rejoined me. "Say, get anything out of it at all? By heck, I couldn't make head or tail of anything. At this rate, it'll take me ten years to learn my A, B, Cs."

I did not confide that I had private reasons for feeling more optimistic than my friend, though I did offer my help, which was refused. Rawson now seemed to revel in lamentations. Hotly he deplored our plight; he no longer saw anything romantic about it, and least of all relished being made to go to school again; and he reminded me time after time of Captain Gavison and the crew, whom we had last seen stranded in the wilderness with the disabled *X-111*, and who were no doubt despairingly awaiting our return. Though I did not share Rawson's dislike of our present quarters, I had to listen when he spoke of our duty to out comrades; and regardless of the forbidding precedent set by Stranahan and Ripley, I felt that we must spare no effort to rejoin our shipmates.

As the doors of our dwelling were open and there was no one to interfere with us, we sauntered immediately into the streets. As usual, we found them almost deserted, hence had no hesitation about retracting our steps towards the city entrance. The various gardens and palaces were unmistakable landmarks; and so—in less than half an hour—we had reached the threshold of the town, before the great statue-like edifice where we had been imprisoned. The path of escape now seemed so wide open that we paused momentarily, a little suspicious at encountering no obstacles. But not a person was in sight, not an impediment was visible as we started up the slope to the colonnades and outlying temples.

We had almost gained the top, and I was already regretting our departure from this charming city, when half a dozen pale-gowned individuals appeared from above the ridge, their cries and gestures warning us back. They carried no weapons, yet could not have been more imperious had they borne loaded rifles; there seemed to be some hidden compulsion, some irresistible magnetism about them, so that our wills quailed and bowed to their wills. I do not know why, but we no more thought of disobeying them than a trained dog thinks of opposing its master. Back to the city we hastened, while they followed with faces stern and set; and; having re-entered the town, we made our way directly to the building we had just left, our actions still controlled as by some superior mind.

Upon our return, our first thought was to look for Stranahan and our three other shipmates. We had expected that they would be occupied, as before, by cards or some other time-killing game; instead, we found them seated in the four corners of the room, each with a native companion. From the peculiar gestures of those companions and their habit of writing occasionally on pads of paper, we recognized that they were giving lessons in the language of the land. Two of the newcomers were ladies, one of them being of matronly years; but one, who sat opposite Stranahan, smiling, making notes with her pen, was not only in the full bloom of youth, but had that singularly sweet countenance, those singularly clear and magnetic large blue eyes that could belong to only one woman in the world.

DISCOVERIES

KEEN AS WAS MY JOY UPON OBSERVING Stranahan's tutor, it was to be long before she would exert her eventual great influence upon my life.

Meanwhile, I was to resign myself to a regular routine, largely prescribed by those whom I had come to consider my masters. Each night (by which I mean the period of eight or ten hours when the golden orbs were quenched and the city was in blackness) I would sleep with Rawson and Stranahan in screened open air rooms on the roof. And each day I would live almost as though by formula. Aroused by the burst of light that marked the underworld dawn, I would take a plunge in a saltwater swimming pool in a court of our apartment. A few minutes later, I would join my companions in a repast of some fragile little native cakes along with a luscious fruit like a cross between the apricot and peach, which were brought to us regularly by well-laden carriers whom I observed likewise supplying neighboring houses. Breakfast over, we were free for a while; and then I would usually ramble about the city with Rawson or Stranahan, or sometimes with all my five former shipmates; and we would have a merry time laughing and chatting, inspecting the palaces, colonnades and gardens, and poking fun at any object that happened to strike our sense of humor.

After an hour or two, we would return to our apartments, to await our tutors, who had a habit of arriving in a band of six sometime towards noon. Stranahan was still the most fortunate of us all, since his teacher continued to be that woman of the Madonna features and magnetic large blue eyes; but the rest of us were also fortunate in a way, for she would always beam upon us with a bewitchingly bright, "Good morning."

At the end of about two hours, the tutors would leave for the day; but they would first provide us with work in the shape of simple exercises to be written, or of passages to be deciphered in textbooks of the kind used for six-year-olds. This "homework" (as Rawson wryly called it) would keep us busy until late in the afternoon, when a native would enter with a tray containing various savory viands: a gray bread made from a grain with a flavor like walnuts; a succulent vegetable like French toast well-browned; a spiced, starchy food reminding me vaguely of baked potatoes; cakes of a hundred varieties, and fruits shaped like tomatoes and tasting like Muscat grapes, or elongated like cucumbers and tart as oranges, or round and large as cantaloupes and substantial as bananas. But although delighted at these appetizing foods, we were not a little surprised and disappointed at the absence of much that we had once considered essential; we wondered why no meat, fish or other animal products enhanced the bill of fare.

After this meal (our second and last for the day), we were once more free; and we would spend the time until dark in strolling about the city, or in sitting around in a little circle exchanging anecdotes, or in propounding theories as to where we were and how we had arrived, or in playing cards or any other game we could devise. Except for our tutors, we had contact with none of the natives; for we were still too ignorant of the language to talk with the few whom we passed on the streets.

But we were much less concerned about the natives than about our old comrades. We were still held in the city by the same mysterious compulsion; and, as the days lengthened into weeks, no word of Captain Gavison and our absent shipmates reached us. For all that we could say, they might have died of starvation or, more plausibly, they might have been discovered by the natives, and led as captives to lodgings miles away. Should we see them soon, or at least have news of them?

Secretly I was determined to find out. But first it was necessary to understand the native language—hence I spared no pains to learn to read and write. Thanks to my acquaintance with ancient Greek, I progressed more rapidly than any of the others, and soon acquired the rudiments of a speaking and reading knowledge. Not only did my own ears tell me so, but my teacher admitted as much by his occasional nods and smiles of approval. But not content with my normal rate of advance, I fortified myself with much secret practice. Often I refrained from joining my comrades in their strolls and pastimes, but remained in my room with a pad of paper and a pencil supplied by my tutor. I would devote hours to writing in the native alphabet; or would jot down a list of words and phrases and repeat them aloud time after time, trying to imitate my instructor's peculiar accentuation.

It was only natural, however, that I should be able to read the language before I could speak it. Not more than two or three weeks had passed before I felt capable of deciphering any average native document. But, unfortunately, I had little opportunity to test my talents, for the only written material I saw consisted of simple, uninformative exercise books.

Consequently, I was grateful for that chance that put me in possession of several volumes intended for adult readers. One afternoon, for lack of better occupation, Rawson and I were examining the picturesque patterns of our veined marble apartment walls; when suddenly I stopped short with a cry of surprise, startled to see a little rectangle faintly engraved in the else unbroken surface of the stone.

Promptly I shared the discovery with Rawson. He echoed my surprise, and excitedly suggested that this was some mysterious trapdoor. Although I only laughed at this idea, I approached the rectangular patch to examine it more closely, and, in so doing, rested one hand appraisingly on the marble surface.

To my amazement, a portion of the wall gave way, swinging inwards on noiseless hinges. The displaced rectangle revealed a little closet or vault about three feet deep—a compartment filled to the brim with treasure! At least, it was filled with what I regarded as treasure, in the shape of scores of books...

Hastily I reached for the nearest volume, a heavy tome bound in a sort of artificial leather. The title rejoiced me; it was a "Lexicon of the More Commonly Used Words."

Aided by Rawson, I examined the entire collection. And as I read and translated the titles, I made discovery after discovery. Not that any of the books were the works of sheer information I desired most of all, but that all contained important hints and clues. Some seemed to refer to some great disaster, as in the case of one entitled, "Artistic Progress Since the Destruction"; another, which was called, "Speculations Concerning the Supermarine World," fortified my impression of being in some inexplicably sunken land; while several were treatises on such difficult subjects as "Inter-Atomic Engineering," "Marine Valves and Their Construction," and "The Creation of Artificial Sunlight."

But the book that most surprised me—a book that seemed at once a priceless find and an insoluble mystery—was the well-thumbed yellowing little volume at the bottom of the heap. Even today, when all that passed in those enigmatic realms is an old and often-repeated story, I am stabbed anew by my original astonishment at that discovery. Imagine the bewilderment of one who, having voyaged all alone to another world, suddenly finds himself addressed in his native language! Imagine this, and you will have only a vague notion of my amazement when, turning the pages of the book in that unknown cavern land, I recognized the name of Homer!

And not only did I recognize the name of Homer; I found it affixed to a poem not previously catalogued among his works. "Telegonus" was the title—and instantly I recalled that there had been a legend among post-Homeric writers of one Telegonus, the son of Odysseus and Circe, who had been sent by his enchantress mother in search of his father, and had slain his sire without realizing the latter's identity.

You may be sure that I wasted no time about plunging into the book. You may be sure that I took little heed of Rawson's surprised questions, but read on and on as fast as my knowledge of the language would permit. Truly, the poem was Homeric in quality. I recognized at once the swing of the inimitable hexameter; the opening passages, executed with epic dash and sweep, convinced me that here was a work not unworthy of standing side by side with "The Iliad" and "The Odyssey."

But how came the poem to be here in this weird undersea realm? How came these submerged people to possess a Homeric work unknown to the modern world? These were the questions that perplexed me as I followed stanza after noble stanza; yet ponder as I might, I could conceive of no explanation, but was as mystified as if I had traveled to Mars and there been presented with copies of Dickens or Shakespeare.

QUESTIONS AND ANSWERS

NOW, OF COURSE, I was doubly anxious to speak the native tongue. Not one of the scores of volumes cast any light on the problems that bewildered me, and least of all on the mystery of Homer's "Telegonus"; apparently I should remain in ignorance until I could converse with the natives. Hence I had need of that rarest of qualities—patience.

Yet, had I not been so eager, I would have found good cause for encouragement. I was still progressing, gaining a speaking knowledge of the language with a speed that spoke well for my training as a linguist. And it was not really very long before I was able to exchange ideas with the natives. At least, I felt that I was able to exchange ideas, and awaited only the opportunity to prove my powers.

The obvious course would have been to speak with my tutor, and more than once I was on the point of doing so; but always he seemed so absorbed in the day's exercises that I decided to wait. However, chance was to send me a more charming informant.

I had, naturally, not forgotten that entrancing woman, Stranahan's tutor. Indeed, how could I have forgotten her? Her exquisite features and bright eyes kept flashing before me at all hours of the day or night. Under her witchery, Alma Huntley was becoming no more than the shadow of a remote, misty past—and this although I was still a stranger to the fair one, had scarcely exchanged more than a formal greeting with her, and had no idea how to further our acquaintance.

Already, however, I had found my first faint encouragement. Was it but the blind fancy of an infatuated man which said that several times I had caught her smiling in my direction? Smiling calmly and yet kindly, with a look of interest that went a little beyond mere curiosity? I knew that I might have been deceived. Possibly I only imagined that once a slight flush had crossed the flawless alabaster of her features as she gazed at me. And, certainly I over-emphasized the fact that one morning, as she was arriving for her day's teaching, she had beamed upon me and pleasantly inquired, "And how do you like our country, my friend? Do you find things down here very strange and difficult?"

In my embarrassment, I had been able to reply only awkwardly and formally. But already my thoughts began to leap all hurdles, to the time when I would enjoy her friendship—though beyond this, as yet, I had not the temerity to venture even in hope. Eagerly I awaited the opportunity to know her better; and the chance came one day when she lingered longer than usual over her work with Stranahan, and did not leave, as ordinarily, in the company of the other tutors. Good fortune was to be with me. When she emerged from the marble doors of our home I happened to be strolling along the colonnade not a hundred yards away.

At first it was a shock to see her come ambling towards me all by herself—a shock of pleasure mingled with something close to dread. I actually had an impulse to hide behind one of the great stone columns! Yet, as she approached, I could scarcely take my gaze from her. Across the noble width of her pale face there was a serenity such as she almost always wore; but the light of a smile flickered about her lips, and her great blue eyes were withdrawn as if they looked only on some calm and perfect inner vision.

Slowly, diffidently, I moved into her path. For a moment she seemed not to see me; then, almost as though she had been expecting someone, her gaze was lifted to meet mine; and no, surprise was marked there, nor any annoyance, but only an un-looked-for pleasure. In low, musical tones, she murmured," Good morning"; while the glory of her whole gracious spirit shone in her eyes and illuminated her features.

"Good morning," I replied in the native dialect, and at the cost of greater effort than I would have cared to admit.

She still beamed on me charmingly, and was about to pass on. But in desperation I strove to detain her. "I beg pardon," I said. "I beg pardon, but please can you spare a minute? There are one or two questions I should like to ask."

She gave a surprised toss of her great golden clusters of hair. But a smile played lightly about the corners of her mouth.

"Of course, ask any question you want," she acceded, evidently puzzled. And, pointing down the colonnade to a circular marble bench enclosed by a ring of slender columns, she suggested, "Let us go over there."

When I found myself seated at her side, her vivid blue eyes looking inquiringly into my own, I felt as one who sees the Venus of some old master miraculously come to life. It was with difficulty that I answered when, in low sweet tones, she asked what it was that I wished to know; and when the first words came to me, they were forced out by an effort of the will, for I should much have preferred to sit there silently, staring in delicious admiration at her exquisite, animated face.

But not being able to continue gazing at her in speechless rapture, I answered her question with some commonplace remarks that expressed nothing at all of the exaltation within me.

"I am a stranger in this land," I began, picking my words with a translator's care, "and many things here perplex me. I wonder, would you not be good enough to help me? Am I imposing upon your kindness?"

"Oh, no, of course not!" As she spoke, I noticed how her upper lip trembled slightly, as though from extreme sensitiveness and sympathy. "We are always pleased to be of aid."

I was enchanted by this reply, for there could be no doubting the candor of her earnest blue eyes, which glowed with a softness equal to the magnetism they sometimes displayed.

Encouraged to the point of boldness, I risked a daring step. "Before I ask any other questions, shall we not know each other's names?"

"Naturally. I am called Aelios."

"Aelios…" I repeated, fascinated. "What a delightful name. And what is your other name, may I ask?"

"Other name?" she echoed, in astonishment. "What other name?"

I saw that I had made a mistake. "Then haven't you a second name?"

"Well, if that isn't the most outlandish idea!" she tittered. "What would I do with a second name?"

"Why, where—where I come from," I stammered, "everyone has two names, or maybe three or four."

"Oh, how perfectly ridiculous!" she exclaimed. "Just as if it isn't enough to remember one name apiece…"

She paused, and I was too much embarrassed to resume the conversation.

"How many names have you?" she continued, after a moment. And the playful light in her eyes told me that she could not have been more amused if asking how many hands or feet I had.

"Only two," I admitted, glad that I had not to confess the crime of a greater number. "I am known as Anson Harkness."

"Anson—Harkness," she repeated, slowly, as if savoring the sound. "Why, if that isn't the strangest I ever heard!"

"No one in my country thinks it strange. Of course, everything there is very different—"

"Yes, I know. You come from above the sea."

"How do you know?" I cried, astonished.

Again she peered at me in surprise, and also, I thought, with something of that puzzled air with which one regards a child who persists in asking the ridiculous.

"Why, you must come from above the sea. Where else is there to come from?"

"Then does everyone here know where we're from?"

A naive seriousness replaced the frolicsome air of the moment before.

"Yes, indeed. That's what we've all been worried about. We thought we were proof against invasions from above, and simply can't understand how you got here. Why, for three thousand years the Upper World doesn't seem to have suspected our existence."

"Three thousand years?" I burst forth. "Three thousand years? For God's sake, how old is this land of yours? And, in heaven's name, what country is this, anyhow?"

"Why, I thought you knew," murmured Aelios, with a look of surprise. "This is Atlantis, of course."

"Atlantis!" I ejaculated, my mouth hanging loose in overpowering amazement. "Atlantis!" And confused visions of a lost continent swarmed through my mind, and I wondered whether this could be the sunken world described by Plato.

But before I could utter another word, my attention was diverted. "Great Shades of Alexander, having a nice little tete-a-tete, are you?" came a familiar voice from the rear. And Stranahan, stalking up uninvited, slumped down into a seat just to the left of Aelios, and grinningly requested us not to heed him, but to go right on with our little talk.

THE SUBMERGENCE

THE ARRIVAL OF STRANAHAN WAS not without its effect. He not only interrupted our conversation at a crucial point, but made it impossible for the discussion to take a personal turn. I realized, to be sure, that his motives were those of good fellowship, but I felt that he displayed remarkably poor sense; and I may have shown my displeasure in the forced welcome that I frowned upon him.

But Stranahan was afflicted with no foolish sensitiveness; he seemed not to notice my frozen greetings. Like a self-appointed chaperon, he remained resolutely with us. He was not discouraged by his slight knowledge of the language, which made him a stranger to most of what we were saying; but appeared content to sit by in gaping ignorance, venturing an occasional remark with such poor display of grammar and pronunciation that I could only smile.

Yet our discussion was so engrossing that for minutes at a time I quite forgot Stranahan's existence. Even the bright kindled eyes of Aelios had for the moment no more than an impersonal interest, for I was making a discovery so strange, so amazing, so unprecedented as to upset my conception of human history.

"Can this really be Atlantis?" I heard myself inquiring, when the disturbance created by Stranahan's arrival had subsided. "Can this really be the famous lost Atlantis?"

"Lost Atlantis?" repeated Aelios, looking perplexed. "I didn't know there was any lost Atlantis."

As briefly as possible, I explained the legend of the ancient continent said to have sunk beneath the sea. "If there's any truth in the story," I remarked, "that was one of the supreme disasters of history."

"Disaster..." echoed Aelios, her perplexity deepening. "Disaster? This is the first time I ever heard anyone call the Submergence a disaster!"

"You mean, then, that there actually was a submergence? That a whole continent sank beneath the waves?"

"Why, of course!" she affirmed, astonished at so self-evident a question. "How else do you think we got here beneath the sea?" And she pointed significantly to the great greenish roof and the bright golden orbs above us. "Where do you suppose we can be now, except in Archeon, the capital of Atlantis?"

At this point Stranahan thought it time to let himself be heard. He drew his lips far apart as if to speak, uttered an inarticulate syllable or two, and then stopped short.

"What is it, my friend?" asked Aelios, turning to the seaman with a gracious smile. But since the latter could only gape idiotically in reply, I thought it my duty to answer for him.

"What I cannot understand," I said, returning to the question that had been puzzling me most of all, "is that you say there was a submergence, and yet seem to think it was not a disaster. Surely, if the whole island of Atlantis was lost—"

"What makes you think the whole island was lost?" demanded Aelios, a quizzical, almost amused light in her great blue eyes, "Why, the better part of Atlantis is safe here beneath the sea!"

"Safe here—beneath the sea?" I cried, in growing confusion, "How is that possible?"

"That is a long story. It goes back very far—thousands of years, in fact."

"And cannot you tell me that story? Remember, I am a stranger here, and everything is very puzzling. What is this Atlantis of yours? How old is it? And how large? And how did it come to sink? How did anyone survive the submergence?"

"Whole volumes have been written on those questions," declared Aelios, her bright eyes turning upwards with a winning smile. "But I'll explain as best I can," and she paused for a moment, while Stranahan craned his long neck forward, as if to take in all that she had to say.

"It is the most romantic tale in history," she resumed, speaking almost with exaltation, while she took on a far-away look, and her upper lip twitched with the same sympathetic quivering I had noted before. "Atlantis is one of the most ancient republics in the world, and at one time it was one of the most populous and powerful of all countries. Our history goes back more than seven thousand years, four thousand above the sea and three thousand beneath. At a time when Egypt and Babylonia were still unheard of, our engineers reared monuments greater than the pyramids."

"But just where was your country located? And how large was it?"

"It was in an isolated position a day's sailing west of the Pillars of Hercules. As for its size, it was large, yet not too large; a swift runner could have traveled around it between full moon and full moon. But today you might look in vain for its plains and snow-tipped mountains. All you would find is the wide foaming waters."

"Ah, how sad…" I could not help lamenting. "What a tragedy…"

"No, not a tragedy," she quickly denied. "There is no tragedy in the history of Atlantis, though, of course, there might have been."

"But is it not tragedy for a whole great country to be submerged?"

"It may be, or may not be," she replied, enigmatically. "In this case, it was not."

Noting my quizzical silence, she continued, with a reassuring smile. "No doubt you will find this hard to understand. In your world above seas, conditions may be very different from those of old Atlantis, doubtless you are spared the perils which compelled us to submerge our continent."

"Compelled you to submerge your continent? You don't mean to say you submerged deliberately?"

"Yes. How else? The Submergence—or the Deliverance, as it is sometimes called—was the most fortunate event in our history. We celebrate it annually at the "Festival of the Good Destruction.""

Once more she paused, as if uncertain how to proceed; while I joined Stranahan in a bewildered silence.

"So as to make things clear," she went on, her upper lip still fluttering, and her eyes smiling with kindly goodwill, "I must describe Atlantis as it was before the flood. Thirty-one hundred years ago, when the Submergence was first proposed, we possessed secrets which the Upper World may not have re-discovered even today. By that I do not refer to our art, literature or philosophy; the thing we were proudest of was our science. This, however, was a very lop-sided growth; it was most developed on the material side. It could, indeed, tell us how to compute a comet's weight and how to talk with Mars; yet, on the whole, it was more interested in such questions as how to create food artificially and how to utilize new sources of energy. In these directions it had done wonderful things. We had long passed the stage when we needed steam, gasoline or electricity to run our motors; we had mastered the very life-secret of matter, and could use the energy within the atoms to produce power equal to that of a tornado or volcanic eruption."

"Marvelous!" I approved, enthusiastically. "What magnificent opportunities that gave you!"

"Yes, that was just the trouble," pursued Aelios, the trace of a frown darkening her lovely cheeks and eyes. "There are some opportunities that no man should have—what would be the gain in giving a wasp the power of a bull? Why do you suppose, for example, that the decline of art was simultaneous with the rise of science? After thousands of years in which beauty had been one of the objects of life, men began to be bewildered by the idea of physical might; they came to build huge, intricate machines, towering but hideous piles of masonry, and miraculous flying boxes for getting from place to place. At the same time, they became ill with a form of insanity that made them want to destroy; they began to swoop down upon foreign coasts, picking quarrels with the people and finding excuses for killing thousands. Oh, it is unbelievable, but the records prove it is true."

"And your enemies struck back ferociously, and there was nowhere above ground to escape them?" I asked, fancying that I saw a trace of light at last. "Is that why you had to submerge your land?"

"No, that is not why," denied Aelios, smiling at my naivete, while a half-suppressed yawn from Stranahan did not encourage her to continue. "Not all our people were savages; not all believed we proved our greatness by the treaties we broke or the foreigners we stabbed in the back. Of course, the objectors were at first mere voices wailing against the waves; but the protest persisted and grew, even though millions continued to judge the cities by their size and science by its deadliness. Yet the time came when the party of rebellion was almost as numerous as the conservatives or 'Respectables.' At that time, the question of limiting mechanical power became an issue that threatened the life of the state. The climax arrived in 56 B.S.—"

"What does B.S. mean?"

"Before the Submergence, of course," explained Aelios, with a slight frown that instantly made way for a broad and glowing smile.

"In the year 56," she proceeded, "the Agripides ministry came into office. First, you see, there had been an open insurrection of beauty—lovers against the 'Respectables.' Then the Anti-Mechanism Party triumphed in a general election, and Agripides, known by his friends as 'Saviour of the World' and by his foes as the 'City-Wrecker,' began to carry out his revolutionary policies.

"I don't know how to tell you briefly about these policies. They were the most daring ever conceived by the human mind, for they called for the overthrow of existing civilization in favor of something better suited to endure. Agripides proved—yes, proved it by the researches of the very scientists he opposed—that the State of Atlantis, under current conditions, could not last more than two hundred years. Its best human material was being used up and cast aside like straw. Its best social energies were being wasted. Its over-rapid scientific progress was wrenching our minds and institutions out of focus. There was only one remedy—a complete change, a metamorphosis such as the caterpillar endures when it enters the chrysalis. We needed an environment of such peace and repose that society might have time to recover from its overgrowth and evolve along leisurely lines."

Another half-unconscious yawn from Stranahan forced a brief interruption. But Aelios had thoroughly warmed to her theme; and, disregarding my comrade's rudeness, she continued, "Agripides had been making much the same arguments for years. Yet I don't wonder that they caused many people to gasp and shake their heads. He declared, in a word, that Atlantis was not enough of an island. It would never be safe while exposed to commerce and worldly affairs; the only course was for it first to lance out its festering sores, and then prevent further contamination by walling out the rest of the planet. But since no sea was wide enough and no fortress strong enough to ward off the hordes of mankind, the one possible plan was to go where no man could follow, to seal Atlantis in an air-tight case—in other words, to sink the whole island to the bottom of the sea!"

"Good lord!" I exclaimed, horrified, "Sounds like a lunatic's ravings."

"No, quite the opposite. Agripides was not a lunatic; he was the greatest man that ever lived. Look, I'll show you," Aelios flung out, almost as a challenge, since I seemed to doubt her hero's greatness. And rising hurriedly and flitting a dozen paces down the colonnade, she pointed to a life-sized marble bust on a panel between the columns.

"See! That is Agripides! Does that look like a lunatic?"

Hastily, I had followed, with Stranahan at my heels; and he joined me in surveying the bust with a show of interest, though his puzzled expression proved that he neither knew nor cared who Agripides may have been. "The glorious saints have mercy on me; if he ain't got a beard like a goat!" was his only comment.

Not deigning to reply, I fixed my eyes appraisingly upon the countenance of Agripides. The hair and beard were perhaps a little long, I thought, unconsciously agreeing with Stranahan; but the features were the most striking I had ever seen. Like many of the faces that have come down to us from classical times, it combined intellect and beauty in a singular degree. The brow was broad as in the representations of Homer, and rose to a majestic dominance; the eyes were large and alert, the lips thin and compressed, the cheeks long and finely modeled, while the features were furrowed with deep lines of sympathy that reminded me of Lincoln and contrasted with a savage, almost tigerish determination more implied than clearly graven on the even contours of the face.

"Agripides was a remarkable orator, and a writer of force," stated Aelios, as we returned to our seats. "Hundreds of his essays and addresses have been preserved. They show such brilliance, vehemence and wit that you cannot wonder that he converted all Atlantis to his views. Or perhaps it isn't fair to say he converted all Atlantis—there was plenty of opposition, and even some armed revolts and insurrections. But Agripides was not a man to be daunted easily; and in the year 48, in spite of the objections of the "Respectables," he published complete plans for the Submergence.

"Those plans were more daring than his worst enemies had foreseen. He proposed, in fact, to cover a large part of Atlantis with a glass wall, reaching hundreds of feet above ground, and thick enough to withstand the pressure of miles of water. Near its base should be two great valves, one admitting the ocean into a broad canal or artificial river, and a second (at the opposite end of Atlantis) allowing the waters to be pumped out again by means of gigantic inter-atomic pumps. Deep wells and distilled sea water were to serve for domestic and drinking purposes; decomposed water would provide oxygen for breathing; and artificial sunlight, synthesized chemically so as to produce all life-giving elements, would supply illumination and support vegetation and human life."

"Yes, yes, that is all very good," said I, feeling that Aelios had not yet touched upon the essential fact. "But how did Agripides propose to sink the island?"

"Now that is a difficult question," she murmured, with a smile that was worth more to me than volumes of knowledge. "It involves technical engineering problems that I know very little about. But as I understand it, what Agripides proposed was to bury enormous tanks under the sea bottom far to the west of Atlantis. At a given signal, the water in the tanks would be raised to boiling point by means of split-atom bombs; and the resultant thousands of tons of steam, in their fury to escape, would cause an explosion that would burst the very floor of the sea. In one direction, there would be a gigantic upheaval and a lifting of the ocean bed; and in another direction, by way of reaction, there would be a sinking of the ocean bottom, since the strata not directly affected would tend to fill in the gap. Thus, while a vast area would rise thousands of feet (although not to sea level), another area would be forced downwards an equal distance; and that area, which would be of enormous extent, would include the island of Atlantis. Maybe I can make this a little clearer by the illustration of a common plank, one end of which cannot be tilted upwards without causing the other end to slant down. One may imagine Atlantis as on the lower slope of such a plank."

"But all of that is mere theory," I pointed out. "Certainly Agripides wouldn't dare put his trust in such unproved calculations."

"Oh, no, of course not. The computations were all tested by actual experiment. Aided by skilled engineers, Agripides made a small model of the continent and the ocean around it, reproducing every detail. Then, having caused an explosion under the proper conditions, he found that the miniature island sank just as he expected the real island to do."

"Even so," I argued, "wouldn't the great glass dome be split and ruined?"

"All that was provided for. The submergence was to be so gradual as to require several hours. Besides, as the explosion was to occur under the sea and not beneath the island itself, it would not shatter the crust of the earth near at hand, and would not be severe enough to affect the glass wall. In other words, the island was to be like a ship that sinks completely after striking the reefs, although only the prow has been damaged."

"Yes, I understand," said I, recalling my recent experiences in the *X-111*. "But even if the experiment was perfectly safe, how could Agripides persuade the people to submerge their homes?"

"It was just there that he proved his greatness," asserted Aelios, with an admiring glance in the direction of Agripides' statue. "Knowing that the most powerful force in life is imagination, he began to work upon the mass mind to show the dangers of civilization. Immediately after publishing his plans for the Submergence, he opened an exhibition palace presenting the most ghastly display in history. He had, in fact, constructed in miniature Atlantis as it would be if his ideas were defeated—and no one could gaze on that Atlantis without praying for the Submergence. Try to picture it if you can conceive of anything so hideous: the landscape blasted and black, and scarcely a green leaf to be seen; steel towers and smokestacks dotting the island like hills; great wheels and chains whirring and rattling in the darkness inside the buildings; poison fumes in the air, and steel jaws chewing at living hearts and brains; and the huge engines fed with the blood of men, and watered with their tears. Countless multitudes—men, women and sickly, pinch-faced children—were bound as slaves to the machines, and moved at their, automatic orders; and after they had served long and their limbs were growing frail, they were crushed and mangled by the very masters they had served."

"What a horrible picture!" I cried, with a shudder, "But, certainly a gross exaggeration...?"

"No. Agripides had no need to exaggerate. He simply showed the logical advances upon existing advances. But this was the least gruesome of the exhibits. The most frightful half of the display was entitled 'The Triumph of Science.' Here again he depicted many-towered cities; but the wheels were not revolving, though clouds of smoke were in the air. At first sight, you would hardly have recognized them as cities at all; they were mere heaps of stone and iron; many of them had been broken to fragments, some had toppled over, others showed bare mangled frameworks of steel. And as for the inhabitants—there was only an occasional sign of them: here one gasping for breath, writhing on the ground like a tormented worm; there one groping crazily through the ruins, with torn limbs, and blinded eyes; yonder a family group lying sprawled across the pavements, with pale faces convulsed in agony.

"If you had looked for the source of the destruction, you would not easily have found it; you might not have known of the invisible poison rays that filled the atmosphere. But far above, so high as to be scarcely visible, you might have seen a mosquito-like fleet buzzing on its way."

Aelios paused, a deep seriousness darkening her features. And as I sat there staring at her in silence, I could not but reflect what unspeakable distances separated the bloody picture she described from the enchanting scenes among which she dwelt.

"It may all seem unbelievable," she continued, smiling across at me with an almost childish confidence. "I know that you will be shocked to learn that men could have fallen so far beneath the beasts. But Agripides proved every assertion. Naturally, the people were not eager for the disasters he pictured; and our great leader, acting at the psychological moment when all Atlantis was aroused, convened the National Assembly, and polled a majority of—three to one for the Submergence. This majority being confirmed by a people's referendum, Agripides immediately began to carry out his revolutionary project.

"Forty-eight years were consumed in the preparations. In that time, Atlantis found herself halfway towards realizing Agripides' direst prophecies. The island of Antiles, a small republic located far to westward, spied out and enlarged upon the schemes of Atlantean militarists, and manufactured a fleet of poison-bearing aircraft capable of spraying death upon whole cities. No one for a moment doubted whom they were aimed against! Unfortunately, the danger could not be averted by diplomacy, since the nations had sunk so far that they could no longer trust one another's promises. On the other hand, to combat the catastrophe by force of arms would be to drive Antiles into striking all the sooner. Thus, the dread of disaster arose to restrain last-moment vacillation.

"Agripides himself, I am sorry to say, did not live to see his plans consummated. Such a happiness was more than he had hope for. He was already old when his ideas won approval. But, dying peacefully in 15 B.S., he lived long enough to supervise the most important parts of the project and be assured of its success.

"In accordance with his directions, a reinforced glass wall many layers thick was erected over the most picturesque part of Atlantis, the rest (including the site of many cities) being held not worth saving. Steps, of course, were taken to ensure the people's health and comfort after the Submergence, to rear palaces and homes, to duplicate the sunlight, and to produce food chemically. Then, just before the Good Destruction, all power-driven machines, except the most essential, were piled up in the doomed part of the island, to be drowned together with the towers of the deserted cities.

"However, don't imagine that all the people were content to be sunken. About one-third emigrated eastward in a great body a few months before the Submergence. This was what made us most sad when Agripides' plans were fulfilled and we sank at last to the bottom of the sea."

"Have you ever heard what happened to them?" I inquired.

"No, how could we? We have never established communication with the earth. But perhaps you, being from the Upper World, can tell us something about them."

"I am not sure but what I can," I replied, slowly, thinking of the ancient Greeks and their resemblance's to the Atlanteans, and wondering whether the immigrants from the sunken island might not have been among the original settlers of Athens and Corinth.

And then, recalling the mystery of the "Telegonus," that powerful lost Homeric epic, I perceived a possible clue. "Tell me," I asked, with apparent irrelevance, "what do you know about Homer?"

"Homer?" she echoed. And then, with the ease of perfect familiarity, "Why, he was one of the greatest poets we know of—almost equal to the best since the Good Destruction. He lived at about the time of the Submergence, in a country far to the east, with which we traded despite its half-barbarous condition. It was, in a way, a sort of dependency of Atlantis; its people acquired their alphabet from us, along with their language and many of their institutions. Sometimes we've wondered if that was where the Atlantean migrants settled—"

"Ah, I see," I said, with a flash of understanding. "Then you mean—"

But even as I opened my mouth to speak, interruption burst upon us from an unexpected quarter, and, with a jolt, I returned from ancient Atlantis to the realities of my own life. "Hello, boys! Hello! Hello! There they are, there they are..." came in loud familiar tones from our rear, followed by a salvo of cheers. And before Stranahan and I could quite realize what was happening, we felt our hands grasped in a multitude of hands, and found ourselves surrounded by dozens, literally dozens of well-known faces. The first I recognized was that of Captain Gavison, who grinned happily in welcome; then I distinguished one after one of the faces of the seamen, apparently all of them, and all of them talking, laughing, crowding about, slapping us on the back, and shouting greetings in a tumultuous chorus.

TRIAL AND JUDGMENT

TO OUR DISAPPOINTMENT, THE arrival of Captain Gavison and his men was not explained at first. A score of the natives, who stood frowning in the background, appeared to object to our conversation, and began motioning the newcomers to follow them. And all, from the Captain down, obeyed as though in response to an absolute master, marching in regular formation and with every appearance of discipline.

Having nothing better to do, Stranahan and I trailed in their wake, for Aelios had murmured a hasty "Goodbye" and had tripped out of sight around a bend in the colonnade.

In a few minutes, we saw our comrades enter a building we well knew: the palace of sapphire and amber. Expecting to be ordered out, we made bold to follow, passed through the gates without attracting any attention, and reached the central amphitheater, where hundreds of natives had assembled as though in debate. Many an eye was turned upon the newcomers in amazement; but there was no audible word at our entrance. And when Gavison and the crew were motioned to seats, Stranahan and I did not hesitate to join them.

But the unlucky Stranahan was doomed to further boredom. For nearly an hour he was compelled to listen to a discussion of which he understood scarcely a word. Certainly, he had cause to envy me, for I easily followed most of what was said—and how enticing I found it!

The leader of the debate was a broad-browed woman, with a firm and distinguished manner, and more than a trace of beauty despite her graying hair. But she spoke comparatively little; six or eight of the audience took turns in standing in the open space in front of her and delivering brief addresses. At first I imagined that they were discussing some question of politics, and was surprised to discover that what they were arguing was no mere practical matter, but concerned the architecture of a new building, the "Palace of the Ten Arts." One of them suggested a lagoon fronting the edifice, a second recommended rainbow fountains, and a third favored an arcade of multi-colored crystal; and all the proposals were heard with equal respect, and carefully noted down by the leader.

When at length all who wished had had their say, the speaker declared the meeting open for further business. And then it was that a tall young man, whom I had recognized as one of the attendants of Gavison and his men, arose and advanced with a determined air. A hush had come over the gathering; all eyes were fastened earnestly upon the young man.

"Fellow citizens," he began, in a deep-toned voice that shared in the musical quality common to his people, "I must bring to your attention today a matter unique in our history. But first let me recall to your minds several momentous facts. A few weeks ago we were astonished to find in our midst two creatures whose sallow complexions, grotesque costumes, and still more grotesque features proclaimed them not to be natives of Atlantis. How they could have penetrated beneath the glass dome of our country we could not imagine, but it was decided that it would be advisable to educate them in our language, and then question them in the effort to solve the mystery. This decision was reinforced by the appearance of two more of the queer creatures a day or two later, and then again by the arrival of a third strange couple. While it was feared that our age-old seclusion had been broken by an invasion from the Upper World, it was agreed that for the present the best course would be one of vigilant silence."

The speaker paused, and cleared his throat. "Only yesterday, fellow citizens," he continued, "you heard the startling sequel. A field naturalist, roaming along the Salty River in the wilderness beyond the Border Colonnades, made the most surprising discovery of his life—a peculiarly ugly, rod-shaped ship of unknown type, fairly swarming with uncouth humans! Naturally, the scientist was alarmed; and, having made his escape, hastened back to the city for aid against the aliens. As he described them, they were in every respect like the barbarians mentioned in ancient annals, great brawny beings of unkempt and ferocious appearance. But we knew that they could be no more redoubtable than their kindred whom we had already captured; we knew that they would be subdued by the irresistible magnetic wills with which nature had endowed our race. And when an expedition of twenty men set out one morning, we had reason to believe that the aliens would be here by evening for trial before this assemblage.

"As you observe, we have not been disappointed. But now, fellow citizens, the problem arises. The prisoners are unclean as well as wanton and unprincipled men. Contrary to regulations, they have been catching fish in the Salty River. They have been slaying innocent crabs and turtles, and—disgusting though the idea be—boiling and eating them! They have been polluting the water of the stream; they have been trampling rare seaweeds, and beating to death the daintiest water-flowers; they have scrawled outlandish designs on the delicate pink and blue of the roof-bearing columns!

"But all of this, criminal though it be, may be overlooked for the moment. The chief problem is of wider consequence. For the first time in more than three thousand years, the principles of Agripides have been violated. Visitors from outside have appeared. We are in danger of contamination by the Upper World... How the invasion was made is now clear: the barbarian ship, equipped to travel under the sea, was sucked into the whirlpool at the ocean entrance of Atlantis, and forced into the valve admitting the waters of the Salty River. Of course, this trespass may have been accidental. But remembering the warlike ways of the Upper World, I suspect that it was cunningly planned, and that other invading craft—if not a whole invading fleet—may be expected to arrive. Fellow citizens, what is your opinion?"

Amid general silence, the speaker took his seat. But in my mind a storm was raging. I was infuriated at the tall young man's misstatements. With a lack of self-consciousness that I can explain only by my blinding anger, I found myself doing the unprecedented.

Springing to my feet, I demanded, hotly, in the native tongue, "Friends, may I say a word?"

Instantly hundreds of pairs of eyes were turned upon me in surprise.

"Certainly, say all that you wish," rang out the clear, well-rounded tones of the lady leader of the debate. "This is the Hall of Public Enlightment, you know, and any person with anything to say will be heard gladly."

"Go on, old sport, give it to 'em good!" whispered Stranahan into my ear, although he could not have caught the drift of what was happening. And, with his words rankling in my mind, I started towards the speaker's space.

But as I took my place before the silent, staring multitude, I wished myself safely back in my seat. What right had I to address this strange assemblage? What reason to expect that I could speak their language intelligibly? Yet somehow, after gaping stonily at the spectators, I began to utter a series of more or less connected sounds. I did not say what I had intended, and I suspect that more than one English word got intertwined with my Atlantean; but I was encouraged to see all eyes fixed upon me in apparent interest.

After a vague, spluttering introduction, I began to find myself on fairly solid ground. I declared that I could answer many of the previous speaker's questions. I explained that my companions and I were not barbarians, but representatives of the highest modern civilization. I stated that we had no evil intentions, having come to Atlantis by chance, and not being the forerunners of a planned invasion; and I offered thanks for the good treatment accorded us, and expressed our intentions to abide by the traditions and laws of Atlantis.

As I took my seat, I could see that I had produced a favorable effect. Many were the nods of approval, and many the sympathetic smiles. Yet I knew that I had not made myself perfectly clear; and when a score of voices simultaneously requested my return to the platform, it was impossible to refuse.

Questions regarding my native land were now rained upon me. But whether because of my limited knowledge of the language, or because of the narrow range of the Atlanteans' experience, I had great difficulty in making myself understood. My description of modern attainments was heard with interest, but with a lack of comprehension that I thought almost idiotic. Thus, when I declared that the United States was a leading nation because of its population of a hundred and fifty million, its rare inventions and its prolific manufactures, my hearers merely looked blank and asked how the country ranked in art. And when I stated (what surely is self-evident to all patriotic Americans!) that New York is the greatest city on earth because of its tall buildings and its capacity for housing a million human beings in one square mile, my audience regarded me with something close to horror, and one of the men—evidently a dolt, for he seemed quite serious—asked what steps had been taken to abolish the evil.

But aside from a few such questions and an occasional murmured "Agripides was right!" my words brought little direct reply. The audience seemed quite unimpressed by my description of the wonders of modern industry and transportation. Someone would ask me, tersely, "And do men know more of love and happiness than of old?" and, thinking of the war, the havoc, the famine and the persecution that scourged the surface of the earth, I would have to bow my head, and answer, "No." Hence I returned to my seat feeling myself in disgrace.

The remaining business of the day was disposed of quickly. Following my withdrawal, the tall young man again addressed the meeting, pointing out that judgment had not yet been passed upon us. "Fellow citizens," said he, in conclusion, "I have a proposal, which, so far as I can see, is the only one possible under the unfortunate circumstances. Whether we like it or not, the intruders are here; and, though we did not will their presence, we must treat them humanely. Since we cannot dispose of them by violence, we must let them remain, while seeing that they are educated and put to work like all other citizens. But one thing above all else we must insist upon: the isolation of Atlantis must be protected, and the countries above seas must never learn of our existence. Therefore none of the aliens must ever return to the Upper World!"

It was with a sinking heart, with the hopelessness of one being sentenced to life imprisonment, that I heard the assemblage endorse this recommendation.

THE UPPER WORLD CLUB

IN THE SPACE OF A FEW hours, Captain Gavison and the crew were all arrayed in native clothes and lodged in sumptuous quarters throughout the city. How comical they looked in their new costumes of light blue, green and yellow. And how they grumbled at the change! But they acknowledged their relief at having left the *X-111*; and this relief was not neutralized even by the prospect of passing their remaining days in Atlantis.

During the past several weeks, they had had a wretched time. A spirit of panic had grown among them when Rawson and I had failed to return from our searching expedition, and neither bribes nor threats could induce any of them to follow us. Anxiously they had remained near the disabled ship, drinking the distilled water of the Salty River and snatching what food they could from the land while exhausting their vessel's reserves. How long they could have held out, none of them could say, but the arrival of the natives was most timely; madness had been overtaking them with the delay and the suspense, and bloody disaster might have broken out.

But this does not mean that they were contented with their new surroundings. For some time they walked about like men in a daze, or, rather, like men who know they are dreaming; they stared with incredulous eyes at the marble columns of the Sunken World, its sculpture-lined thoroughfares and statuesque palaces. And what wonder if they were dazzled and a little frightened at this beauty, which seemed so cold and alien? What wonder if the more superstitious shuddered a bit at times, and muttered to themselves? What wonder if they missed the familiar things of the earth, the scenes and faces they had left behind them, the habits they had discarded, and all the old, remembered life?

Fortunately, they were not always free to brood over their misfortunes. Like the six who had preceded them to Archeon they were at once supplied with tutors to teach them the Atlantean tongue; each received at least two hours' instruction a day, and each was required to devote several hours to prescribed written exercises. And although most of them grumbled and swore at this enforced application, the tutors persisted, and prevailed by means of that magnetic dominance I had often noted in the Atlanteans; so that all the crew, from grizzled old McCree to callow young Barnfield, were soon plodding over their grammar and spelling.

But among a group of nearly forty men, it was only natural that some should make abler students than others; natural that, while the more backward still struggled with their A, B, Cs, others should stride towards a speaking knowledge of Atlantean. Among the latter was Captain Gavison, who still had a position to maintain and could not let himself be outdone by his men. Whether because of a natural aptitude or of diligent application, he speedily outdistanced all the others, with the exception (I must modestly admit) of one whose pre-war speciality had been Greek. And partly on this account, but more largely owing to the force of habit, he remained our acknowledged leader; his word was still law, his approval a favor to be courted, his anger a thing to make one quail, although his commission from the United States Navy could give him no authority here in Atlantis.

I believe that it was at Gavison's prompting that we took the step that was to band us more closely together. At all events, the step was inevitable; for we were like kinsmen isolated among strangers. One afternoon we found ourselves convening—the whole thirty-nine of us—in a little colonnaded court in one of the city parks. All were waiting expectantly, for it had been whispered that important events were in store; and there was a buzzing of excitement when Gavison arrived, and, taking the center of the stage, launched into an address.

"The proposal has been made," he announced, beginning without formality, "that we all join forces by forming a social club. We're all in the same boat still, you see, even though we're out of the X-111. Most of us feel pretty much out of place down here in Atlantis. We find the people strange, the land stranger still, and the customs strangest of all. So the best way will be to stick together and try to make things pleasant for one another." And in this vein he continued for five or ten minutes.

When he had finished, he asked for opinions—and received them in abundance.

"If we got together and started a club," summarized Stangale, whose views were those of the majority, "things might begin to look a little less dead. Seems to me every day down here is Sunday."

"Sure, and they've got lots of Sunday closing laws, too," Stranahan contributed, with a wry grimace towards the massive columns and tinted statuary.

Very tactfully Captain Gavison reminded Stranahan that the question to be decided did not concern Sabbath regulations. "Now how many are in favor of a social club?" he demanded, in his most official tone, by way of keeping the discussion to the point.

This proposal having been accepted by unanimous acclaim, the next question was one of nomenclature. Various names were suggested: "The Franklin D. Roosevelt Club," "The U.S.A. Club," "The X-111 Club," "The Underseas Association." But finally, after much debating, we decided that since we were the sole representatives of the Upper World in Atlantis, the most appropriate title would be "The Upper World Club."

Having threshed out this important matter, we felt it necessary to elect the officers of "The Upper World Club."

Obviously, there was only one possible nominee for President. It seemed almost a matter of form to propose the name of Gavison; and once this name had been mentioned, the election was settled, for who of us would be daring enough to run in opposition, or even to propose another candidate?

After being duly installed in office, the Captain made his inaugural address. It was brief and to the point. He began by thanking us for the honor and promising to try to run the club as well as if it were a ship under his command. And he concluded with a declaration of policy...

"We're all caught like rats in a sinking hull, you know, so there's nothing to do but make the best of our prison. The Upper World Club should be the means. It should, first of all, bring us together in a social way. Secondly, it should give us the chance to discuss our problems, and express our views to the Atlanteans. Lastly, it should keep us all together, so that we can act hand in hand if the time ever comes to make a dash for liberty."

"That time will never come..." I surprised myself exclaiming. And seeing all eyes bent upon me inquiringly, I felt bound to continue.

"Let's not fool ourselves! We're buried beneath thousands of feet of water, and for all practical purposes America is as far off as the moon. Even if there were a way back, what good would that do us when we can't leave this city without permission? No, boys, we'd better look facts in the face. We'll all remain here till we're gray and toothless, and never see the U.S.A. again. But let's reconcile ourselves to our fate. Let's try to become citizens of Atlantis, and share in its life..."

But there was one effect of my words that I had not anticipated. When I had taken my seat again, the President turned to me, and said, "Harkness, I appoint you a committee of one to confer with me in drawing up the constitution of the Upper World Club." And with that the meeting adjourned.

And thus began my intimacy with Captain Gavison. I do not know how seriously he took the Upper World Club and its constitution, for at most times his grim, firm face was inscrutable;

but he acted as if he took it seriously indeed, and he and I spent hours together planning for the club, almost as though we had to arrange a pact not for thirty-nine individuals, but for thirty-nine sovereign states.

How much the club profited from our zeal shall always be a question in my mind; but I know that I, personally, profited a great deal, and believe that even Gavison was not without benefit. Although he had a habit of shutting his thin lips stoically and glaring upon the world with a set, impassive air, an occasional look of weariness and even melancholy in his stern gray eyes told me that he was lonely; and while he would have been the last man in the world to admit this openly, he admitted it tacitly by the amount of time he spent with me over the constitution of the Upper World Club.

As a result, we were drawing together by degrees; he was emerging from the shell of his reticence, as I was emerging from mine. We began quite naturally by discussing Atlantis and the Atlanteans; and gradually we wandered into more personal subjects. There came a day when I went so far as to tell of my former life, my training in ancient Greek, my love affair with Alma Huntley; and, responsive to my confidences, he offered one or two glimpses into his own past, and made himself appear more human than ever before, by stating that he had a wife and little daughter in New York, who, no doubt, were even now mourning him as lost.

"You know, Harkness, that's the hardest thing of all to bear," he said, while his slim fingers stroked his bristly beard ruminatingly, and the drawn lines of his gaunt face enhanced his habitual gravity. "If only there were some way of getting word to them... But I might be dead for all they know—and would you believe it, Harkness, sometimes it seems to me as if I actually am in my grave." And the Captain averted his eyes, and after staring into vacancy for an indeterminate period, he continued, more rapidly and almost with brusqueness, "Now you see why I'm so anxious to get back. For my own part, it wouldn't matter so much, but I can't help thinking it must be Hell for them up there." And he concluded with vivid pictures of blue-eyed Martha, his wife, and auburn-haired, six-year-old Ellen, who was waiting for the father who would never come back.

74

To all this I listened earnestly; and when Gavison had finished, I said what I could by way of consolation. In order to make his woes seem less by comparison, I exaggerated my own, and, in particular, dilated upon my grief at losing Alma Huntley—although, to tell the truth, she had been almost driven out of my thoughts by one even fairer than she.

It was from the time of our mutual confessions that my real friendship with Gavison dated. Naturally, we now lost sight of our former positions as superior officer and subordinate, and began to act as man to man. Often of an afternoon, when he had completed the day's studies, or of an evening before the great golden orbs had been extinguished, we might have been seen strolling together along the colonnades, or seated on seaweed cushions in a marble hall, discussing the art or the odd ways of Atlantis, practicing the Atlantean speech, exchanging reminiscences of the world we had left, or merely absorbed in one of those long silences that marked our queer acquaintanceship.

THE PAGEANT OF GOOD DESTRUCTION

WHILE MY INTIMACY WITH Gavison was ripening, I had not forgotten one whose friendship meant more to me than that of any man.

In the exhilarating moments of that first interview with Aelios, I had had visions of speaking with her often—visions of an Atlantis made bright by her presence. But, before long, I began to feel that I had been too sanguine. I did still catch glimpses of her when she gave Stranahan his daily lesson, and she would always nod ingratiatingly; but it was long before I had another opportunity to speak to her alone. Day after long, uneasy day dragged by until they had piled into a week, and slow, protracted weeks until they had accumulated into a month, before at last we had another conversation.

Then by chance I observed her in one of the great festooned courts at the base of a towering campanile. She saw me first; and—approaching—flashed upon me a smile that seemed to make the universe stand on tiptoe with joy. As I glanced at her glowing, graceful young form, I felt—as more than once before—as if some ethereal radiation emanated from her and enfolded her, making her appear almost as one of the immortals. But mingled with the very sweetness of my adoration there was a trace of sadness, for her beauty seemed to have a touch of the unattainable.

But evidently she had no idea of the thoughts that disturbed me. "I'm glad to see you, my friend," she said, simply and with unaffected kindness. "I have been waiting to tell you about our coming pageant. I know you will not wish to miss it, for it will explain many things you have wondered about."

"What pageant do you mean?" I asked, although Aelios alone occupied my thoughts.

"The Festival of the Good Destruction. Every year, as I've told you, we hold a celebration on the anniversary of the Submergence. This time it will take the form of a pageant. It will be the Three Thousand and Thirty-fifth anniversary."

"And when will the pageant be held?"

"In eight days. It commences at noon in the Agripides Amphitheater, which you will easily find, since it is the center of town. I certainly hope to see you there."

"I certainly hope to see you," I seconded. But at the same time a shadow crossed my thoughts—the shadow of a practical consideration that could not be thrust aside. Hesitatingly I had to confess that, after all, I would not be able to go.

"Not able to go?" she demanded. "What other engagement can you possibly have?"

Since some definite excuse appeared necessary, I explained—very reluctantly explained—that I could not pay my admission.

"Pay admission?" echoed Aelios, in such shrill surprise that I thought she had misunderstood. "What on earth are you thinking of? Do you imagine we are barbarians?"

"I'm afraid I haven't made myself clear," I hastened to state. "Where I come from, it is customary to pay upon going to a theatre."

"Really?" ejaculated Aelios, incredulously. "What for?"

"Why, what is there so queer about that?"

"By our lights, it is very queer. Almost outlandish, in fact! Of course, I do remember reading that people had to pay for everything before the Submergence. But that was so long ago… I thought the world had outgrown all that?"

"I don't see anything wrong about paying for what you get," I argued. "Don't they really charge for going to theatres down here?"

"Of course not! Fancy being charged for beauty or ecstasy or dreams… Why, you would as soon think of paying for the air you breathe, or the light that shines upon you! The State recognizes the theatre as the birthright of every citizen, just as it recognizes poetry, music and education. We all take part in giving the performances, and everyone is invited."

"Do you yourself take part?" I queried, my personal interest in Aelios overshadowing all thoughts of the native customs.

"Oh, yes, I try to do my share," she acknowledged, with a faint blush that only accentuated her beauty. "Sometimes I lead in the dances."

"And a most exquisite dancer you make!" said I, recalling my first enchanting glimpse of Aelios on the colonnade outside the city.

I would have liked to prolong the conversation, and fumbled in my mind for things to say. But before I had had time for further compliments, she had whispered a light "Goodbye," and had gone tripping across the court and out of sight through a little half-concealed door at the base of the campanile.

Needless to state, I eagerly awaited the day of the pageant. Not that I was thinking of the entertainment itself; I remembered only that Aelios had invited me, and that I should see her again. So utterly out of my head was I that her bright face now appeared to me constantly; her least smile, her slightest gesture, her most careless nod, was re-enacted a thousand times in my memory. And what if somewhere in the past there had been an Alma Huntley whom I had admired and fancied I had loved? She was now no more than a ghost amid the twilight of a vanished world.

When at last the day of the pageant arrived, I was so jubilant at the prospect of speaking with Aelios again that I could hardly restrain my impatience, but left for the festivities an hour earlier than necessary. My eagerness was such that I could not even walk at a normal pace, but unconsciously hastened my steps as when, in my native land, I had feared to miss a street car or be late for an appointment with Alma.

And as I hurried through the streets, striding more rapidly than ever before in this land of leisure, I heard a well-known voice shouting behind me, "Hey, wait a minute! Where's the fire?" With a sinking heart, I wheeled about—to face the grinning Stranahan.

"Great Jerusalem, you were racing so damned fast I could hardly catch up!" he panted, as he joined me. "Where you bound for, anyway?"

"Where you bound for?" I countered.

"To the pageant, of course." And, amiably unconscious that he might be interfering with my plans he suggested, "Well, we both seem to be heading in the same direction, so what you say to going together?"

"Fine." I had to acquiesce. And so it happened that Stranahan and I reached the Agripides theatre arm in arm.

As I might have known, we were much too early. The whole enormous open-air theatre was occupied only by a few children who danced about the stage and romped from tier to tier of the seaweed-cushioned marble seats.

Upon entering, I paused for a view of the theatre. Large enough to accommodate an entire community, it was constructed with a simple and yet majestic art. The seat arrangement was typically Greek, but the stage surprised me, not only by its size but by its appearance, for it was two or three acres in extent, and was enclosed by a ring of columns bearing a dome inlaid with ebony and gold. But what particularly caught my attention was an object which was evidently not part of the building—an amorphous mass many feet in height and covering more than half of the stage, but completely mantled in a linen-like, white cloth.

To my annoyance, Stranahan would not halt to view the building. Impetuously he started down the sloping central aisle, and did not stop until he had reached the front row, where he took the best seat as nonchalantly as though it had been reserved for him. Of course, I had to join him, but I could not help wishing he had chosen a less conspicuous position.

Before long, the theatre had begun to fill. Singly and by whole family groups the people were arriving, children and gray old men and bright-faced girls and youths; and all wore happy, expectant smiles, and all were clad in pastel-tinted gowns that made them look like animated flowers. I had a chance to observe the Atlanteans as never before; and, as never before, I was struck by the exceptional number of well-formed and beautiful faces; by the fact that everyone seemed tranquil and contented, and that there was little, if any, sign of tragedy or sorrow. Here was no evidence of the torn and withered, the distorted, the grotesque, the wolfish, the weasel and the bovine types so common on earth; even the old seemed to wear a sweet and placid, and at times, a beautiful look; and most of the faces bore the imprint of something akin to poetry and music, the exalted something that I had first noted in Aelios, and that set the Atlanteans apart from every other race I had ever known.

Even to be among these people seemed to produce a strange uplifting effect. I do not know what mysterious psychic currents were at work; but I remember that, as the theatre gradually filled, a singular sense of well-being and almost of thankfulness came upon me, a feeling of tranquility and repose, as though by some subtle transference of thought I had shared the mood of the multitude.

Nevertheless, there was a shadow across my happiness. As I scanned the faces that thronged down the aisles, I sought in vain for one countenance. Surely, Aelios had not forgotten the day, nor overlooked her implied promise to see me here. Yet till the last seat was filled, I scrutinized the faces of the newcomers without catching any glimpse of her.

Then, after about an hour, my thoughts were forcibly called to the spectacle in the amphitheater. A flickering of the great golden orbs attracted our attention; we noticed that they were being dimmed to less than half their usual brightness. At the same time, long shafts of light began to shoot out from all points of the horizon—multicolored shafts of every hue in the rainbow. In wide ambling curves they met the dark glass of the roof, splashing it with red and purple, orange and green, lavender and violet; and for many minutes the play and interplay of light continued, the searchlights seeming to work out all manner of patterns and arabesques which endured for a moment and vanished.

The one thing to which I could liken this pageant of light was the music that sometimes precedes theatrical performances in our own land. The flashing colors had all the ethereal loveliness of music; and, like music, they prepared one for a mood of rapture and contemplation. And when at length the original lights had faded out, to be replaced by others that shone directly down upon the open stage, this mood was intensified; yet all the while I knew we had seen but an introduction to the real exhibition.

Suddenly, in the illumination of the many-hued searchlights, a white-gowned woman appeared upon the stage. She was very young, scarcely more than a girl, and her face had something of the same sweetness and radiance as Aelios; while by the glow of the ever-changing lights she seemed some shimmering, fairy thing, some apparition as unreal as rainbows or moonlit cloud.

Therefore I was just a little surprised when the elfin creature began to speak. Or perhaps it would not be correct to say that she spoke; her words came in a soft, wonderfully melodious voice half like song.

"Fellow citizens," she began, while a hush overspread the assemblage, "fellow citizens, for this year's celebration we have decided to offer a historical pageant. Imagine yourself borne backwards almost thirty-one hundred years, to days when the Submergence was not yet accomplished, and Agripides stood before the old National Assembly urging the Good Destruction. Agripides shall now appear before you, as he appeared to your forefathers above the sea; you shall be the National Assembly before which he speaks, and he shall present his views to you as he presented them to our ancestors, and depict for you, as he depicted for them, the reasons why Atlantis should become a sunken continent. Behold, here comes Agripides!"

With a wide-sweeping bow, the speaker ceased, retreating from view through some unseen door. And at the same instant an invisible instrument sent forth a sound like a trumpet blast, and from the rear of the stage a tall figure appeared, walking slowly with head bent low as though in thought.

"Agripides! Agripides!" came one or two indistinct murmurs from behind me. And all eyes were fastened upon the newcomer, and I found myself a partner in the excitement of the multitude.

Even had I not heard the name, I should have recognized the advancing figure from the bust shown me by Aelios—there was the same bearded countenance, the same broad and noble brow, the same furrowed and sympathetic features. But one characteristic there was which the bust could not show, and which, while merely incidental, struck me with peculiar force. The garments of Agripides were not gay-hued, like those of modern Atlanteans, but were of a somber brown, and clung to his body so closely as apparently to interfere with his walking.

But I forgot all such irrelevancies the moment that Agripides—-or rather, his living representative—had uttered a word.

"Fellow members of the National Assembly," he opened, with a low bow, while I could almost hear the awed silence of the audience, "for the hundredth time I address you regarding the proposed Submergence. For the hundredth time, I remind you that we have no choice; it is a question of the Submergence either of the land of Atlantis or of its soul. Let me prove this to you. Members of the Assembly, let me show you how near the soul of Atlantis already is to submergence. Watch carefully as a stream of typical modern men and women passes by."

The speaker ceased, and from invisible corridors on both sides of the stage there came a noise as of shuffling feet, chattering voices, horns, bells, and clattering wheels.

"By the Holy Father, if we're not back in the old U.S.A!" muttered Stranahan, so loud that many of the audience could hear him. And he leaned forward so far I feared he would fall over the railing into the stage.

Truly, Atlantis before the Submergence must have been hideous! From both sides of the stage a slow procession of men and women began to file, the two streams passing each other and trailing out in opposite directions; and the faces and figures were the most repulsive I had ever seen. Some were so lean and scrawny as to remind me of walking skeletons; others, fat and bloated, waddled along like living caricatures; the majority had an unnaturally sallow, flushed or mottled complexion. And their clothes accorded with their appearance: they were all dressed in a drab brown or black, some with a peculiar steely collar that encircled their chins and ears, some with strange metallic waistbands that prevented them from turning, some with ornamental brass spikes that elevated the soles of their feet inches above their heels and converted their walking into a form of hobbling.

But what chiefly interested me was the faces of the people. Not a few, with heavy paunches and baggy cheeks, reminded me of nothing so much as of a certain bristly domestic beast; not a few others had features grotesquely like those of baboons, wolves, foxes, weasels or tigers. And a majority looked like nothing so much as the prey of tigers, weasels and foxes. Their eyes wore a hunted expression; they seemed continually confused and frightened, and had the look of cowed and beaten creatures.

All the while, as they proceeded across the stage, they produced a pandemonium of squeaks, grunts, hoots, rumblings, howls and snarls, some of which seemed quite familiar to me, while others sounded like voices of the wilderness. The acting, I thought, was marvelous; it was executed so perfectly that I quite forgot it was acting at all. Hearing the uproar and peering at the dark-clad multitude, I could not but think by contrast of Aelios and the grace and beauty that surrounded her; and I missed her even more keenly than before, and wondered if I should not see her at the pageant.

At last all the uncouth mob had gone trooping off the stage, and only the tall figure of Agripides remained.

"Members of the Assembly," he resumed, "you have viewed some typical citizens. Do you not believe them more deeply submerged than if a thousand fathoms of water rolled above them? But if you are not yet convinced, let me show you these people in their normal occupations."

As though at a pre-arranged signal, three or four huge instruments with long segmented oblong belts moving on wheels, were dragged to the center of the stage by half-invisible wires. I recognized these machines as forms of treadmills, for on each of the belts a man had been deposited, and each man was forcing his legs back and forth as though running in a desperate hurry. But no matter how furiously they worked, all the men remained in exactly the same places, for the belts slid backward precisely as fast as their feet pressed forward.

"Saints in heaven," opined Stranahan, with a puzzled frown, "they'd get there just as fast if they took their time!"

After a minute or two, the treadmills were pulled off the stage and Agripides briefly spoke once more. "My friends, I will now illustrate for you another leading occupation of our times."

I do not know what rare art of stagecraft was then applied. As if by wizardry, a bright bed of flowers sprang to life before us, and long-stemmed purple and yellow blossoms resembling tulips and hollyhocks waved above some retiring white-budded plant reminding me of the violet. Then from one side of the stage, before we had had time to enjoy the gorgeous blooms, there came a series of oaths, growls, curses, shrieks, hisses, and mutterings, gradually increasing in volume; and soon an amorphous mass of squirming, twisting, embattled men writhed into view. I could not tell how many of them there were, except that they were numbered by the dozen; and I could not make out what they were like, except that they were all soberly dressed. But it was as if a storm had been let loose among them; they were tumbling over one another, wrestling with the ferocity of wildcats, snatching violently at one another's arms, legs and necks, until they seemed little more than a blur of convulsive, wildly agitated trunks and limbs.

"Holy Methuselah, it's a new kind of football!" cried Stranahan, as he poked his long neck far forward.

Before I had had time to reply, the struggling men were pressing across the stage, and intruding upon the flowerbeds. But none seemed to notice, and the pandemonium continued until the actors were beating down the flowers on all sides and not a hollyhock, tulip or violet remained.

Then suddenly one of the men was thrust out of the wild multitude, and lay as if dead, his clothes ripped and torn, his body gashed and bleeding. But no one appeared to see him, and the shrieks and howls rang forth until another had been flung aside with broken limbs, and then another, and another. In the end only two remained standing, both grappling for a little metallic disc that glittered a deep yellow. With brutish snarls and screeches they wrestled over this trinket and at length, still wrestling, and with blood red, distorted faces, they tumbled moaning off the stage.

After this exhibition, there was silence for several minutes. I was glad when finally Agripides seemed to feel his audience ready for a change of mood, and again took the center of the stage.

"Members of the National Assembly," he proclaimed, "you have now observed modern life in two of its more common phases. You will find something no less familiar in the third phase."

This time a gigantic clattering black machine was rolled on to the stage, its innumerable wheels, belts and chains in rapid motion, some of them vibrating so swiftly as to look like whirring shadows. All about its sides, in a long even row, stood scores of grim-faced, sooty men, their feet clamped to the ground by iron vices, their arms fastened by long rods to the wheels above. And, meanwhile, those rods were moving, moving with rhythmic, clock-like regularity; moving up and down, up and down, pulling the arms of the men with them, first the right arm and then the left, then again the right and then the left, as though they had done so for all eternity and would do so for all eternity to come.

"The devil take me," muttered Stranahan, who still had to have his say, "it ain't the men that work the machines... It's the machines that work the men..."

I am afraid that these remarks diverted my attention and made me miss part of the performance, for when I next turned my eyes to the stage the scene was much changed. A great clawed steel device was reaching from the interior of the machine, seizing one of the men, wrenching him from his position like a misplaced screw, and casting him bleeding to the floor. And while he lay there moaning, a clamor of shouts was heard from off stage, and a score of battered men came rushing in and threw themselves down before the machine as if in reverence. And the machine, as though endowed with intelligence, seemed to hear, for it extended the same great clawed hand, clutched one of the men, and thrust him into the place of the rejected one. And now the arms of the newcomer began to work up and down, up and down, up and down, accompanying the steel rods in the same even and automatic fashion as the arms of his predecessor.

The next feature on the program was an oration delivered in Agripides's most celebrated words; following which the actor prepared us for the climax. "Members of the National Assembly," he said, still using the phrases first uttered three thousand years before, "I wish you to look carefully at Axios, which, as you know, is one of our leading commercial cities. First gaze upon its domes and towers as they are now; then behold them as they will be when the unleashed waters sweep across them; then open your eyes for a fore-glimpse of the golden era after the Submergence."

As the last words were uttered, my attention was drawn to the huge amorphous mass, which lay cloaked in white at one side of the stage. Invisible hands seemed to take hold of the covering, which slowly was lifted into the air, then slowly moved to one side and out of sight. At first I could gape only in astonishment— distinctly I was reminded of the paintings in various halls of Archeon. A city in miniature stared before me, but a city such as I would have expected no Atlantean to conceive! Not the faintest resemblance did it bear to this undersea realm of statue-like temples and many columned palaces; rather it was like a city of the modern world... Row upon row of box-like edifices, apparently of granite or brick, loomed at irregular heights and with flat, ungarnished roofs; tier after tier of little oblong windows looked out from the smoke-stained sides of the towers; slender defiles, so narrow that they reminded me of light-wells, separated the opposing ranks of masonry; and, at the base of these dreary gray pits, swarmed masses of dark-robed men and women.

"By the Blessed Mother, if it ain't little old New York," sputtered Stranahan, nudging me knowingly in the side.

Even as he spoke, I was startled by a noise as of a thunderclap. And instantly the midget men and women scattered pell-mell, vanishing through little openings in the walls. Meantime, new thunderclaps dinned, loud-rumbling and resonant, one crash pealing and reverberating before the echoes of the last had died away; while miniature lightnings darted from the great greenish vault above. As the display proceeded, it grew constantly brighter and more vivid; and I was wondering where it was all leading, when suddenly there came a blast so loud that I clapped my hands to my ears in terror. Simultaneously, a blade of light cut dagger-swift through the toy-like buildings, wrapping them in sheets of flame; the walls heaved and trembled as though in an earthquake's claws, and there came to my ears the rattling and crashing of falling masonry.

Then, while the clamor increased and the buildings heaved with the motion of ships tossing at sea, the ground beneath them gave a sharp lunge downwards; and, like child's castles, they all at once collapsed, some falling over their neighbors in smashing confusion, some shaken into dusty piles of mortar and stone, some peeled of their walls and showing great contorted steel ribs, some erupting into flame that crackled demonically and poured out dense black spirals of smoke.

Scarcely had the thunder of the overthrown walls died down when a new, more ominous roaring came to my ears, a tumult as of Niagara or of sea-waves splashing the cliffs. Out of the great earthen basin into which the ruined city had subsided, there issued a foaming chaos of waters, as though a reservoir had burst its dam; and, from all sides a white-flecked torrent plunged down upon the wrecked towers, which were rapidly sinking from sight. Heap after gigantic heap of debris dipped its head into the waters and was lost to view; edifice after edifice, dismantled and battered, were engulfed by the insatiable flood. And now the fires no longer burned and the smoke no longer soared; now only two or three tortured steel columns reached out of the indifferent sea; now only one was left, one lean and crooked metallic shaft like the agonized clutching hand of a drowning man. But soon even this had vanished, and the frothy-tongued blue waters gave no sign that a city had ever barred their path.

And as the last trace of old Atlantis faded, a grayness as of twilight suffused the scene; the golden lights became dim and dimmer, until they had fluttered out, and blackness blotted all things from our gaze.

But as we sat there spellbound in the dark, feeling like men who had beheld the end of all things, there came an airy change to break the dreariness of our mood. From far, far away, apparently whole worlds away, issued a faint tinkling music, half like the loveliness that one hears in dreams, half like the remote ghostly melodies borne to one across the wind. But gradually it grew nearer, gradually louder and more distinct, although its ethereal and elfin quality remained. At length I recognized that it came from a chorus of voices, a wonderfully sweet womanly chorus whose members may have been human, but seemed little less than angelic. For it was with a divine exaltation that they sang, and their tones were the tones of immortal sweetness and hope, and they seemed to assure us that all was well with the world and with life.

As the singing continued, the darkness was slowly dispersed; yet the great orbs above did not resume the full brightness of the Atlantean day, but remained subdued to a rose-tinged twilight glow. And in that twilight a troop of shimmering-gowned dancing maidens appeared, swinging from side to side with superbly harmonious movements of arm and waist and ankle until they seemed not so much individual dancers as parts of the eternal rhythm of the universe.

But whether or not the singing proceeded from them was more than I could judge; for my eye was caught by the leader of the dancers, and my thoughts were as if paralyzed. As she glided across the stage with motions like music, she smiled a gloriously sweet smile; and that smile seemed bent full upon me, though here my imagination may have borne false report. But with furiously thumping heart and a surge of tender feeling, I realized that Aelios had kept her promise to see me at the pageant!

AN OFFICIAL SUMMONS

THREE OR FOUR DAYS AFTER the pageant, I was surprised to receive a visitor in the shape of a serious-looking, gray old man. In one hand he bore a little green, sealed scroll, on which my name had been inscribed; and his grave manner, and particularly the meaningful way in which he held the document, filled me with alarm. Had I unwittingly violated some law?

But this fear was swiftly dissipated. "I congratulate you, young man," said my visitor, having made sure that I was the person he sought. "This is an occasion that comes but once in a lifetime." And with a sedate and deferential air, apparently not aware that the nature of his mission was a mystery to me, he passed me the document; then congratulated me again, and bowed his way out of the room.

I now suspected that I was the recipient of some high honor though I could not imagine what or why. No wonder that my fingers trembled when I ripped open the green seal! But again my expectations were to prove ill founded. The message proved to be very brief, and far from providing cause for exultation or dismay, it served merely to puzzle me.

"To the respected Anson Harkness," ran the handsomely formed words, "the Committee on Selective Assignment announces that it is ready for the hearings and examinations in his case. If he will be so kind as to present himself at the Committee offices any noon during the next ten days, he may be assure that the investigations will be carried out with a minimum of delay."

And that was all, except for the signature of the Head of the Committee. Not a word as to what the Selective Assignment might be. Not a word as to the nature of the "hearings and examinations." Time after time I re-read this message, scrutinizing it until I had memorized it in its entirety; but the more I read the more perplexed I became. Just what was to be investigated and what decision was to be reached?

As I could think of no plausible answer to these questions, I determined to ask one of the natives. However, I was acquainted with only one Atlantean aside from my tutor, and that one (whom, of course, I was doubly anxious to consult) was Aelios.

But how isolate Aelios long enough for a conversation? After some thought, I decided on the most obvious idea: to learn where she lived and visit her, and so solve the mystery of the Selective Assignments at the same time as I furthered a still more desirable end.

Yet only by a severe effort did I find the courage to carry out my plans and follow Aelios one afternoon at the end of her day's instruction. Through many curving lanes and avenues I trailed after her and her fellow tutors, pressing close to the columns and the walls of buildings, like a detective tracking his prey. At length, as we approached the outskirts of the city, Aelios waved farewell to her companions, and started off alone down a little path bordered by a deep-red, geranium-like flower. Thinking this to be my opportunity, I hastened my footsteps. But before I could overtake her, she reached the end of the path. Unaware of my approach, she entered the arching doorway of a house (or should I call it a palace?) with curving convex walls of the color of pearl.

For several minutes, I stood wavering without. Then, hesitantly, I forced my feet to the threshold, and rapped at the violet, stained-glass door.

It was but a minute before I was answered by the sound of approaching footsteps, and the door swung open, bringing me face to face not with Aelios, but with a young man of about twenty-five, broad-browed and sparkling-eyed like most of the Atlanteans.

"Pardon me, is this—is this where Aelios lives?" I gasped, in embarrassment.

"Yes. Aelios lives here," he returned, with a winning smile. "You would like to see her?"

I mumbled in the affirmative, and was admitted into the house. Having passed through a broad hallway or vestibule illuminated by large swinging orange-colored lamps, we entered a tapestried sitting room featured by lanterns of pale blue. The young man bade me be seated on the seaweed-decorated sofa, and left me momentarily; and in my brief snatch of solitude I was assailed by storms of jealous questions. Who was the young man? What was his relationship to Aelios? Was he her suitor? Or merely her brother? Or was she already married, and was this her husband?

At the latter question, I experienced in advance all the pangs of unsuccessful love. My head swam with senseless fury; I was weighed with despair, and saw myself the victim of hopes that could never be fulfilled.

I had just reached the darkest point of my broodings, and was telling myself that, of course, I could never attract so admirable a woman as Aelios, when I heard a well-known melodious voice murmuring, "What is the matter today, my friend? What are you so depressed about?"

Recalled from my dejection as from a bad dream, I sprang up to face Aelios, who was smiling graciously.

What I next said I can't recollect. No doubt it was some bit of nonsense not worth repeating; indeed, it might have been some bit of sentimental nonsense, had it not been for the unknown young man. But since I was not bold enough to inquire whom he was, and yet could not banish the thought of him, I held back from all personal advances in this our first private meeting. Nevertheless, whenever her live blue eyes flashed, they drew me towards her like magnets; and whenever she smiled her tantalizingly bright smile, I hungered to dash down all barriers in one long fervent confession.

Through all the epochs of adventure and terror that separate me now from that enchanted interview, I can recall the sparkling eagerness with which her words poured forth, like the wavelets of a rapid crystal stream. I can recapture the sage nodding and tossing of her head, the ripples of deep feeling that passed and re-passed on her mobile countenance, the luminance as from some inner sun that would make her whole face shine as she uttered some rare bit of wit or fancy. But it was she who did most of the talking, while I looked on in awed worship; and she was either blind to my reverence for her or else chose to ignore it.

"You can't imagine how strange it seems to be sitting here talking with you," she began, dazzling me with the radiance of her glance. "If anyone had said, even a few months ago, that I would actually speak to an Upper World man...why, I would have thought it was like chatting with the dead."

"To you our Upper World is dead, is it not?" I returned. "What do we represent but your discarded past?"

"It is odd," she continued, meditatively, "after all these centuries, many of us had come to think of the Upper World as scarcely real at all. Of course, we know it existed; but it was dwindling to a dim, remote, golden legend—as fairy-like and fabulous as the voyages of Odysseus. We were no longer able to imagine what the Upper World was like. Some of our antiquarians had even argued that such things as the sun, moon and stars were no more than myths. And then you arrived to make the Upper World once more real."

"Are you sorry we came?" I asked. "Sorry we interrupted your dream?"

The smile that darted at me was vivid with the illumination of her whole personality. "No, I am not sorry," was all she said. And little she knew how my heart fluttered at that simple statement.

"As for me," I asserted, "I am glad—very glad to be here!" And I longed to tell her why, in particular, I was glad—and why Atlantis meant more to me than the Upper World could ever have done.   But, somehow, the thought of the unknown young man intruded, and a wave of irrational jealousy checked my words as they were about to be uttered.

Yet for at least an hour we talked delightfully enough, despite my supposed rival; and not until I rose to leave did I remember the subject that had brought me to see Aelios.   And then, since the hour was late and my mood no longer prosaic, I did not care to discuss that topic long.   I merely showed Aelios the letter, which she glanced at briefly and with a smile; after which she surprised me by congratulating me just as the gray-haired message-bearer had done.

But she was very chary of information.   "When you go to the Committee offices," she suggested, "the whole matter will be made much clearer than I could make it."   And, after directing me where to find the offices, she added, "I'd advise you to waste no time, else you may lose your turn and have to wait another half year.   You know, that's what happened once to my cousin Argol, who met you at the door."

Gratified to have my doubts about Cousin Argol dispersed, I thanked Aelios and turned to leave.   My heart pattered happily when she accompanied me to the outer door; and I felt an electrical thrill of joy when she pressed her little hand in my great one, and murmured in tones that could leave no doubt of her sincerity, "Come again, my friend.   Come whenever you wish someone to talk with, I shall always be glad to see you."

It was with a triumphant glow that I found myself ambling down the flower-bordered walk towards the main avenue.   Aelios was even more friendly than I had had any reason to expect! Considering all things, I had every cause to be thankful, and who knew but that some day— But here again my thoughts reached a dazzling veil beyond which I would not allow them to penetrate...

THE HIGH INITIATION

PROMPTLY AT NOON THE following day I presented myself before the Committee on Selective Assignments.   The offices, which I found without difficulty, were located on the lower floor of an imposing blue-tinted granite edifice; and the Committee itself occupied a hall reminding me vaguely of a courtroom, except that its ornamental columns, busts and statues were unmatched in any courtroom I had ever seen. Before a long marble railing sat fifteen men and women, some old but several conspicuously young. All were perched on cushioned marble seats before little marble pedestals or writing stands; and to the rear were cases lined with parchment-bound volumes that lent the place a scholarly dignity. In front of them, across the railing, were half a dozen tiers of blue stone benches; and on each of the benches stood a pile of books, as though the spectators were expected to make use of their time during delays in the proceedings.

But I was not admitted at once into this great hall. First I was escorted into a small anteroom, where three Atlanteans—two youths of about twenty, and a girl of the same age—were seated studiously reading. Each carried a little green-sealed document, which made me wonder if they were not here on the same mission as myself; but all were so preoccupied that I had no opportunity to question them.

Hence I turned to inspect the room; and was delighted to observe a heap of books on a reed stand in one corner. The very titles proved alluring; some were works of information dealing with subjects so various as "Post-Submergence Mural Art," "The Rise of Government by Selection," "History of the Abolition of Crime," and "History of the Decline of the Upper World." Others were essays on topics such as "The Cultivation of Genius," "Is Altruism One of the Human Instincts?" and "How Atlantis Found the World by Losing It"; still others were works of literature, and included an epic poem on "Agripides," a volume of lyrics by some unknown writer of two thousand years ago, poetic drama destined for performance at the annual celebration of the Submergence, several novels, a collection of stories, and a romance of the far future entitled "Super-Art."

But what particularly caught my attention was a genial little satire known as "The Prisoner." This story, written in a crisp and simple style that I found delightful, recounted how an Atlantean of a thousand years before had been sentenced, as the penalty for his sins, to pass his remaining years in the Upper World. Having been sent above seas in a little water-tight craft propelled by inter-atomic engines, he had set about to seek his fortune; and, finding that the way to win distinction was to accumulate gold, he applied his superior Atlantean intelligence so well that he became fabulously wealthy. But, after attaining what was reputed to be success, he discovered that his wealth meant nothing to him; he was hungry for the art and beauty of Atlantis. Even though he could have purchased any treasure on earth, he took to morbid repining and brooded until he went completely out of his wits, which were finally restored when the Atlanteans took pity and let him return. And so the sufferer went back to his native land, after forfeiting his riches; and this was the last case of insanity ever known among the Atlanteans.

I had just finished this little story, when I was roused to reality by hearing a strange voice pronouncing my name. Looking up, I saw a lavender-gowned man motioning me towards the main Committee Room; and I observed with surprise that the youths and the girl had disappeared.

I found the central hall empty, except for the fifteen men and women sedately seated behind the railing.

"This is Anson Harkness, is it not?" rang forth the high-pitched, yet not unpleasant, voice of an aged man whose proximity to the railing declared him to be the head of the Committee. And after I had replied, the Head Member continued, earnestly, "Be seated, Anson Harkness. It is an important matter that brings you here. More than the usual amount of time and thought will be necessary before we can reach a decision."

The Head Member paused, cleared his throat, and slowly proceeded, "I trust that you will cooperate with us, for only so can we expect satisfactory results. Just as the ordinary man is betrothed but once in his life, so he appears but once before the Committee; and since, as in the case of a betrothal, much may depend upon the proper choice—"

"I beg your pardon, sir," I interrupted, unable to endure these long-winded sentences that added only to my confusion. "Would you mind telling me why I am here?"

The Head Member peered at me in mild surprise; his fourteen associates darted inquiring looks at one another.

"Why, yes, that is a proper question," he resumed; blandly. "I had forgotten; you are a foreigner, and unacquainted with our ways. You understand, of course, that foreigners were so totally unknown before your coming that the necessity for explanation has not occurred to me. However, the whole matter can easily be made clear. You are summoned for the High Initiation. In other words, this should be the happiest day of your life, since you are now regarded as having reached maturity and may enter upon your career of service for the State."

Having been a voter in the United States for eleven years, I was not flattered to be told that I had reached maturity.

None the less, I held my tongue, and listened patiently as the Head Member continued. "Your tutor reports that you have acquired an elementary knowledge of our language and customs, and suggests that you be assigned to service. Acting on his recommendation, we shall promote you to duties that accord as nearly as possible with your capabilities. But first a word as to our methods. Ever since the great social revolution of the second century A.S., which for a time threatened to engulf us in chaos, we have employed what is known as the Beehive System of Labor—which means that every citizen is required to perform a certain minimum of work for the State, in order to accomplish indispensable tasks. Fortunately, inter-atomic energy and the elimination of waste have reduced the essential work to one fifth of that thought necessary before the Submergence; and the average citizen now labors only two or two and a half hours a day. While there have, indeed, been occasional men and women so enamored of their employment as to insist on four or five hours, such excessive application is not encouraged, since it is believed to blunt the mind and overcast the aesthetic sensibilities."

"Then for heaven's sake," I burst forth, thinking this country wholly without "push" and energy, "what do people here do with their time? If they don't work, they must be simply bored to death!"

The Head Member regarded me with a tolerant smile, as one might regard a harmless lunatic.

"That is where you misunderstand the word work," he explained. "Our people *do* work, and work diligently, and sometimes work many hours a day—but not on those barren practical duties that are assigned to them merely in order that the community may exist. As soon as any man or woman has passed the period of elementary instruction and is given service by this committee, he finds himself with many leisure hours a day—and those leisure hours constitute the most important part of his life. It is on their account that he is congratulated on reaching maturity. For now he has the opportunity for self-expression and for the better sort of service to the State, he may devote himself to study, research or creation in any field that suits him (there is no restriction in this regard, although everyone is expected to apply himself to something definite). One, for example, may elect to paint landscapes; a second to conduct some philosophical inquiry; a third to write poetry; a fourth to investigate the ways of marine animals; a fifth to be an actor, or a musical virtuoso, or the author of historical essays, or a critic of architecture, or a designer of fine tapestries."

"But what if you find nothing at all that you can do?" I inquired, wondering how I could possibly fit myself into this superior scheme of things.

"Oh, but you must find something!" declared the Head Member, while his colleagues eyed one another with looks implying that I was really too naive for belief. "It would be a disgrace to do merely one's practical duties. It would mean that one had been a failure in life; that one's existence had added nothing to the world. Why, there isn't more than one such case a year—and then it's usually found that the poor sufferer has been the victim of some accident blunting his mental faculties."

The Head Member paused; and I had horrific visions of myself as the first failure in a year.

"Well, now that we have made all the necessary explanations," he continued, "let us get down to the actual assignment. What sort of work do you believe you would prefer, young man?"

Having no reason to believe that I would prefer any work at all, I did nothing but gape blankly.

"I am surprised at your hesitancy," resumed the Head Member, severely. "There is so much to do that I should think you would overwhelm us with suggestions."

But I fear that I continued to do nothing but look blank.

"You will pardon me," I pleaded, when the suspense had become embarrassing, "if I leave the suggestions to you. I really know so little about Atlantis."

"True, you do know little about Atlantis," coincided the Head Member, with a smile, "but there is something which you undoubtedly know a great deal about, and of which we Atlanteans know nothing at all."

"You mean—my own country?" I asked, while the entire Committee leaned forward with interested glances.

"Of course—your own country, and the Upper World in general," the Head Member nodded, approvingly. "Remember our latest news of your world was received some three thousand years ago. Even for a leisurely people like us, that is a long while. You cannot imagine how curious we are as to all that has happened since."

"And that's what you want me to tell you?"

"Naturally. Not that anyone man could tell us everything, but that we'd like a general outline of events. So we are thinking of appointing you Official Historian of the Upper World."

"Official Historian—of the Upper World?" I repeated, like one in a daze.

"Yes. Why not? Judging from the fact that you've out distanced all your companions in learning our language, we think you would be the one best qualified."

"But I have never specialized in history—"

"That doesn't matter. What we're most interested in is a sort of knowledge any educated man might give us. You're not altogether unacquainted with civilization up above, are you?"

"No, not altogether."

"And you've been taught a reasonable amount about the past?"

"I've done a little reading—and have taken some history courses at college."

"Excellent! Excellent!" The Head Member beamed upon me ingratiatingly. "Then the rest should be a mere matter of application. You don't object to the appointment, do you?"

I confessed that I did not object.

Whereupon, turning to his associates, he inquired, "Do you all approve of the appointment of Anson Harkness as Official Historian of the Upper World?"

Since there was no dissent among the Committee members, my lifework was apparently settled.

"But just what do you expect me to do?" I queried doubtfully.

"You are to write a history of the Upper World, of course," explained the Head Member, surprised that I should ask obvious. "How to proceed will be for you to decide; but remember that this will be your assigned task, to which you are expected to devote not less than two hours a day. However, yours is one of those rare cases where the assigned task is so important that you might combine it with your optional work; and so dedicate your time exclusively to your duties as historian."

"Perhaps that would be the best way," I agreed.

But at that instant an important question occurred to me. Evidently the examiners had overlooked something essential.

"Now as to practical returns," I ventured, mildly, not wishing to seem too commercial. "I know, of course, that I cannot expect to be paid very much—"

"Paid?" repeated four or five of the Committee members all at once, with looks of such amazement that I knew that I had blundered. "Paid?"

"Oh, then perhaps I must show results first?" I suggest, so bound down by my Upper World habits of thought that I could perceive no other alternative.

For two or three seconds there was silence—an ominous silence which made it clear that I had given deep offence.

"Young man," the Head Member at length broke forth, severely, "I fear you are under a grave misapprehension. But possibly you are not wholly to blame; it may be that your own country still labors under those primitive social arrangements which we Atlanteans abolished three thousand years ago. Know, then, that there is no such thing as payment in our land. There is no money; there is no medium of exchange; there is no private property, except in a few personal effects. You do your work, and receive all the necessaries of life; your meals are brought to you by State employees; you are lodged by the State, educated by the State;

the State works of art are at your disposal; you are admitted to all State entertainments, and are granted periodic vacations to break the monotony of existence. What more could any man desire?"

"No more, of course," I conceded, feeling crushed.

"Very well, then," said the official, with an indulgent smile. "Now there is only one more matter to be decided. How would you like to start out on your travels the day after tomorrow?"

"What travels?" I gasped.

"Why, evidently you haven't heard about that, either," remarked the Head Member, noting my surprise. "You see, every Atlantean, upon receiving his assignment and before taking up his duties, goes on a tour of the country, so as to acquaint himself with it at first hand. Otherwise, how expect to voice himself intelligently on national affairs?"

Having nothing to say in reply, I gaped and remained silent.

"Ordinarily, the journey requires nearly a month. The trip is made entirely on foot, so that one may observe the country thoroughly. There is a party leaving in two days—perhaps you would like to join them?"

"Why not?" I assented. And, after being advised on a few details of the trip, I went away feeling more puzzled than ever, for how could Atlantis show me anything more marvelous than it had shown already?

THE JOURNEY COMMENCES

TWO DAYS LATER I SET out on what was to prove one of the most curious excursions of my life. Arriving early in the morning at the appointed meeting place—an open, flower-bordered "circle" or park near the western end of town—I was greeted by a score of eager young men and women, who introduced themselves as my travelling companions. They were all in an excited, highly animated condition, roving about restlessly, chattering and jesting continually; and all, without exception, were conspicuously and vividly youthful.

I was wondering whether these were to be my sole companions, when I was surprised by the sight of four newcomers—two men and two women of somewhat maturer years. Upon their arrival they were surrounded so enthusiastically that I had not a chance for a clear glimpse of them; but even the partial glimpse was enough—among their number I detected two sparkling, familiar blue eyes...

"Aelios!" I cried, feeling my heart begin to pump hard and a pleasurable thrill run down my spine. "Aelios—what are you doing here?"

She smiled her bewilderingly sweet smile, but did not answer directly. "What are you doing here?" she countered.

"Why, you ought to know," I reminded her. "Didn't I show you my summons from the Assignments Committee?"

"Yes, I remember. Only I didn't know your travels would begin so soon. But I'm very glad. Now you'll be a full-fledged citizen."

"And are you going with us, Aelios? Are you going, too?" I asked.

"Yes, I am going." And, observing how quizzically I was regarding her, she continued. "You see, three or four tutors are assigned to each travelling party, since we have made the journey before and are able to explain the sights."

"But how can you leave so suddenly?" I questioned, remembering Stranahan's daily lessons. "How about—how about your work—"

"Oh, I'm excused, of course. Some other tutor is substituted for me, and my students don't suffer in the least."

"Their loss is our good fortune," I said.

A few minutes later, we were under way. We crossed the Salty River on a long bridge overarched with a crystal arcade and lined with friezes. Opposite us, across the stream, stretched the low contours of the colonnades and temples I had inspected soon after arriving in Atlantis; and at our feet the waters shot swiftly by, with a gentle swishing and murmuring, a green-gray expanse several hundred yards across, but differing from all other rivers in that it was of an even width and flowed without any twists, turns or meanderings.

All this, of course, I had already observed; and my first surprise did not come until after the road had bent abruptly northward away from the river. Then, as we advanced into what for me was virgin territory, the vegetation became denser and more curious; tall reeds, bushes and trees began to cluster about us until I had the impression of being lost in a jungle. But it was a jungle such as no explorer had ever viewed in the wilds of Africa, New Guinea or Brazil. The plants were so fantastic that even the strange undersea vegetation I had already remarked seemed commonplace by comparison.

Here, for the first time, the trees were of a vivid green, and a normal foliage abounded. Yet how much looked abnormal... Some of the trees had branches symmetrically woven into the likenesses of great cobwebs from which dangled clusters of grape-like fruits; other trees were cactus-like and leafless, with huge round protuberances along their spiny boles; still others were almost concealed amid the thick meshes of vines, or were adorned with multi-hued, cup-shaped blossoms larger than a man's head, or were dominated by scores of succulent-looking stalks like gigantic asparagus. Then, again, some were little more than great rounded masses of leafage, reminding me of ten-foot cabbages; and some would have seemed but ordinary mushrooms, had they not reached as high as my waist; and some of the shrubs and creepers bore pods resembling beans and peas, except that they were over a foot in length. The most conspicuous fact about the plants as a whole was that the vast majority were fruit-bearing; on every side I could observe multitudes of green fruits of all sizes and shapes, as well as a profusion of the ripening and ripe product.

As we entered this peculiar jungle, I detected a change in the atmosphere. For the first time, I was aware that there could be such a thing as climate in Atlantis. The air was growing dark and hot, as if we had entered the tropics. Simultaneously, I observed a dazzling increase of light, and felt as if a torrid sun burnt directly above. Yet the source of the added warmth and illumination was no mystery—brilliant white lamps shone at intervals along the great roof-supporting, tinted columns, glaring down like miniature suns, and combining with the larger golden orbs to lend the scene a dream-like and unearthly beauty.

Soon I noted that the vegetation was interrupted every few hundred yards by ditches five or ten feet across and filled with sluggish brown water-ditches whose even width and geometrical straightness brought me reminders of the irrigation canals I had seen on the semi-arid plains of Arizona and California. Then, as we crossed a little arching bridge over one of the widest of the waterways; I saw a long flat boat anchored just beneath my feet; and four or five men, clad in close-fitting gray instead of the usual long-flowing, tinted robes, were busy loading this barge with clusters of fruit.

But these queer jungles still contained a multitude of mysteries; and, accordingly, I listened eagerly when one of the tutors, besieged by an enthusiastic, questioning coterie, launched forth upon an explanation.

"From the earliest times, as you know," he said, speaking informally, and yet with something of the manner of a professor, addressing his class, "we Atlanteans have been skilled in horticulture. To begin with, nature provided the stimulus; the flora of an island such as Atlantis is apt to be unique, and that of our country was particularly so. But long before the Submergence we had outdone nature by developing innumerable new plants; and, since the Submergence, our botanists have been incessantly busy. It is well known how they have experimented, trying the effect of new soils and environments, grafting the limbs of bushes and trees, cross-fertilizing and encouraging desirable chance growths or 'sports.' In these pursuits, they have been aided by our altered environment, which is favorable to rapid variation, and has given rise to countless species unknown before.

"I need not tell you how essential all this has been to the maintenance of life, for our land is limited in extent, and much of it is unsuited to agriculture. It has been necessary to evolve food-plants that would produce more prolifically than any known before; and, at the same time, we have had to develop a light which was the chemical equivalent of sunlight, and so would stimulate the chlorophyll of the leaves, the original source of all organic matter. This, to be sure, was accomplished even before the Submergence; but since the Submergence there has been a constant improvement in the quality of the artificial sunlight. In fact, in the eleventh century the great chemist Sorandos produced an illumination actually superior to sunlight. At least (for some reason that Sorandos himself never made plain) it stimulates plant life to an extraordinarily rapid growth, even though it has the corresponding fault of inducing swift decay. It is this illumination which you see shining now from the great stone columns."

The speaker paused, and I thought it opportune to put a question.

"You tell me that you have need for intensive crop production. Yet have I not heard that you can produce food chemically?"

"Yes, indeed," admitted the tutor, with a shrug. "The same light that develops the chlorophyll in plants may be employed for the synthetic manufacture of starch and sugar out of charcoal and distilled water. But that is an old-fashioned method, and not very successful on the whole, for we have found that this artificial food lacks some element essential for good health."

"Perhaps what we call vitamins," I ruminated. "Even so, why rely wholly upon plant life? Do you never eat meat?"

"Eat what? Meat?" The tutor's tone was one of astonishment; half a dozen pairs of eyes were staring at me in shocked surprise.

"There has been no meat consumed in Atlantis since the Submergence," declared my informant, sternly. "Flesh eating has been discarded along with other uncivilized practices. How could we deem ourselves superior to the beasts and yet live at the cost of blood?"

"But are there no animals at all in Atlantis?"

"Oh, yes, though naturally we couldn't take care of many after the Submergence."

My companion paused, and pointed to a little red-breasted feathered thing perched amid the dense green foliage.

"There are birds, of course; we could not dispense with them. Then there are a few insects, such as the butterflies, and the bees, which give us honey and are necessary for plant pollenization—all harmful insects were long ago destroyed. Also, there are squirrels and chipmunks and other small creatures; and in the Salty River and the canals there are many fish. And in some places along the Salty River there are hundreds of bullfrogs."

"Bullfrogs!" I exclaimed. "Bullfrogs..." And suddenly I understood those strange noises that had terrified my shipmates and myself during our first night in Atlantis.

THE GLASS CITY

FOR FIVE OR SIX HOURS WE WANDERED through the fruit-bearing jungles, which seemed limitless in extent and yet constantly displayed unexpected, new features. But the journey was by no means arduous, for twice we paused for rest and refreshments at little open-air inns that fronted the road. Most of the party seemed still eager and energetic when, towards mid-afternoon, we emerged from the thickets and saw a group of fairy-like towers gleaming ahead.

"That is the city of Thalos," explained one of the tutors. "It is there that we stay for the night."

Half an hour later, having passed through a glass wall by means of a minute gateway, I found myself in what might have been a city out of the "Arabian Nights." I cannot say with certainty whether I beheld a single building or a hundred, or whether I stood in an open court or in a street; a wide expanse of masonry, of arches and covered galleries, of steeples and cupolas and winding balconies, was spread before me; and all this masonry was of glass and seemed joined in a unified whole. There may have been individual edifices, but there was no edifice not connected with its neighbors by arching walls or overhead passageways. There may have been streets winding through this wilderness of glass, but it struck me that there were only open spaces alternating with twining glass-roofed corridors. Yet the various segments of the city, in their garments of amethyst or pale blue or turquoise or vivid ruby, fitted together as perfectly as the parts of an intricate and beautiful mosaic.

We had barely entered the town when half a dozen natives ran forth to greet us. Like the members of my own party, they were all dressed in exquisite light-tinted gowns; and, like all the Atlanteans, they were well-built, and prepossessing of appearance; while there was a perfect natural courtesy in their manner when they greeted us and bade us accompany them to their lodgings.

Still speechless with wonder, I followed my companions through long crystal galleries, around the base of jewel-like towers, and across flowered parks where fountains splashed and bubbled. "This is typical of the latest in architecture," I heard one of the men saying, as he pointed up at the curving, inter-linking stained glass porticoes and domes "Thalos in its present form is only five centuries old, and is wholly a product of post-Submergence art."

Almost before these words were out of the speaker's mouth, we were led up a long flight of stairs and through an elliptical doorway into a chamber walled and roofed not with glass, but with marble. Here we were treated to a sumptuous repast, consisting of a sort of vegetable steak, native cakes and bread, honey and fruit, which lay spread for us on a dozen little tables. And, after we had dined, we were each shown to a room on the roof, where if we wished, we might rest from the day's exertions.

Some of our party may have welcomed this opportunity; but, for my own part, I was so excited to be in Thalos that rest was out of the question.

Having washed myself clean of the dust of the journey, I hastened down from my roof apartment. And as I stepped towards the outer door of the building, I rejoiced to see a familiar, blue-clad figure preceding me. "Aelios!" I cried; and when she turned at the sound of my voice, I joined her with the suggestion that we take a little stroll together. And—quite unexpectedly—she smiled consent.

"Luckily, I've been here before, and know my way about," she said, as we started. "If you went alone, you might get lost."

"I wouldn't mind—not in such a place. But, of course, I'd much prefer having such a companion."

A faint blush overspread her countenance. But she made no reply; and I was not quite sure how to pursue the topic.

Hence for a time, as we followed streets dominated by glass turrets and domes, I let the conversation drift to indifferent themes. First we spoke of the wonders of Thalos; then by pleasant degrees the discussion turned to subjects more nearly concerning us. Aelios asked me about the world I had come from, and whether it had any architectural marvels rivaling those of Thalos; and I replied that it had not, though the skyscrapers of New York were considered wonderful enough. But I was reluctant to talk about my own world. I did not wish to be disturbed by remembrances; I desired only to walk with Aelios as I was walking now, and to hear her speak, and be permitted to glance into those glamorous bright blue eyes of hers, and feel the glow of that sweet presence wherein, for me, love and joy and gentleness and the pain of an insatiable longing were strangely, deliciously mingled.

Like one in a sorcerer's spell, I listened as she told of her life, and how she was the eldest child of two celebrated artists and had never lacked anything she really wanted, and how from her earliest years she had loved music and the dance, but particularly the dance, and had followed her childhood inclinations in her chosen work for the State, though in her prescribed work she was a tutor. All this and much more Aelios told me about herself, while I heard with adoration that must have been all too apparent in my gaze, and now and then felt a wild temptation, which I suppressed with difficulty, to fling out my arms, and clasp her close, and not let her go.

After an hour's stroll through the rambling thoroughfares, we seated ourselves on a cushioned marble bench at one corner of a wide court. "If we stay here until dark," suggested Aelios, "you will see one of the oddest exhibitions of your life."

Only a few minutes later, the golden orbs above us flickered and slowly faded into blackness. At the same time, other lights gleamed from the city's unseen pinnacles; and their rays darted in colored streamers against a glass wall directly across from us, illuminating it with fantastic designs. They shed definite patterns, I might almost say pictures, upon the broad glass screen: first the form of a man, life-sized and with palely tinted robes, would start forward in agile cinematograph fashion; then the two would engage in various significant motions or gesticulations, to be joined, perhaps, by others; and in the swaying and blending of the lights, the weird mingling and intermingling of myriads of shades and colors, the background of shadows and the foreground of lithe and active figures, I realized that I was witnessing the representation of scenes from Atlantean life!

What those scenes were I cannot recall; I fear that my mind was upon more personal subjects. Although the seats about us were being occupied, I felt as if Aelios and I were alone together; and under the enchantment of the shifting and pictorial lights I pressed close to her, until not a fraction of an inch divided us and it seemed that we breathed not as two persons but as one. A thrill as of some exquisite, forbidden joy crept over me; I trembled a little with the realization that the soul of all things desirable sat so near, so very near to me; I am sure that my face, had there been light enough, would have appeared deeply flushed. Very cautiously, like one who creeps into some prohibited shrine, I reached out my hand, until it touched hers and the palm closed over her fingers. She did not return the pressure, yet did not withdraw her hand; and, encouraged, I let my arm enfold her slender waist.

Her head swayed towards me. With a sudden dizziness, I had the sense that her whole form was leaning towards me. But instantly, with some swift power of self-command, she had straightened up, and was gazing at the pictured display as attentively as if her life depended upon her acquaintance with every detail extra white.

EARLY NEXT MORNING we were again under way. After leaving Thalos through a little arched gateway under the western wall, we trudged for several hours across a flat green countryside. Here and there at irregular intervals, we observed edifices that my companions described as "farmhouses," although, with their statue-lined walls and marble columns, they seemed little less than palaces. These dwellings, of which there must have been four or five to every square mile, were conspicuous from a distance, for there were no obstructing trees, but the landscape was dominated by a hardy reed that grew shoulder-high in impenetrable clusters.

Except for the size of this plant, I might have fancied it to be a variety of wheat. Not only were its leaves long and grass-like, but it bore a rich crop of some grain that closely resembled wheat, in spite of seed-clusters as large as ears of corn. That it was cultivated for food was obvious, for brilliant white lamps were beaming from the tinted columns as in the fruit-jungles, and every few hundred yards we passed irrigation ditches, where gray-clad men were at work here and there amid the green thickets.

But while this scenery had many points of interest, I was relieved when the landscape showed a change and the cultivated plains gave way to long, low-lying, grass-covered hills. From the beginning, I noticed something peculiar about these eminences, for they were rounded with geometrical evenness; and beyond the furthest heights a clear rapid stream flowed out of the ground, and, after rambling to the edge of the reed-covered plain, divided into half a dozen diverging irrigation canals.

Even as I stood staring at the stream in wonder, a huge rock at the base of the nearest hill suddenly thrust itself outwards, and a man emerged as if from the center of the earth!

Startled, I turned to my companions for an explanation—but not a murmur issued from them.

"Here is where we enter," one of the tutors declared, in matter-of-fact tones. And, followed by the rest of the party, he plunged through the aperture made by the dislodged boulder.

More bewildered than ever, I trailed with the others into that hole on the hillside. As I approached the entrance, I found that what I had taken to be a rock was not a rock at all but a cleverly disguised bit of metal; and, upon reaching the doorway, I was amazed to view, not the tunnel-like corridor I had expected, but a wide-vaulting hall.

With the exception of the Sunken World itself, this was the largest enclosure I had ever entered, for it occupied the entire interior of the hill. Along the full length of a half-mile gallery, the white-lanterned ceiling arched to a height of two hundred feet; and rising almost to this ceiling, on each side of a broad passageway, was a series of gigantic boilers. All were connected with innumerable wires and with pipes thicker than a man's body, while at the further end of the gallery the tubes were interwoven in intricate loops, coils and convolutions like the exposed entrails of a Titan.

As I stepped through the doorway, a warm breeze swept my face, bearing the odor of oil, and reminding me of the furnace-dry air of steam-heated apartments. "What place is this?" I asked. But I was sorry to have spoken, for four or five pairs of eyes turned upon me in astonishment at so obvious a question.

"This is a distillery, of course," answered one of my young companions.

"A distillery?" I echoed, amazed. And all at once—although the Atlanteans had seemed a sober people—I had visions of the manufacture of intoxicants on a scale inconceivable to the most bibulous of my own countrymen.

"Yes, this is where we prepare our distilled water," continued my friend, surprised at my surprise.

I stared at him without comprehension. "But why so much distilled water?"

"That's easily explained," said the young man, with a smile. "The water is necessary for irrigation, without which Atlantis would be a desert. The supply from our deep wells, which serves for drinking purposes, is limited in quantity; and, on the other hand, the Salty River is limited in quality, for it is ocean water, and the brine would kill all land vegetation. And so the only possibility is to distill the water. This was arranged long ago by Agripides, when he built this distillery and eleven others, which keep our irrigation system supplied, and incidentally, provides salt for domestic and chemical purpose."

"That may all be very well," I objected. "But the amount of heat necessary to evaporate so much water—"

"Why, that's no problem at all," my companion interrupted. "By means of inter-atomic energy, we could generate power enough to distill the entire ocean."

This statement, I felt sure, must be an exaggeration; but before I had time for further questioning, my attention was diverted. Our party had paused before a circular slit in the floor; and a brown-clad workman, stepping forth from amid the boilers, applied a key to a little hole near the edge of the slit, and removed a steel disc five feet in diameter.

Instantly we were bathed in a brilliant copper light, so dazzling that I had to turn away abruptly. Then, as my startled eyes gradually accustomed themselves to the vivid illumination, I peered through a glass partition far down into what remotely reminded me of a furnace, except that no flames were visible, but from a vague, fire-bright background great sheets and rods of a shining red or a blinding brassy yellow stared at me steadily with unbearable incandescence.

"Those are the inter-atomic generators," explained the workman. "They constantly liberate energy which is transformed into electrical power by means of giant induction coils. It is this electricity that is wired to the boiler room and heats the water from the Salty River."

"But how terrible to work down there— How can any man—"

"It is not necessary to work down there. The generators operate automatically so long as they are supplied with fuel."

"And what fuel do you use?"

"Various metals, of course. Any of the heavier ones will do. One of the cheapest is gold, whose high atomic weight makes possible extensive dissociation. Sometimes, however, we use silver, palladium, platinum, or lead—although the latter is ordinarily regarded as too valuable for such purposes. A supply of lead will run the generator for twenty-seven years, of silver for thirty-three, and of gold for forty-five. When new fuel is required, we simply shoot it in through the tube over there."

The speaker paused long enough to indicate a rod about as thick as a man's wrist, which projected several feet above the floor between two of the boilers.

I thought that I had now seen enough of the distillery, and was not disappointed when my companions prepared to leave. But there was one problem that still troubled me: why did the building look so much like a hill from without, and why had such evident pains been taken to conceal its existence?

To these questions I found a ready answer. "If this edifice had been erected in the days before Agripides," said one of my young friends, "it would have been an ugly mass of steel and stone. But Agripides, seeking a way to beautify such structures, hit upon the plan of covering them with earth and sowing the earth with grass, so as to give the appearance of a green hill. All our factories, you will find, have likewise been concealed or made beautiful."

This, indeed, I discovered to be the case. We had now reached the industrial center of Atlantis, and all the rest of that day we were busy inspecting manufacturing plants. But nowhere was the air clouded with smoke or dust; nowhere was there a dingy or soot-blackened building; nowhere were my ears assaulted by the shrieking or droning of whistles, or by the hammering, pounding, screeching, whirring or grating of machines. In the midst of pleasant, grassy lands, an occasional tree-bordered building arose with glittering steeples, or stainless marble facade, or august columns of granite; and within each building, which one might have mistaken for a mansion or a temple, electrically driven wheels and levers were operating noiselessly, preparing the food of the Atlanteans or weaving their clothes from the fiber of a flax-like plant, manufacturing farm implements or fertilizers, scientific articles or household wares. And in every factory a few workers (never more than a score) were serenely tending the machines, occupying thus their hour or two of assigned daily service for the State.

The building that most interested me was the one where chemists were at work renewing the air supply of Atlantis—or, rather, the oxygen supply. Here, in a long hall dominated by great vats connected by pipes and wires reminding me of the distillery, a continual stream of water was being disintegrated by a process of electrolysis, the hydrogen being diverted to form various compounds, the oxygen being released into the atmosphere to replace that consumed by respiration and combustion. Thanks to the air-gauge—a finely adjusted apparatus whose index was a flame that varied with the amount of oxygen—chemists were able to determine how much of this vital gas was required at any time; but some oxygen had to be provided continually, for, large as Atlantis was, it was not so great that nature would preserve a balance.

But if the Atlantean industries were arranged with a regard for the aesthetic sensibilities of the people, scarcely less pains had been taken to insure the health and convenience of the workers. I will not speak of the safety devices, which had been so perfected that accidents were virtually unknown; I will not dwell upon the precautions to vary the monotony even of the brief working day, and to guard against fatigue and strain. But what I must mention, because it impressed me as unique, is that the workers were housed in dwellings not less imposing than the city homes. The road took us through half a dozen villages reserved for factory workers; and each seemed in itself a work of art, with many-columned residences, arches and connecting colonnades, flowered parks, statuary and fountains, all coordinated in a tasteful and elegant design.

THE WALL AND THE WIND MAKERS

THE FOLLOWING DAY, AFTER sleeping in Arvon, a town huddled amid vegetation so thick it resembled a forest, we were to penetrate some of the salient mysteries of Atlantis.

Even though I did not know what was before me, I had a hint of something unusual very early in the morning. We had hardly left Arvon when I observed that the golden-lighted dome seemed lower and nearer than usual, and curved gradually down to westward until it appeared to merge with the ground.

"That's where the glass wall begins," said one of the tutors, pointing.

A little further on, the road turned abruptly southwards, and for several miles we merely paralleled the wall. Then, to my joy, a familiar gurgling met my ears—we were back again near the Salty River... Straight across the stream we passed on an arching bridge. On the further side we again started westwards and followed the river directly towards the green glass wall.

As we advanced, I noticed that the waters were becoming white and foamy, with great briny patches as if a passing steamer had churned up the waves. Gradually these frothy expanses grew wider and more conspicuous, and the entire river became a seething, effervescent mass; troubled waves sprang to life, with a turbulence that increased as we moved upstream, until the bubbling white was mingled with the green and gray of leaping surges, and the waters were agitated as if by a storm wind. Yet only the faintest of breezes was blowing.

At the same time, a disquieting sound came to my ears—the continuous, droning sound of thunder, dull and muffled, but gradually growing louder despite the clamoring of the waves. So deep-toned was it, so voluminous, that it reminded me of a din I never expected to hear again—the booming of the ocean along resisting shores.

All of our party moved without a word now, moved rapidly and with faces straining westward, as if eager for some long-awaited event. In their very speechlessness there was a contagious tension; and, held by their mood, I, too, was expectant, though I could not guess what lay in store.

Yet, I did not have long to wait. "Look! There it is!" exclaimed one of the youths, suddenly. And he paused, and pointed straight ahead; and all his companions paused, and pointed straight ahead, joining in his awed cries of, "Look! There it is!"

Of course, I strained my eyes as earnestly as any of them. But at first all that was visible was a broad sheet of white, looming just above the river almost for its full width, as though there were falls a mile or two upstream.

Then suddenly the path bent away from the river at an acute angle; and, as we followed our new course, the distant thundering grew louder, while a cold wind began to blow over us and the supposed waterfall took on unexpected dimensions. By degrees it lengthened until it resembled a long jet of water shot horizontally out of some colossal hose. Intensely white, with misty, spray-blurred edges, it went hurtling with the impetuosity of an arrow from the nozzle of a gigantic pipe, plunging outwards hundreds of yards in a graceful parabola and giving rise to the Salty River.

Almost as remarkable as this torrent was the tube from which it was discharged. This great pipe, which may have been of steel or lead, was well over a mile long, and was a hundred yards across at the opening; but it narrowed gradually as it crept westward along the ground and disappeared where the green horizon met the earth.

Needless to say, I did not have to ponder as to the meaning, only one explanation was conceivable: the metallic tube was the valve through which the *X-111* had found entrance to Atlantis, the valve that admitted the sea water and kept the Salty River supplied. The aperture at the ocean end was doubtless not very wide (I was later told that it was but twenty-five feet across); but such was the pressure at these depths that the waters burst through with the force and swiftness and tremendous volume I had just observed, and had to be diverted through a long, gradually widening tube before the current could be controlled and safely emptied into the river channel.

As we approached the glass wall, the hoarse, resonant roaring was continuously in our ears, thudding and crashing with reverberations like the combined monody of a hundred Niagaras. But, forgetful of the tumult, I kept my eyes fastened straight ahead, where the great green dome sloped down to meet the ground in a curve like that of the actual heavens. Except for the dark, weird coloration, I might have fancied that I was staring towards a horizon of the earth; and so close was the resemblance that the illusion persisted until I was within a stone's throw of the barrier. Only then could I persuade myself that I actually beheld a solid mass; and, even so, the curvature was so graceful and so elusive that I could not be sure that a mere wall stretched before me. Rather, I had the feeling that it was some ultimate boundary, the dividing line between reality and nothingness.

This impression was confirmed by the fact that the wall at close range looked opaque. Olive-green and of impenetrable thickness, it seemed impervious to the rays of light; though, remembering my experiences on the *X-111*, I knew that it was really transparent.

Almost breathlessly the members of our party approached the wall, held out their hands, and touched it in silence—a procedure that may have had some ceremonial importance, or may have resembled the actions of persons who, seeing the ocean for the first time, gravely dip their hands in the salt water. At any rate, I followed their example, and found the surface of the wall to be just as I had expected—smooth and polished, and of a substance that would have been apparent to a blind man.

After the twenty students had inspected the wall, one of the tutors lifted his voice so as to be heard by the entire party.

"My friends, we have now reached the borderland between Atlantis and the outside world. A rim of glass fifty feet thick divides us from the ocean; and that glass, as you know, is composed of dozens of layers, one above the other, several of them strengthened with interwoven strands of fine wire, and all of them composed of a special pressure-resisting glass devised at the orders of Agripides. You understand, of course, that the wall does not end where you see it, but penetrates five hundred feet underground, lest the ocean overwhelm us from beneath; you also understand that the glass is ribbed with steel, which holds it together in a latticed framework, with girders, beams and stanchions like the skeleton of a great building.

"The construction of the wall represents the supreme accomplishment of Atlantean engineering, and required the labors of thirty thousand men for thirty-four years. But Agripides, with his unusual foresight, has seen that the work, once done, has never had to be renewed; for glass is one of the most durable of substances, and is virtually immune to dissolution by water. We have our immersible vessels, of course, which range the seas around the glass dome in search of any possible fault or fissure; but no serious damage has ever been discovered, and it is safe to say that the wall will serve us and our descendants forever."

The speaker paused, as if for effect; then, seeing that his audience remained silent, he concluded, "Would anyone like to ask a question?"

"Yes, I would," I surprised myself by saying.

All eyes were bent curiously upon me, and I was forced to continue. "Glass is, as you say, exceeding durable, but it is also very fragile. Is there no possibility that the wall will ever be cracked?"

"Cracked?" echoed the tutor, with a surprised smile. "Do you think that, if there had been such a possibility, Atlantis would not have been inundated long ago! Granted, if any very heavy object were to collide with the wall, it might be broken. But how could there be any such object here in the deep sea? Certainly, the fishes can't break through—"

At this there arose such a peal of mirthful laughter that I withdrew, feeling that I had made myself ridiculous. Yet how often my words were to be recalled in the tempestuous days that followed...

For the next hour, we pursued a little path that clung close to the glass wall. Before we had covered more than a mile, a brisk breeze began to blow; and the further we walked the sharper it grew, until it had gathered to a gale, and for the first time since reaching Atlantis I was cold, almost as if I were back on earth. Why we continued in the face of this blast I could not understand, nor whence it came, nor how it was produced. But while I was fighting my way through the wind, a singular whirring sound came to my ears, a buzzing as of gigantic flies; and gradually that sound grew louder, until, from resembling the murmuring of insects, it came to remind me of the flapping of colossal wings.

That this noise was connected with the quickening wind was apparent. And the relationship became clear when the path abruptly swerved away from the wall and I glanced back, to behold a series of queer-looking machines supported on pedestals high up against the glass. It would be impossible to say just what the machines were like, for they were in such rapid motion that the parts were not visible; but there were six or eight of them and they were round and probably each a hundred yards across, and were rotating so swiftly that each formed a gray blur through which the green of the wall was vaguely discernible.

"Those are the electro inter-atomic wind generators," explained one of the tutors, while all the students listened earnestly. "By means of these great fans and others like them, the atmosphere of Atlantis is kept in circulation. Without them the air would be stagnant, and the climate sultry and unhealthful. These generators are in action all the time with great air-wheels that make ten or fifteen revolutions a second. It is estimated that the daily energy consumed by each of them would suffice to boil a thousand tons of ice water."

We did not linger long near the great fans, for the wind was annoying. But we started away at a brisk pace across a moss-covered plain, and did not pause until we had reached the city of Lerenon, our destination for the day.

This town, which was located some miles from the wall, had one striking feature all its own: it was dominated by two colossal bronze figures, one of a man, the other of a woman, which reached far above the city towers halfway to the green-glass sky. Both statues were carved with irresistible majesty, the man's face that of an Apollo, the woman's that of a Diana; and their right hands were extended high over the roofs and joined in a firm clasp, so life-like that I might almost have expected them to move and speak. At first I thought that they represented mythological characters, but an inscription at their base informed me that the man was meant to typify Wisdom, and the woman Beauty; and in their union above the spires of Atlantis I thought I could read the meaning and purpose of the entire land.

THE JOURNEY ENDS

DURING THE TWENTY-SEVEN DAYS of our journey I was the witness of marvels so numerous that, if I were to dwell upon them all, I might fill hundreds of pages. Yet while there is much that I cannot record and much that I have forgotten, there are some observations that have stamped themselves indelibly upon my memory, and that are so essential for an understanding of Atlantis that I could not well overlook them.

Thus, I found that the wall enclosing the country formed a vast circle, of a diameter impossible for me to determine precisely, but probably in the neighborhood of two hundred miles. Thus, also, I learned that the glass dome was at an average height of five hundred feet above the ground, although the distance varied with the level of the land; and I discovered that it was everywhere supported by myriads of the huge tinted columns—columns with steel interiors, and surfaces of concrete or stone. I ascertained, likewise, that the Salty River followed an unbending course, flowing in a straight line and on an even grade from the western wall of Atlantis to the eastern (for it was really a canal rather than a river); and I was amazed and dazzled by the sight of the inter-atomic pumps that forced the torrents back into the sea.

Since they were expected to overcome a pressure of many tons to the square foot, these pumps had to be powerful indeed; and powerful they certainly were, with their labyrinths of levers and revolving chains, and three-hundred-foot pistons and rods that pounded against the waves like gigantic pile-drivers, pressing them slowly back into the sea to the accompaniment of a roaring and thundering that could be heard for miles.

The cities of Atlantis, according to the count I made, were eighteen in number (exclusive of the smaller towns and villages). But an Atlantean city, although always occupying considerable space, was what we in America should scarcely regard as a city at all, since it never had more than twenty or twenty-five thousand, inhabitants. This limited population, when considered along with the liberal amount of territory allotted each town, accounted for the fact that no great crowds were ever seen on the streets; and it also explained how it was possible for efficient popular assemblages to debate and decide public questions.

But what most surprised me about the Atlantean cities was not so much their small population as their almost unbelievable variety. No town in Atlantis was like any other; the only characteristic they all had in common was their unfailing beauty. To give some idea of their diversity, I might mention Atolis, which, when seen from the hill that surmounted it, formed a definite pattern, resembling some colossal Grecian temple of which the streets and avenues were the columns. Or I might picture Aedla, which was built along a series of canals connecting with the Salty River, with a lake in the center, giving a Venetian effect. Again, I might depict the small town of Acropolon, in which all the houses were connected in a colonnaded quadrangle surrounding a flowering park; or I might describe Mangona, another small town, whose, houses were all roofless and collapsible, and were generally taken down during the day and put into place only at night or when the inhabitants desired seclusion.

But more interesting to me than any of these was Sardolos, one of the few cities that had survived from before the Submergence. Although, of course, the town was not at all the same as in ancient times, yet some relics of the old days had been preserved.

Thus, in one corner of the city, guarded in a statue-lined bronze enclosure, were the remains of buildings said to date from the second century B.S. Yet, oddly enough, my first impression was that there was something familiar about the ancient ruins. The most conspicuous among them was a stone wall, five stories high and with gaping, rectangular holes where the windows had been while to the rear was a mass of rusted and distorted steel, reaching the full height of the wall with twisted, spidery arms that had once lent it support.

"A splendid specimen of pre-Submergence architecture," stated a placard. "This was the seat of the Stock Market of old Sardolos—a wholesale gambling house abolished by the Anti-Corruption Act of the first century A.S. The mass of shapeless and desiccated stone opposite is all that remains of the Inter-Atlantean bank, which owned a controlling share in this gambling resort; while just to the right one will see the ruins of the shrine in which the owners of the bank worshipped, and of the clubhouse in which, late in the second century B.S., they convened in the interest of their lotteries and decreed the fifth Atlanto-Bengenese War."

But when I looked for the latter ruins, all that I saw was a series of irregular stone walls, not over three or four feet high, and brown with the lifeless parchment hue of extreme age. Somehow, it made me uncomfortable to observe these vestiges of the past. Nor was I relieved when I gazed at a picture of Sardolos as it had been, and saw two long opposing rows of geometrically regular five-story buildings. To think of these, and then to turn to present-day Atlantis, was merely to shudder at the contrast. Yet all the while I could not fight down that indefinable sense of being in the presence of something familiar.

Now let me speak of something even more interesting to me than the sights of the Sunken World. My continued joy in the trip is not to be explained merely by the engrossing scenes along the way, nor by the companionship of the twenty eager young students. For could I forget even for a moment the presence of one who meant more to me than all else in Atlantis? My opportunities of speaking with Aelios were not plentiful, as she seemed always occupied with some other member of the party; but occasionally we exchanged a few words, and occasionally she darted a bright smile in my direction, thereby reassuring me when at times I gave way to disturbing doubts.

It was not until our travels were drawing to a close that I had another long private talk with her. The morning of the last day had arrived, and we had set out through fields of the wheat-like reed towards Archeon, which we hoped to reach shortly after noon. But, absorbed in somber contemplation, I took no part in the merriment of my companions; almost from the first, I lagged moodily behind them. What a relief, then, to hear light footsteps suddenly at my side, and to find a golden-curled head nodding a greeting and a pair of kindly, bright blue eyes peering at me inquiringly.

"Aelios!" I exclaimed. And I returned her greeting in terms that could not half express my pleasure.

Although I would have liked to discuss only sweet and intimate things, she wasted no time about plunging into the subject that had brought her to me.

"Today our journey ends," she reminded me. "And tomorrow you take up your duties as a citizen. You may find matters a little strange at first. Perhaps there are already some things that puzzle you."

"Indeed there are," I admitted. "I really have very little idea what I am expected to do."

"Oh, but you must have some idea," she remonstrated. "Haven't you been appointed Historian of the Upper World?"

"Yes, I'll have to admit that honor."

"Then you must set out at once upon your duties. No record will betaken of the hours you employ, but you have a moral obligation to work not less than two a day."

"That doesn't seem excessive."

"Yes, but remember you have also an obligation to work on your own account for the State."

"The real problem," I acknowledged, hesitantly, "is that I don't know the language well enough to write a history."

Aelios frowned. "Oh, but you have already a good speaking command of Atlantean, and with practice you'll be able to write. I'd advise you to go to the government library, and read all you can to familiarize yourself with our language—and our life."

I thanked Aelios for the suggestion, and promised to visit the library very soon.

"But don't forget that there are other things," she continued. "I hope that you will make friends of many of our people, and participate in our intellectual contests and recreations. You might even join a political party."

"Political party? I didn't know there were any parties in Atlantis."

"Of course, there are! There are always several of them to present their views at the Hall of Public Enlightenment."

"What parties are those?"

"Well, let's see. First of all, the Party of Submergence, so-called because it was founded by Agripides, and has been the ruling group ever since the Good Destruction. Then the Industrial Reform

Party, which contends that all machines are out of place in Atlantis and should be reduced far below their present number. Then again, there is the Party of Artistic Emancipation, which is really literary rather than political, and appeals for freedom in art. Also, there is the Party of Birth Extension, which holds that the government should relax its restrictions on population. And, finally, there is the Party of Emergence, which is the smallest of them all and has always been very unpopular, since it believes we should forsake the principles of Agripides, enter into communication with the Upper World, and send some of our people to live above seas."

"That sounds quite interesting," I commented, for the Party of Emergence seemed to me the most understandable of all. "But you say this last party has never had much success?"

"Fortunately not. Its members have always been looked upon as anti-social agitators, who would transgress against the principle of 'Atlantis for the Atlanteans.' Few respectable citizens have ever supported them."

"Too bad," I found myself remarking, with unguarded frankness. And the shocked expression on Aelios' face showed me how I had erred. "At any rate, you must know something of the parties before you choose among them," she concluded.

I assured her that I would try to choose wisely.

"If ever you're in doubt about anything," she urged, "don't be afraid to come to me and ask. I know that things aren't easy for a stranger in a strange land."

Delighted at this invitation, I thanked her fervently, and declared that I should not hesitate to consult her.

"I'm glad to hear you say that," she returned. And her eyes shone with a warm light; her lips quivered sympathetically, and her whole face radiated kindliness. And once again I felt that powerful sweet, mysterious prompting to reach out my arms, and—

But at this point, as if unaware of my feelings or else intent on thwarting them, she pointed imperatively through a break in the dense green foliage. "See, over there!" she exclaimed. "The towers of Archeon..."

I looked eagerly, and, far across the plain, I observed a minute glittering spire, more than half obscured by the intervening columns—the first sign of that city which I was this day to enter, and where I was to make my home, and seek the fulfillment of my love, and undertake my duties as a citizen of the Sunken World.

XANOCLES

AS AN ACCREDITED CITIZEN OF ATLANTIS, I WAS assigned to permanent lodgings immediately upon returning to Archeon. The housing representative of the government (the only substitute in the Sunken World for our "realtors") accompanied me on a leisurely tour of the city, allowing me my choice of fifteen or twenty apartments. The task of selection was by no means easy, not because it was hard to secure suitable quarters, but because it was difficult to choose between so many desirable places. Never before had I realized how utterly superior the Atlantean homes are to our own—out of all the houses I visited, there was not one that was not separated by wide spaces from its neighbors, or that did not enjoy a full share of light and air, or that did not look comfortable and alluring. The grim and musty interiors of many of our own dwellings, the furniture-littered rooms, the glaring bad taste of gilt and tinsel chairs and adornments, had no parallel among the Atlantean residences. Instead, each apartment was so artlessly inviting that I might have claimed it at once as my home.

The distinguishing feature of most of the houses was a central court that reminded me of the dwellings of the ancient world. Usually the court was square or rectangular in shape, though in some instances it was hexagonal or round; and more often than not it was completely enclosed. Some of the courts were surrounded by stalwart columns, but the majority were plain; some had walls of granite, some of marble, some of a peculiar bluish plastic; some were marked by fountains, some by flower gardens, some by swimming pools; and the most distinctive of all was arranged as an art gallery, with a dominating statue in the center. But whatever the particular contents of the court, it was accessible by four or five doors leading into the several apartments.

After inspecting the various lodgings, I finally decided in favor of a three-room suite (three rooms, that is, in addition to the sleeping chamber on the roof), which looked out over a tree-lined avenue towards the sapphire dome of the Hall of Public Enlightenment. I was persuaded to take these quarters largely because of the fascinating, frieze-lined adjoining court, featured by finely modeled images of gods, nymphs and satyrs; but I was captivated by the rooms themselves, with the seaweed tapestries on the walls, the high vaulted ceilings, the arching doorways and great elliptical windows, and the removable partitions capable of transforming the entire apartment into a single, good-sized hall.

It was fortunate that I chose these particular lodgings, for otherwise I might never have known Xanocles—Xanocles, who was to be my one intimate among all the men of Atlantis. It happened that he—that fiery spirit, audacious thinker, and trustworthy friend—was living in the same building; and it also happened (since fate works in inscrutable ways even in Atlantis) that he and I were early thrown together. Our meeting occurred, indeed, on the very day after my return to Archeon.

I had just settled in my new home, and had gone out into the court to examine its mural decorations, when a door across from me slid open and a tall, white-clad figure emerged. One glance and he knew I was out of place in Atlantis. He paused in surprise, and for an embarrassed instant we stood staring at one another. In that first glimpse I had the impression of a powerful personality: a large head poised squarely over a pair of broad and capable shoulders; two vivid blue eyes deeply set beneath a massive brow; a beardless oval face dominated by flowing chestnut locks; classic features, with chin and nose consummately sculptured. But I did not notice then what I was often to observe later: the ironic glitter in the alert eyes; the forceful and determined lines into which the face would habitually settle; the air of overflowing vigor tempered by an easy self-command. Judging from the smooth contours of the man's face, I took him to be not over thirty years of age; and I was later surprised to learn that he was well past forty.

"By Agripides! You must be one of those visitors from up above," exclaimed the newcomer, recovering from his astonishment. And he approached with a winning smile, and held out both hands by way of greeting. "My name is Xanocles. We seem to be neighbors, you and I. Maybe we can get to know each other."

"I hope we shall," I seconded, as I took his hands. "My name is Harkness. I've just finished my tour around Atlantis, and now I'm to begin as a citizen."

"That's quick work," nodded Xanocles, approvingly. And then, after an instant's pause, "So you're the one they appointed Historian of the Upper World?"

Smilingly I pleaded guilty to the accusation.

"I knew it must be so," explained my new acquaintance, "because only one of the immigrants has been admitted to citizenship so far."

"Won't you come in," I suggested, with a gesture towards my apartments.

Xanocles needed no second invitation. A minute later we were seated opposite one another on seaweed cushions in the little room that was to be my study.

"It seems to me, Harkness," he urged, using my name as familiarly as though he had known me all my life, "we might as well be frank with one another from the beginning. At least, I might as well be frank with you. I'd better warn you that you'll not gain much from my acquaintance. I'm none too popular."

"No?" I demanded, wondering what offence he had committed.

"No," he confessed. "I'm so very unpopular, in fact, that it might damage you even to be seen in my company."

"But why?" I demanded, incredulously. "You don't look as if you've blown up a building, or stolen someone's jewels, or killed a man—"

A frown of disgust passed across Xanocles' face.

"Such primitive forms of violence," he reminded me, "are unknown in Atlantis. No, I haven't stooped to anything so low. But I've done something bad enough in the eyes of the people."

"I'll have to give it up."

"It shouldn't be hard to guess—not if you know the ways of Atlantis. I've joined the party of Emergence."

"Party of Emergence?" I echoed, remembering what Aelios had told me of this minority group.

"I've not only joined the party," he acknowledged, completing the indictment, "but I've let them elect me one of their Debating Delegates."

"But I don't exactly understand—"

"You would understand if you knew more about Atlantis. Every people has to have its pet aversion, I suppose. Ours down here is the Emergence Party. That's because it opposes the hundred percent Atlanteans."

"But just what is the Emergence Party?" I inquired, still in doubt as to the nature of this detested faction. "Is it anything so very terrible?"

"That all depends upon the point of view."

Xanocles paused long enough to flash me an instant's scrutiny with keen and quizzical eyes.

"I am not sure that you'll understand," he decided, speaking as much to himself as to me. "But the main thing is that we oppose compulsory limitation of population."

"Oppose—compulsory limitation of population?"

"Most certainly. You've heard, perhaps, that our population is limited by law to six hundred thousand?"

"But how is that possible? Why, I should think population is one thing you can't limit by law."

"Experience has proved quite the contrary."

For a moment I did not reply. I merely sat staring at my companion, trying to fathom the secret hidden in those deep grave eyes of his.

"What do you do with your extra inhabitants? Do they immigrate to the center of the earth? Or do you prefer to shoot them or drown them, or perhaps asphyxiate them humanely?"

"There are no extra inhabitants," was the surprising reply. "Do you know nothing of the Milares' Compulsory Population Law?"

I had to confess my ignorance.

"Then let me enlighten you. First let me take you back a few thousand years, to the days just after the Submergence. At that time the population numbered several millions, and the swarms were so dense that long hours of labor were necessary, living quarters were crowded and unsanitary, and there was little time for the creation or appreciation of beauty. This state of affairs endured for over a century, when, after much discussion, the Milares' Compulsory Population Law was passed, and the citizenry was gradually reduced to its present satisfactory numbers."

"And what was the Milares' Population Law?"

"It is the law that is still the backbone of our life. According to Milares', a great social philosopher of the second century A.S., the most important public question is that of parentage. He maintained that the parents of each generation might either poison or uplift the next; and all his numerous pamphlets and books bore the warning that persons congenitally deficient in mind or physique should not be permitted to breed.

"In pursuance of these views, Milares proposed a basic innovation in social customs; he recommended that the institution of marriage be dissevered from that of parenthood. In other words, while marriage—and likewise divorce—should be permitted to all, parenthood should become a subject of drastic regulation; any young couple wishing children must have their fitness examined by a carefully selected State Board. Since effective methods of birth control were known, this system was quite practicable, and, in fact, has proved—"

"But what if the orders of the board were disobeyed? Certainly, the unlawful newcomer couldn't be punished."

"Certainly not. But a stigma would attach to the parents the stain of illegitimacy."

"You mean—the parents would be considered illegitimate?"

"Exactly. And the disgrace is so great that few have ever offended in that way. Hence, we have never exceeded the prescribed population by more than one or two percent."

"Even so," I contended, rather vaguely, "wouldn't such a system be too arbitrary to succeed?"

"The answer is that it has succeeded for nearly three thousand years. Do you think that, at the time of the Submergence, our men and women enjoyed such perfection of physical beauty as today? Or do you imagine that the intellectual and artistic types predominated? Far from it! Thousands were sickly and stunted in body; thousands were imbecile, weak-minded or insane. But thanks to the rigidity of the selection, these types have been eliminated, and the average life has been lengthened from the pre-Submergence figure of sixty-five years to a hundred and twenty—which means that a man has a whole century of mature service to render instead of a mere four or five decades."

I had no choice except to applaud the results. But, at the time, I noted a vital oversight in Xanocles' recitation. "All this," I pointed out," tells me nothing of the party of Emergence. In fact, if the Milares' Population Law has worked so successfully, why should you oppose it?"

"It would not be quite correct to say that we oppose it," he explained. "We recognize its benefits, but believe the time has come to modify it. Not that we would increase the population of Atlantis beyond the present mark; but we hold that many deserving persons are being denied parenthood, and that many more children of the highest quality might be born. To give you a simple illustration, the Board seems to dislike to perpetuate the radical strains, and rules with suspicious frequency against members of the Party of Emergence."

"But precisely what does your party advocate?"

"Just what our name implies…to let our surplus population emerge into the Upper World. That would be easy enough, for the submersible repair ships that range the ocean about the glass wall could convey us above seas. Of course, there might be no way to return, but a return would not be desirable. It would be sufficient if we could insure life for thousands of our unborn sons and daughters, and remake the Upper World by an infiltration of our superior blood and standards. Besides…" here Xanocles hesitated perceptibly, "…there is another reason."

"What is that?"

Xanocles remained silent for a moment, staring abstractedly towards the romping fauns and mermaids on the seaweed tapestries of the wall.

Then slowly he resumed, "We hold—and in this we are violently combated by the Submergence Party—that there was one minor flaw in the plan of Agripides. In a thousand respects his projects were perfect, but in the thousandth and first he made an oversight—perhaps an unavoidable oversight. He did not leave room enough in Atlantis for adventure. Everything here is so well designed that there is little chance for daring, courage, the unknown—little chance for sheer primitive rashness and hardihood. Our games and recreations, our art, our political contests, of course consume much of our surplus energy; but, after all, we are the children of savage ancestors, and among our young there is a craving for keener experience. Hence we of the Emergence Party favor the increase of population, so, that those who wish may enjoy the greatest adventure of all—may launch their vessels towards unknown worlds!"

"You would find that adventure well worth taking," I commented.

"Then you—you perhaps agree with the Party of Emergence?" cried Xanocles, rising and coming towards me, enthusiastically.

"Perhaps I do," I admitted, also rising, and taking his extended hands. And as I felt his hearty clasp, it seemed to me that I had not only gained a friend, but found my political allegiance.

WHAT THE BOOKS REVEALED

AMID ALL THE excitement of my return to Archeon, I had not forgotten Aelios' advice to visit the library. Nor had I forgotten my official duties as Historian of the Upper World, nor the necessity for acquiring more explicit knowledge of undersea customs before I could hope to interpret my own country to the Atlanteans. Therefore I was determined to accomplish a double object: to prepare myself for my prescribed work and at the same time to gratify my curiosity by extensive reading.

As soon as I was settled in my new apartment, I set out for the main government library, a many-domed edifice of granite and white chalcedony, located in a large flower-bordered square near the center of town. Had I not been able to identify it from the descriptions, I might have recognized it by the streams of people constantly flowing in and out, giving me the impression that it was the business heart of the city.

Yet my first impressions were merely bewildering. Not only was the building one of the largest I had seen (covering all of five or six acres), but its contents were amazing in their profusion and variety. My first surprise was at the discovery that there were no railings, fences or locked doors, and that the visitor was admitted without question to every room and corridor; my second surprise arose from the queer arrangement of the books. For the volumes were catalogued and stacked, not alphabetically, but chronologically. There was a gallery reserved for each century of Atlantean history, down to the seventh century B.S., and within the galleries the books were arranged by authors and subjects in a pleasingly novel way. In a niche among the books, for example, you would observe the bust of a stern-browed, bearded man; and, coming close, you would note that this was the poet Sargos; and just below the bust you would find the complete collection of the poet's works, as well as the commentaries upon them. Or in another corner of the room you would pause to admire the painting of a crowded ancient seaport, and the inscription below the painting would tell you that this was the vanished maritime city of Therion. Just beneath this inscription would be the books wherein Therion was pictured and discussed.

The sheer abundance of the volumes was a source of great astonishment to me—it seemed as if every era in Atlantean history had been a literary one. As nearly as I could determine, an average of several hundred books a year had been thought worthy of preservation—and the high period of productivity had already endured for twenty-five centuries! Nor were the favored works merely stored on dusty shelves—every one of the scores which I opened had been well thumbed, and the crowds browsing along the alcoves and aisles testified that literary interest was not purely a thing of the past.

It was not long before, seated in company with twenty or thirty Atlanteans before the long marble table in the most modern of the galleries, I began to taste the contents of several books I had selected at random. And these proved so delightful that it was hours before I thought of leaving.

While all were richly diverting, the one that interested me most was a little volume entitled, "Social Life in the Thirty-First Century." When I recall the unusual size of the type and the extreme simplicity of the style, I feel sure that this book was meant for a juvenile audience; but this fact did not then occur to me, and I found the work admirably suited to my needs. Questions that had been perplexing me ever since my arrival in Atlantis were explained; and I gained a clearer idea than ever before of Atlantean beliefs and institutions.

I had been wondering, for example, about the statue-like palace wherein Rawson and I had been imprisoned; I was now informed that this, "The Temple of the Stars," was among the oldest buildings in Atlantis, having been erected just before the Submergence so that the people might bring to mind the aspect of the skies. I had been wondering, likewise, about the "Hall of Public Enlightenment," that amber-hued and sapphire amphitheater in which I had listened to several debates; I now read that such a building had been erected centuries before in every Atlantean city as a place of popular assemblage; and I learned that any citizen might attend the meetings there and take part in the discussions, and that at such popular gatherings the few laws of the country were proposed and most important problems settled.

The discussion of the Halls of Public Enlightenment naturally paved the way for a description of the country's political system.

"The State of Atlantis," I read, "is neither a monarchy, an oligarchy, nor a republic. It is a Commonality, which means that everything, except a few personal articles, is possessed in common by the people. At the head of the State is the High Chief Adviser, whose principal duty is to counsel the citizens, but who decides certain specified minor State questions, and is empowered to assume dictatorial authority in case of a national crisis (although such a crisis has never occurred since the riots of the second century A.S., following the passage of the Milares' Compulsory Population Law).

"Like all the other officials, the High Chief Adviser receives his position neither by appointment, nor by heredity, nor by election, but by Automatic Selection. In other words, he takes office after defeating all rivals in a series of debates and competitive examinations. His term of service is indefinite, but every three years he must prove his fitness by engaging in contests with qualified aspirants for the Advisership; and unless he can still outdo all opponents, a new chief executive is installed."

It occurred to me that such a system would detract from the dignity of the High Chief Adviser; but the book informed me that, on the contrary, it added to his dignity, since he was assured of governing on a basis of merit only. In fact, he was bound to keep fit and even to improve while in office; and most High Chief

Advisers did actually remain so well qualified that they stayed in power for an average of thirty years. For example, Icenocles (the incumbent at the time of the publication of the book) had already ruled for forty-five years, and now, at the mature age of one hundred and seven, he still regularly put all competitors to shame.

To my astonishment, I learned that there was no such thing as a legislature or law-making group in Atlantis. "Ancient experience has taught us," said the book, "that representative government usually represents only a faction. And in a community whose members are few and all of whose citizens are intelligent, there is no necessity for delegated authority. Local statutes and ordinances were abolished at the time of the Submergence; and the few national laws are proposed in the Hall of Public Enlightenment of any of the cities. Having been debated and approved by an assemblage of a hundred citizens or more, the measure is submitted to a referendum of all the Atlanteans after a lapse of thirty days and a majority vote suffices for its passage.

"At the head of each city is a Local Adviser, selected in the same manner as the High Chief Adviser. Aided by a corps of from five to fifty assistants also chosen competitively, he decides all questions not settled in the popular assemblies—questions such as the amount of energy to be devoted to the erection of new buildings, the time and nature of local festivals, the adoption of local hygienic measures, and the number of public physicians required to attend the ill and aged. Equally important, theoretically, though in actual practice far less so, is the court of eleven judges which resides in each town, settling disputes among citizens and reprimanding law-breakers. No doubt there were such persons as law-breakers three thousand years ago, when these courts were planned, but today such offenders are virtually unknown, for the only crimes are those of impulse and passion, and these are exceedingly rare. Occasionally, indeed, some diseased person will break an unwritten rule of society, such as that against trapping or slaying fishes or small animals; but the government hospitals care for such unfortunates, just as they care for the criminals of impulse, and ordinarily effect a cure. As for disputes among individuals, they are as obsolete as embezzlement or highway robbery, for now that the ownership of property has been abolished, what is there left to quarrel about?"

At a single sitting, I read the book from cover to cover. It mentioned innumerable other facts of high interest: how the great golden lamps of Atlantis were atomically lighted, and were switched on and off at specified intervals by countrywide clockwork; how all Atlanteans, old and young, ill and healthy, were cared for by the State, so that no man was weighed down with dependants; how disease had been almost wiped out, since all the commoner noxious germs had been conquered; how religion in the organized sense had ceased to exist, for the reason that each man was expected to arrive at his own philosophy; how the temples that littered the country were without theological meaning, but were sanctuaries of beauty whereto anyone might come for worship amid the solitude of his own thoughts; and how education was one of the prime pursuits of the people, and was participated in by all from childhood to old age.

From the few pages that the author of the "Social Life" devoted to the latter subject, I realized that the Atlanteans would have been horrified at our system of herding forty or fifty children together in subjection to a glowering pedagogue. Their theory was that friendly personal contact with the teacher was the important thing; hence their boys and girls were taught in small groups, and never for many hours a day, nor with more than a minimum of restraint upon their natural spirits, nor in a specified or unvarying place, for as often as not their schoolroom was a marble colonnade, or the court of a temple, or even the open fields. And, in the same way, the higher education (except in the case of scientific work requiring laboratory training) was much less formal than among us. There were no such things as universities and degrees, but men and women of recognized wisdom and learning were chosen to commune with the young, somewhat like Socrates presiding among his disciples; and these "Guardians of the Mind," as they were called, would counsel and direct their young charges, and guide them in that reading which constituted their chief source of information.

HOPES AND ANXIETIES

IT IS FROM MY FIRST VISIT to the library that I date my real initiation into the affairs of Atlantis. From that time forth I was no longer a stranger in a strange world; I became involved in such a round of activities that I began to feel almost at home.

First of all, of course, there was my "History of the Upper World," on which I consumed much time in planning. The introductory section was to be devoted to a description of the modern world, its customs, languages, social systems, scientific discoveries, and wars; and having begun with this grand resume of modern achievements, I intended to show the steps by which we have advanced, and to picture the course of those social fluctuations, those invasions, battles, slave-raids, civil conflicts, religious persecutions, crusades, economic revolutions, industrial tumults and international blood-feuds that have brought civilization to its present proud estate.

But while I was mapping out my book, my thoughts were frequently on more personal subjects. And having completed the outline, I could not forget the invitation made me by the most fascinating woman in Atlantis.

Late one afternoon, when her day's tutoring would be over, I paid my second visit to her home. I went just a little hesitatingly, yet not without some justifiable hope, for I recalled vividly the delicious, all-too-brief contact of our meeting beneath the pictorial lights of Thalos.

It was Aelios herself who came tripping to the door in response to my knock; and it was Aelios who escorted me into the house with cordial greetings and hospitable smiles.

"Well, my friend, I thought you would be coming," she said, simply, as we took seats side by side on the seaweed sofa we had occupied on my first visit.

"What made you think that?"

"Why, didn't you say you would come?" she returned; in transparent surprise. "You're undertaking a difficult task, you know—to write a book in a strange language. Isn't it only natural to want advice?"

"It certainly is," I confessed, and should have liked, to add, "...when I can have such a charming adviser."

"I suppose you've been working hard," she continued, evidently unaware of what was in my thoughts. "And, of course, you've brought something to show me."

"Yes, indeed," I admitted; and unfolded the paper that contained the plans for my history.

For several minutes she gazed at it intently, her features furrowed with thought.

But all the while my own mind was far, how far from anything so mundane as the annals of the Upper World! I was noticing again the exquisite grace of my beloved's countenance, with the golden hair piled above the pale brow and the large, divinely blue eyes. I was wishing that I was a sculptor, to set in imperishable marble the perfect, sharply-chiseled contours of her face. I was thinking how blessed above all men I would be to enjoy continually the glow of that dear presence, the fragrance that seemed to surround her like a sweet emanation of her personality.

Is it any wonder, then, that I scarcely heard her comments on my outline? Is it any wonder if, in my loving fervor, I let my attention drift from her words, but drew near her, and then a little nearer, and was about to let my arms once more plead for me, when she herself, with a decisive gesture, stopped me?

Had she some clairvoyant perception of my thoughts?

At all events, she drew away from me—not abruptly, but with a dance-like, sudden movement that took her quite out of reach.

"Keep greater control of yourself, my friend," she counseled. "Here in Atlantis we are used to holding our emotions more in leash."

But instantly, when she saw how downcast I was, how my head drooped at the sting of this rebuke, she approached me once more, and spoke in low musical tones that had some power of instant healing.

"Forgive me, dear friend, if I have hurt you. I forgot that you come from another world—a less disciplined world, where men keep less restraint on the fluttering of the heart. But try to behave like one of us, Anson. You are here now to discuss your History of the Upper World. Let us talk of that—only of that."

"As you say," I conceded. But in her soft smoldering eyes there was a sympathetic, a kindly glow that lent renewed strength to my hopes.

What if, for the rest of that visit, our conversation was confined to my proposed book? Despite the temporary check I had received, I could not keep exultant thoughts from my heart. And when I left, it was with her last words ringing in my mind, like the refrain of a song.

"Come again, my friend. Come again. Perhaps I can help you some more. Our doors, you know, are always open."

Yet, with one of the swift, gusty alternations that so frequently disturbed the course of my love, I was exalted only to be immediately cast low again.

This time it was something quite external—and quite accidental—which hurled me back into the fog of depression. It was my friend Xanocles who was responsible for the change; though he was quite unconscious of the damage he caused. Somehow, during one of his discussions of Atlantean social life, he had chanced to touch upon the marriage system. And he had mentioned the Milares' Population Law, and stated that this alone had not been responsible for the superiority of the Atlantean stock.

"Another cause," he continued, "is what is called marital selection. This is regulated by custom, and is mostly in the hands of the women, yet is so rigid that an inferior man can hardly find a mate. Indeed, a superior woman would be disgraced by linking herself to a weakling."

"Just what do you mean by a weakling?"

Xanocles looked at me in surprise. "A weakling, of course, is one with nothing to give to society. A great poet, for example, could never be thought of as a weakling; nor a competent painter, philosopher, musician, or biologist. But any man whose contributions show no skill or individuality is regarded as a weakling. Naturally, he is not condemned so long as he does his best; but he is not considered fit for marriage except with another weakling—and, needless to say, weaklings are not encouraged to propagate."

How little Xanocles suspected that these words were thrusts direct to my heart! I do not believe that, in my own world, I had ever suffered from what is known as an inferiority complex; but among the Atlanteans, with their higher standards, mere honesty demanded that I question my own qualifications. And what, I wondered, had I to offer a woman such as Aelios? Must not my meager attainments appear childish to her? Would I not, by comparison with the natives, justly be rated as a weakling?

For many days I was harassed by such thoughts, while consoled to some extent by the companionship of Xanocles. The friendship begun at our first meeting was strengthening and solidifying; the proximity of our lodgings made it easy for us to see one another, but there was also a proximity of mind, which gave each of us pleasure in the other's company. Despite the gulf of race and experience, we actually had more in common than many people who have spent all their lives in the same home. And so we would often seek each other out, and spend hours exchanging ideas in the seclusion of our rooms; and frequently we might have been seen strolling arm in arm about the city, while I pictured to him the wonders and vastness of the Upper World, or while he regaled me with colorful anecdotes, and told how he was employed by the State as a binder and designer of books, but spent his spare time in writing economic and philosophical treatises or delivering lectures in favor of the Emergence.

But my friendship with Xanocles did not make me forget certain older acquaintances. Even after being elevated to the dignity of citizenship, I saw as much of my former shipmates as before; indeed, I saw some of them more than ever, and in particular Captain Gavison, who frequently visited me to exchange reminiscences; and I rubbed shoulders with the whole crew at the regular bi-weekly meetings of the Upper World Club, which were now held in my apartment.

These meetings were sometimes exciting affairs, perhaps because there was little else in Atlantis which offered much prospect of excitement. Looking back today, it is not easy for me to recall just what there was to be agitated about; but certain it is that there would be fiery debates, which occasionally became so heated that President Gavison would rap and rap with the bit of stone that served him as gavel, raising his voice until he almost shouted. Sometimes the disputes were due to conflicting opinions of Atlantis; sometimes the altercation would concern some proposal for improving our status. Many and curious were the views expressed. One of our members would suggest that we attempt to make life more endurable by constructing a motor boat or automobile; another would be convinced that all would be well with Atlantis were it not for the absence of radio and movies; and a few would toy fondly with wildly impractical ideas of escape.

As time went by, it became more and more apparent that the majority would never be reconciled to Atlantis. They felt estranged by its art, overwhelmed by its majesty, and bored by its peacefulness. While they still studied the native language for several hours a day, and at times were delighted at being allowed a part in the native pastimes and athletics, all in all they felt as much out of place as ever. "Sacred Jehovah, you can keep all your kings' palaces and pretty pictures, and give me a good old corncob pipe and a whisky jug!" Stranahan would express the fervent view of the majority. Here amid the ideal surroundings of Atlantis, the men were coming to look upon the Upper World as a lost Elysium!

CURIOSITIES, FREAKS AND MONSTROSITIES

ALTHOUGH MY FORMER SHIPMATES were still ill at ease in Atlantis, as the months went by they were becoming better trained in the native tongue, and one by one were being summoned before the Committee on Selective Assignments and ordered to some specific daily task.

Captain Gavison, one of the quickest to master the language, was among the first to be graduated into citizenship. But his advancement brought him no great pleasure, since his prescribed duty was to spend two and a half hours daily in a bureau engaged in compiling statistics of population and industry; and his chosen work for the State, which was to write a comparison of Atlantean and Upper World civilization, gave him no end of trouble owing to his inexperience in authorship.

Meanwhile, Stranahan and Rawson had also matriculated into citizenship; and each had his assigned work. Rawson, as a well-formed and brawny youth, was permitted to exercise his muscles for an hour and a half daily in a marble quarry north of the city, while Stranahan, who had had his choice of several occupations, decided that it would suit him best to serve three hours daily as doorman at the Archeon City museum.

It was as if this position had been made to order for him. When he stood at the museum entrance, robed in an official red while politely directing visitors to the various aisles and departments, he had the dignity of one born to a lofty station. His work was not wholly easy, he asserted, for the exhibits were many and confusing; yet to see him as he swayed commandingly from side to side of the great arched doorway, with chest thrown well out and arms folded behind him, one would scarcely have believed him anything less than the owner of the building.

Indeed, the interest that he took in the museum seemed almost personal. He summoned the whole Upper World club to inspect it as though it had been his own handiwork; and directed us from gallery to gallery and from exhibit to exhibit with the serenity of expert knowledge. Thus we had him to thank for introducing us to some extraordinary displays.

Unquestionably, the museum was one of the things most worth seeing in all Atlantis. The contents were remarkable; I could not view them without astonishment at the beauty of some exhibits, at the strangeness and ghastliness of others. I might describe the department of science and invention, with its odd contrivances, its machines for preventing earthquakes, machines for regulating the undersea temperature, machines for detecting and isolating noxious bacteria, machines for transforming iron into copper or tin into lead, machines for boring through the ground as a submarine bores through the water. But what interested me even more was the historical department.

Never shall I forget my first visit to this section. Imagine, to begin with, a glass case containing nothing but the fragments of a brick wall—yes, a commonplace wall of red brick! Imagine reading that this was "a substance employed for building purposes in the days before the Aesthetic Renaissance." Or, again, picture yourself in contact with half a dozen gold coins, larger than silver dollars and each worth several days' wages, yet left unguarded where anyone might seize them! And fancy reading that these bits of metal had "once been considered valuable" and had even been fought for and hoarded. Or, to take another illustration, conceive of your surprise at seeing a carefully treasured speck of coal, and being informed that this was used for fuel in the days before inter-atomic energy. Or paint for yourself the shock of coming across a case of fine jewelry, of rings, earrings, brooches, bracelets, and the like, and finding them represented as "typical of primitive taste…"

But while all the historical department proved most entertaining, there was one section that interested me more than all the rest. This was known as the "Hall of Horrors." Somehow, there was something about the "Hall of Horrors" that seemed familiar, even though a placard at the entrance assured me that all the exhibits dated from a remote antiquity. Thus, the first thing that I noticed was a gas mask credited to the third century B.S., but looking as if it might have served in the First World War. Besides the gas mask was a steel helmet of the fourth century B.S., yet had it not been for the card identifying it, I might have suspected that it was a relic of Europe of the Nineteen Forties.

Such a suspicion, however, would not have applied to the other military implements ranged about the room. Most of them were so crude of design as to make me smile. Even as I write this, I can recapture the mood of exultation I felt at the proof of our own superiority! The rifles of the second century B.S., were so puny-looking as to appear primitive, and the bayonets were half a foot shorter than our own; the machine guns of the first century B.S. had obviously not half the killing value of ours, and the cannon were not constructed for long distance firing; while the absence of the armored tank, the hand grenade and "liquid fire," and the small range and bomb capacity of the military airplanes as compared with Upper World types, showed that the ancient Atlanteans would not even have been in the competition with the war-makers of our own day.

From the "Hall of Horrors" Stranahan led us into a scarcely less interesting department whose miscellany of ancient oddities would have defied classification. "Here's where you'll feel at home," grunted our guide, as with a gesture of welcome he preceded us through the doorway. But we did not feel in the least at home. I had never had a more distinct reminder of my exile than when I gazed at great brick and iron chimneys, catalogued as typical of

"The Age of Steel and Fire"; and it made me almost homesick to see pictures of long-vanished cities wrapped in clouds of smoke and soot, and described as "Representative of the tubercular era in old Atlantis."

But much more surprising were the huge ancient furnaces, resurrected in detail, with puppet stokers in the act of pitching coal into the flames. An explanatory card declared that, "These were once considered necessary evils, not only for industrial reasons, but because the Submergence had not yet made possible the automatic regulation of the weather."

There was, however, an apparently insignificant object, which aroused far greater interest among my companions. Carefully guarded under a glass cover, where it had evidently undergone some special process of preservation, was a flat little rectangle of some shriveled brownish substance, beneath which appeared the following placard:

"A fragment of a narcotic, variously known as tobac and tobaccan, which was imported into old Atlantis from across the western ocean. It found favor at one time among the women of the country, and to a lesser extent among the men, although its use was considered a mark of effeminacy. There were several common ways of absorbing the drug, the most popular being to suck the smoke into the lungs by means of a little paper tube. Happily, this disgusting habit has long ago disappeared; the elimination of this plant at the time of the Good Destruction is not the least of the benefits conferred by Agripides."

I am afraid that my companions did not sympathize with the latter statement. They cast longing glances in the direction of the tobacco; it was fortunate that it was safely guarded beneath glass!

With the memory of the tobacco still rankling in our minds, we were escorted into the "Department of Human Evolution." Here was depicted the rise of man from savagery to the height of present day Atlantis. A series of skeletons indicated the gradual transformation from a broad-boned, ape-like thing to a big-skulled modern—and, to my surprise, the large cranial capacity was represented as belonging almost exclusively to the aboriginal and Post Submergence eras! While I was wondering why this should be, I chanced to overhear the words of a sagacious-looking bearded man, who accompanied a party of youths, evidently as their tutor.

"Observe this skull," he said, pausing and pointing to one of the most ancient of the group. "This is the fossil of a Paleolithic pre-Atlantean, who inhabited our island forty-five or fifty thousand years ago. You can see for yourself how much higher and ampler is the skull than that of your own ancestor of thirty-two hundred years ago, whose mental decline was fostered by the reverse selection of that age, which encouraged the average and sub-average man at the expense of the exceptional individual. Fortunately, this tendency was counteracted by the measures of Agripides and his successors, and we can now boast of being on the same high mental plane as the men of fifty thousand years ago…"

The speaker withdrew with his students towards a further exhibit; while I passed on with my companions down several long corridors to the department known as "Curiosities, Freaks and Monstrosities," where Stranahan, with an odd twinkling expression, warned us to be ready for a surprise. Certainly, he warned us with good reason. As we glanced towards the further wall, we were shocked by sight of something startlingly familiar—so familiar, indeed, that several of us uttered little cries of amazement. Neatly arranged behind a glass case, flattened against the rear panels so as to afford a better view, were dozens of well-known blue uniforms! Among them, from the Ensign's stripes, I recognized my own; and among them, also, was the decorated uniform of the Captain. And above them all, on a large-lettered placard, appeared the statements that these were "the clothes worn by the only aliens to enter Atlantis since the Submergence," and that they were "interesting as specimens of the grotesque and unsightly garments fashionable in the Upper World."

THE WARNING OF THE WATERS

ALTHOUGH AT TIMES DURING MY FIRST months in Atlantis I may have wished that the waters would open above me and bear me back to my own land, my longings were never mixed with misgivings, and my regrets were never tinged with fear. Even in my most pessimistic moments, I had no doubt but that the Sunken World was secure; that no menace to life or tranquility lurked in its well-ordered depths. Hence, I was all the more shocked at the discovery of that peril that was to give Atlantis the aspect of a beleaguered city, and to overcast its beauty with foreboding and horror.

I had been below seas little more than a year when the crisis occurred. It was a crisis as startling and unexpected as the flaming of a meteor out of a calm sky; and yet, had we but known it, it had been preparing its way insidiously during the days of fancied safety, like some mortal disease burrowing through tissues that are apparently sound.

I remember that one night, after many onerous hours devoted to my "History of the Upper World," I slept but poorly, with an intermittent slumber disturbed by nightmares of huge towers crashing to destruction. And during the wakeful intervals my thoughts framed other nightmares, and I was agitated by a vague alarm and excitement, though I could not understand why. Not until much later did it occur to me that some telepathic force may have conveyed to me the deep unrest that surcharged the atmosphere.

But whether or not this was the case, I know that in the morning, when I had dressed and stood in my roof-bedroom gazing down into the streets, I became acutely conscious that something was wrong. Every few minutes a native or group of natives could be seen streaking by at a speed I had never before observed among the unhurried Atlanteans; and it seemed to me that their faces were convulsed with pain or fear, while their voices had the nervousness, almost hysteria, of men in a panic.

What could have happened? Had the Atlanteans all suddenly gone mad? Or were they facing an insurrection, or a civil war?

These suppositions, as I turned them over in my mind, seemed utterly fantastic. Yet I was still filled with apprehension to observe the natives wildly scurrying about the streets.

I was just going out to investigate, when there came an excited rapping at my door. "Come in!" I cried, and the door swung open to admit—Captain Gavison!

He was far from his composed normal self. His pale blue costume was all ruffled; his long hair hung disheveled over his narrow bronzed brow; his face looked all hot and sweaty; his gray eyes burned with a vague distress.

"Have you—have you heard?" he gasped, not waiting for a formal greeting as he strode into the room.

"Heard what?"

"Don't see how you could help hearing," he snapped, and began slowly to pace the floor, his brow wrinkled in thought.

"But what is it?" I demanded, impatiently. "Just what have you heard?"

"One of the natives told me strange things last night," he rattled forth, as he continued his restless perambulations about the room. "I haven't slept a wink, not one wink!"

"What strange things? Not going to be sent back home, are we?" I inquired, with an abortive effort to be facetious.

"Lucky if we're not sent to a damned sight worse place," he growled, bristling into his old military manner. "The glass wall has cracked!"

"The glass wall—cracked?" I cried, stupidly, stunned by the horror of the words.

"Yes, the glass wall has cracked! One of the patrol boats discovered the damage late yesterday afternoon. There's a dangerous fracture near the entrance of the Salty River."

For reply, I could only groan. The glass wall of Atlantis cracked! The whole Atlantic Ocean bearing down upon the Sunken World! Too well I understood what that meant, too well to require comment.

"But how—how in the name of heaven—"

"That's not hard to say," Gavison took up, hastily. "At least, there are suspicions—"

"Suspicions?"

"Suspicions that you and I and the rest of us are to blame."

"But that's not possible!"

"Oh, yes, it's possible enough. It all happened before we got here. The *X-111*, caught in the whirlpool outside the Salty River, was hurled by the force of the waters against the glass wall, probably striking with its steel prow, which, as you know, was built for ramming our enemies. The wall, luckily, was too stout to be shattered but it was cracked, and the crack has been growing all this time without being noticed."

"Merciful gods! Then if—if anything happens to Atlantis, it will be all on account of us…"

Before Gavison had had time to reply, there came another rapping at the door. And, hardly waiting for my summons, a wild-eyed Xanocles burst in. Like my other visitor, he wasted no time on greetings. "You—you know?" he faltered, with a lack of self-command most unusual in him.

Solemnly we nodded.

Without delay, he plunged into the subject that had brought him to us. "Maybe you'd like to go and see for yourselves?"

"But how can we see—"

"The government—that is to say, the High Chief Adviser—has ordered the inter-atomic river boats put at the people's disposal. Several of them are now plying back and forth, bearing thousands to the glass wall. The Adviser thinks the people should see for themselves just what has happened."

"Very well then, let's go," decided the Captain.

Without another word, the three of us set out together. In silence we strode down the long avenue that meandered towards the river. And as we sped along we encountered dozens of the natives, all of them in as great a hurry as we, and all with flushed, excited faces.

Upon reaching the piers, we found that hundreds of Atlanteans had preceded us, most of them so transformed that I could hardly recognize them as citizens of the Sunken World. Many were chattering wildly, or pacing back and forth distractedly, or uttering half-hysterical exclamations; and one or two were mumbling and muttering to themselves, or moving their lips silently in what might have been prayer. But they did not fail to notice our arrival; angry exclamations broke forth at sight of us, and several of the men and women withdrew visibly…until, in my surprise, I did not know whether to ascribe their hostility to the unpopularity of Xanocles or to the part that Gavison and I had played as unconscious agents of disaster.

To calm the excited multitude, a vigorous-looking young man raised his voice. "Friends, there is no cause for alarm. We do not yet know how serious the damage is, but the glass wall still holds, not a drop of water has broken through. There is reason to believe that the break will soon be repaired, and that we will go on living just as usual…"

These words, I was glad to see, had a soothing effect. Yet I was relieved when at last the boat hove into view, a slender affair as long as the longest river vessel, but not more than twenty-five feet from beam to beam. I did not pay much attention to its details, though I did note how low-lying it was, with but one visible deck, one small cabin, and no smoke-stack or mast. But after it had drawn up to the pier and the gangplank was flung down, I wasted no time about boarding it with my two companions. Benches and chairs were strewn about the deck, sufficient to accommodate the crowd; and we had hardly taken seats when the boat commenced to shiver and throb and we started upstream with the velocity of an express train.

So rapidly did we move that in less than an hour we were approaching the head of the Salty River. All during the interval I scarcely ventured to break the brooding solitude of my own thoughts. My silence, I am afraid, was encouraged by that of all the hundreds of passengers; for, now that they had embarked upon the voyage, their excitement had died down to a mood of solemn waiting, a tense and painful waiting all too apparent in the rigid, staring faces of the men and the women's pale cheeks and frightened eyes.

It was with much inward trembling that at length I saw the river grow white and agitated ahead of us, and knew that we were not far from the valve where the torrents were hurled in from the sea. I was quivering with impatience when finally we swerved into a little side canal and our boat landed at a low granite dock whence a sister ship was just leaving. No need to state that I lost little time in stepping across the gangplank, as soon as the thronged state of the deck permitted. And that I was thankful at being able to walk the remaining three or four miles to the glass wall!

To watch my two companions and myself set out along the clay footpath towards the wall, you might have thought us athletes training for a race. But rapidly as we moved, there were scores who kept pace with us.

For many minutes we hastened parallel to the Salty River. We passed the long, white rapids; we passed the gigantic jet of water that shot thundering out of the pipe-like valve; we saw the wall itself sloping down before us, and near the wall we could make out a long black mass, which ultimately resolved itself into a human multitude.

The crowd, as we drew near, proved to be in a wildly agitated condition. Frantically men and women paced to and fro, swarming and squirming like worms or ants, some were gesticulating vehemently, some speaking in high-pitched tones audible from afar, some merely standing petrified like men dealt a stunning blow.

Yet, as we took our places among them, we could observe no tangible cause for alarm. To our right loomed the elongated steely gray valve, a great tube as high as a three-story building, which narrowed as it approached the wall, and passed through it on a level with the ground. And just before us sloped the wall itself, now roped off so that we could not come within a stone's throw, but apparently still the same smooth dark greenish barrier I had viewed months before. No sign of any break was visible.

But while I stood there watching, I heard a faint swishing sound, like the lapping of sea waves against the rocks. I may have been mistaken, for amid the clamoring of the mob and the distant roaring of waters from the valve, it was difficult to be sure just what one heard. But Gavison and Xanocles seemed to note that same ominous noise and both paused to listen with anxious expressions. "It's the water working through the inner layers of the glass," I thought I heard Xanocles remark. But again I could not be sure, for even as he spoke a tumult of shouts arose, and I turned from him in sudden fright.

On one of the great roof-supporting stone columns, a searchlight had been mounted, and was slowly swinging around, casting a piercing illumination upon the wall from a bright yellow eye glaring like a locomotive headlight. For a moment it wavered as if it could not find a focus, then it became rigid and still, and a circle of the wall many yards across stood out in brilliant relief.

Instantly the people began to press forward, so excited that for a moment I almost lost touch with Gavison and Xanocles, and could catch no glimpse of the illuminated patch of wall. At the same time, cries of terror and dismay broke forth. A man behind me groaned, a woman gave a half-suppressed sob; somewhere from the rear came a hysterical wailing. Then, when the circle in the wall again became visible, I was wedged in so tightly that I could I scarcely observe it. Only by degrees could I make out its features, and see what resembled an enormous piece of cracked crockery.

From an amorphous central blur several feet across, great seams and fissures ran in a hundred directions, with spidery arms that reached out like the roots of a tree, gradually growing thinner until they vanished in vacancy. It seemed a miracle that the water had not already burst through, for each of the scores of diverging cracks was rods long and must have been many feet deep.

I do not know how long I stood staring blankly at that tragic break in the glass. I was as one divested of power of thought or movement. I merely hovered there transfixed, listening to the muttering and sighing of the multitude. Strangely enough, it did not occur to me to ask whether the damage could be repaired; it was as if I had known all the while that it was beyond remedy. For the moment, my attitude was curiously detached, almost impersonal, as though I were the external witness of some prodigious catastrophe.

Yet it was a highly personal thought that startled me back to myself. Out of some dim, subconscious depth, there swept across my mind the vision of two bright blue eyes and, with that vision, acute fear seized me. That Atlantis should be in danger was appalling enough—but that Aelios should be imperiled was a thought almost too terrible for belief. And, accompanying that first wild stab of alarm for her, there came a sharp desire to see her, to be with her, to speak with her; and, hopeful that she might be somewhere in this crowd, I began to search all about me, and then to thread my way at random through the dense masses of people, scanning all the faces in my anxiety, until Gavison and Xanocles, following me with difficulty, began to ask whether the crack were in the wall or in my head.

But no Aelios was to be seen; and at last I had to abandon the quest.

A dull, settled sadness had fallen over me; and driven by motives that I would have not acknowledged, I expressed my purpose of returning at once to Archeon, saying that I had already seen everything.

"But you haven't seen a thing yet," demurred Xanocles. "The submersible repair ships still haven't arrived. When they come, they will be a sight worth watching."

And he slipped his arm into mine, and drew me with him towards the wall, while I continued to protest that I must return to Archeon.

No doubt in the end I should have had my way, had another hubbub not arisen to distract my attention. Once more the thousands of voices were lifted in excitement; but this time a note of joy was manifest. Many hands pointed eagerly towards the illuminated circle in the glass; and from just behind me I heard a thankful murmuring. "The repair ships— They're here! They're here!"

Indeed, the repair ships had arrived. Even through the darkest sections of the wall, half a dozen faintly phosphorescent cigar-shaped forms were dimly visible. They were all rather small, hardly a quarter the size of the *X-111*; but they were exceedingly agile and were darting back and forth like great fishes, or else were whirling or pirouetting or standing almost on end, as though stricken with giddiness and unable to control their movements.

"They're having the devil's own time!" muttered Xanocles as he stood watching. "That's the worst danger-spot in the ocean; the waters are in a constant whirlpool because of the torrents emptied into the Salty River. But our men are brave, and somehow they'll manage it."

"But how?" I inquired, unable to imagine any way of making repairs.

"It's far from easy, but can be done. One of the ships will press itself against the wall, so closely that there is no space between. Once all water has been excluded between the vessel and the wall, the pressure on the ocean side will keep the ship in place. And after the ship is in position, a porthole will be opened, through which the men will pour cement into the crack."

Even as Xanocles explained, an anchor was dropped from one of the ships into the slimy sea bottom; and the vessel, having steadied itself, began to drift slowly towards the wall, until it was tightly pressed against the cracked glass. Then a little circle of light opened on its side; and in that circle I could make out the rigid, determined faces of half a dozen men; while in their hands I could observe a variety of rods, tubes, and lantern-like contrivances.

Pessimistic as I had been, I could not but feel a burst of hope to watch the capable, courageous way in which these men set to work. Evidently the waiting throng had become hopeful, too, for murmurs of admiration and approval were on their lips; and as they saw tube after tube of cement emptied into the cracks, they became almost mad with relief. Some began to clap their hands and caper childishly, some sighed in thanksgiving, and some wept silently. After all, Atlantis was saved!

Then, with the suddenness of a thunderbolt, their hopes were dashed out. So swiftly did disaster come that none had a chance to say how or whence. Perhaps it was that the anchor-chain of the submarine had snapped, or that some water had seeped in between the vessel's side and the glass wall. At all events, the submarine was plainly visible one moment, the men pumping the viscid cement through long tubes to the extremities of the crack; and the next moment, there was only a dim shadow flitting away into a watery obscurity.

For an instant, there was an awed silence. Then, as comprehension dawned upon the crowd, a convulsive shudder swept it through and through, and a howl of terror and dismay rang forth. Men glanced askance at their neighbors, blank terror gaping from their eyes; and all at once, as by a common impulse, hundreds pressed confusedly towards the wall, as though thus to succor the unfortunates lost in the briny wastes. But many, conscious of the futility of action, sadly remained in their places, and mutely bowed their heads—a tribute of respect for the drowned.

THE WATERS RETREAT

THE EIGHT DAYS THAT followed were among the most harrowing I had ever spent. Indeed, they were among the most harrowing any resident of Atlantis had ever spent. The acuteness of the peril had become more and more apparent as time went by and the damage was not repaired—the submarine disaster which I had witnessed was but the precursor to other and equally frightful catastrophes. Vessel after vessel battled with the waters; vessel after vessel was shaken away like a twig by the fury of the maelstrom. Sometimes, fortunately, the portholes were shut in time to save the lives of the crew, but on other occasions the ocean snatched its prey; and before a week had gone by Atlantis was mourning seven lost parties of rescuers.

All the country was now in a tumult, I might almost say in a delirium. The regular currents of life had stopped short; men no longer went about their daily duties; the libraries and art galleries were deserted; the young were without tutors, the government departments without clerks; and the cities would have been without bread had it not been for the drastic orders of the High Chief Adviser. Citizens who once had been amply occupied would loiter aimlessly about the streets, or would flock to the Hall of Public Enlightenment to hear the latest reports; or else would restlessly pace along the colonnades, or stand discussing in small groups, nerve-wracked as men under sentence of death. Though I never heard them mention the fear that was uppermost in their minds, yet their pale faces and shuddery manner were eloquent. My former shipmates and I had reason to know how overmastering was their terror, for we saw increasing signs of that aversion I had already noted; the people would glance at us with hostility and even accusation in their eyes, looking mute reproach as though our coming had been responsible (as indeed it had been) for the threatened end of their world.

Every morning five or six of the little inter-atomic submarines would leave Atlantis through the valve in the eastern wall, where the waters of the Salty River were forced back into the sea. And in the evening (if they survived until evening) they would return through the valve in the western wall, where the waters of the Salty

River found entrance. In the interval, their occupants would work as courageously as I had ever known men to work, warring against apparently insurmountable odds; while all Atlantis would stand watching and waiting for news of their progress. It seemed wrongful to my comrades and me that these men, brave and willing as they were, should risk their lives to repair an injury which we had caused; hence several of us volunteered to join the rescuers. But the High Chief Adviser, although expressing his gratitude, refused our offer in terms admitting of no reply; for the repairing crews, as he explained, consisted of specially trained mechanics.

On the eighth day, the officials decided upon a change of tactics. And then it was that the "Acrola," an emergency submarine provided with five anchors and an extra battery of inter-atomic engines, made its way out of the Salty River and around the glass dome to the scene of the damage. Truly, it was time that something desperate be done, for, according to official measurements, the crack had already expanded between nine and ten inches since its detection. But the "Acrola," thanks to its unusual powers of resistance, withstood the buffeting of the waters and remained pressed against the wall while Captain Thermandos and his crew pumped the cement into the innumerable fissures. Except for the extraordinary courage of the men, they, too, would probably have failed, for the task occupied them for more than six hours, any moment of which might have been their last; and they not only had to fill the cracks, but had to hold to their post until the cement had began to harden and was no longer in danger of being washed away.

But the important fact is that they succeeded. Though worn and haggard from their exertions, they had succeeded magnificently. They had saved Atlantis! After all, the floodgates would not burst and the devouring waters would never race along the streets and colonnades!

Such, at least, was the general impression. And so great was the public relief that the pendulum swung violently from a crisis of despair to an extreme of joy. Like men awakened from a nightmare, the Atlanteans refused to believe that the peril had not been utterly wiped away. And for a while, amid the sudden snapping of the tension, their emotions controlled their heads, and their desire to feel safe was converted into a conviction that they were safe. Later, many of them were to awaken from their self-hypnosis; but during the celebration that followed the repairs, the people almost without exception acted as if convinced of their rescue; and all the speakers at the great public gatherings referred in positive terms to the deliverance of Atlantis.

Yet, even at the time, at least one dissenting voice was heard. Among the seven government experts sent to investigate the repairs and report on their soundness, there was one who strenuously challenged the views of his colleagues. While the other six agreed that the damage had been remedied beyond possibility of recurrence, the seventh (Peliades by name) submitted a minority report contending that the relief was only temporary.

"For three or four years—possibly even ten or fifteen," he maintained, "the repairs will prove adequate. But, after that period, the damage will re-appear in an aggravated form. For the cement constitutes a foreign element in the glass, and produces an abnormal bulge, which places too much strain upon those portions which are still sound. At first the wall may be able to endure the strain; but before long it will become too great for the brittle material to resist; and inevitably small new cracks will appear, and then larger, growing by inches and fractions of inches, until the break spreads towards the surface and the tremendous pressure of the ocean shatters the remaining barrier. This effect, of course, will not be noticeable in the beginning; but when it does become apparent, the crack will have spread so far that only heroic measures can save Atlantis.

"The one remedy, therefore, is the immediate erection of a new glass bulwark against the affected portion of the wall. Prodigious though the effort involved, we will probably be able to complete the work in time, *if we start at once!*"

Unfortunately, Peliades' warning was scarcely heeded. In some quarters, he was denounced as a crank, a mad alarmist; in other quarters, he was openly laughed at, or derided as the victim of hysteria; while the majority paid no attention to him at all. Least sympathetic of his hearers were his fellow specialists; these, in response to an inquiry by the High Chief Adviser, testified at great length as to the scientific unsoundness of Peliades' theories, and combined to disprove his views to their own satisfaction.

And so the dissenter's motions were tabled, and Atlantis returned confidently to its normal duties.

THE PARTY OF EMERGENCE

ALTHOUGH ATLANTIS resumed its usual aspect soon after the wall had been repaired, things were never again to be quite as before. It was as though there were some unseen fissure in the life of the Sunken World as well as in its glass boundary; as though the people subconsciously realized that they hovered on the brink of a fathomless abyss. Something seemed to be lacking that had been there before, perhaps because something was present that had never been there before; the corrosive of fear, injected for the first time during all the centuries of the Submergence, seemed to dissipate the charmed tranquility of life and to suggest that inimical and even treacherous forces lurked beyond the marble fountains and palaces and the weird green-golden dome.

But the one tangible result of the discovery of the crack was the rise of the Party of Emergence. This despised minority group, whose very name had been a phrase of contempt, now burst into a prominence as surprising to its members as to the people as a whole, and for the first time threatened to become a power in Atlantean politics. Was it that there were thousands who, beset by a secret dread, looked to the Party of Emergence as their salvation? At all events, a host of disciples flocked to the Emergence banners; and among these were many persons of influence and position, including Peliades, the engineer who had declared the wall unsound.

And now began an aggressive campaign, conducted incessantly in the Hall of Public Enlightenment of every town and village—a campaign that threatened to develop into a life-or-death struggle between the regenerated Emergence Party and the more venerable Submergence group. It happened that I myself took an active, if minor, part in the contest; and it also happened that the entire Upper World Club was implicated, since we all realized that the cause of Emergence offered us our only chance of returning to the earth.

Innumerable were the meetings we attended, and innumerable the pleas we made. To recount all our activities would be impossible, even if I could recall them all; rather let me describe a particular gathering, which stands forth in my mind, not as more striking or noteworthy than the others, but merely as typical.

One afternoon, months after the crack in the wall had been sealed, Xanocles and I prepared for a strenuous session in the Hall of Public Enlightenment. Arriving at the sapphire and amber amphitheater and finding almost all the seats occupied, we took chairs in the rear, and quietly awaited our turn. A discussion was in progress regarding the award of honor to be made to a 'certain lyric' poet; but after this question had been settled, a hush came over the audience and many pairs of eyes were bent towards us inquiringly.

Then it was that Xanocles rose. At a gesture from the same broad-brewed, elderly woman who had presided when Gavison and his crew were brought to trial, my friend stepped out into the aisle and down to the central platform, while all glances followed him intently.

"Fellow citizens," he said, not taking time to pause after reaching the foot of the stairs, "I am here today with one of the most important proposals ever presented since Agripides pleaded for the Submergence. It is not a proposal that has never been put forth before; it is, indeed, at the very backbone of the Party of Emergence, and will continue to be argued and preached until it achieves success. For it is impossible, my friends, that Atlantis should retain its age-old isolation; modern progress makes such backwardness inconceivable, as the arrival of thirty-nine men from outside has demonstrated. I am certain that if Agripides himself were with us now he would agree that our policies must be revised."

Here Xanocles paused for emphasis; but the audience remained silent.

"The question of emigration, my friends," he continued with increased forcefulness, "deserves fresh consideration. Our prohibitions on the subject have been a form of intolerance unworthy of the high traditions of our people; free emigration, if forbidden by the arbitrary conventions of society, is justified by the mandates of nature and the normal craving for romance and adventure.

"Therefore I suggest that the law be modified. But for the sake of those who fear to be too radical, I recommend that we proceed cautiously. Let us begin by allowing three or four of our people to visit the Upper World; and let these, having investigated, return with their reports, so that then, on the basis of definite knowledge, we may weigh the advantages of further emergence."

"No, no, no," rang forth a dozen voices in sharp disapproval. And Xanocles gracefully resigned the floor to one of the dissenters—a tall, stooped man with a sallow face fringed with a white beard.

"Citizens of Atlantis," he declared, in a voice surprisingly resonant and vigorous for one of his age, "I have lived long enough to follow the debates of a hundred years, but never have I heard such folly as has just been advised. Under the influence of Agripides, Atlantis has been beautiful, and it has been happy—and what can life give us more than happiness and beauty? Would you let yourselves be stampeded by the ravings of these modernists, who would trample on every sacred thing, seeking panicky escape from some imaginary peril, or misled by a childish lust for adventure or romance? Take an old man's word, in all the Upper World there can be no romance like that spread beneath our green glass dome, and no adventure like that of our golden-illumined ways. Agripides was right, perhaps more marvelously right than even he could have known. For Atlantis can remain Atlantis only so long as the outer universe is excluded, along with all its bickerings, greedy strivings and ruinous stupidities. Need I do more than to remind you that already the first shock of contact with the Upper World has almost shattered the foundations of Atlantis?"

The old man ceased, and stalked majestically back to his seat, amid nods and murmurs of approval. The Submergence Party had scored, and scored heavily; and, therefore, the time seemed ripe for the address that I had prepared.

I had no difficulty in gaining the floor; and after a few remarks expressing my sympathy with the ends, if not with the methods, of the Submergence Party, I launched into the main body of my speech.

"You are all building without ample knowledge," I said. "And that must necessarily be so, for what can you have learned of the Upper World? But it happens that I, thanks to some years of experience, do know a little of the Upper World; and it is for this reason that I venture to address you on behalf of Emergence."

I paused, in order to pave the way for my next point; and observed hundreds of pairs of eyes straining towards me, in a silence so intense that one might have heard the dropping of the proverbial pin.

"I shall not dwell upon the physical advantages of my own world," I continued. "I shall not describe its wide spaces and splendid vistas, its tree-mantled valleys and sun-burnished lakes, its white-splashed oceans and billowy dark mountains. I shall not discourse upon these sights, for even in the Upper World they are little noted, save by an occasional nature crank or poet.

"But what I shall point out are those advantages familiar to every thinking citizen of the earth. Let me, for example, briefly picture the life of the typical dweller in our greatest city. Both in his home and in his work he enjoys the benefits of the most progressive civilization ever known. To begin with, his dwelling may be of almost any type, for if he likes high places and can afford them, he may enjoy the privilege of looking down upon his neighbors from the seventeenth story. Or, if he prefers exercise, he may walk up to the sixth floor whenever he goes home. Or again, if he be of a sluggish disposition, he may take lodgings at street level or below—and all without extra charge.

"Now as to the daily routine of such a man. After being aroused in the morning by a little clock that is almost human in its faithfulness to habit, he slips hastily into his clothes and consumes a breakfast, perhaps featured by refrigerated beefsteak, grown half a world away, and by coffee made with the condensed milk of cows that lived far away and long ago. Having thus fortified himself against the day's exigencies, he loses no time about leaving the house; and in company with thousands as fortunate as himself, he enters a little hole in the ground, and twenty minutes or half an hour later emerges from another and precisely similar hole five or ten miles away.

"But this is the least of his conveniences. After climbing from the second hole, he wedges his way into a little movable electric box in one of our downtown buildings, and promptly finds himself delivered opposite his office on the fifteenth or twentieth floor. He is now ready for the day's duties; and so marvelously simple is modern civilization that, no matter what those duties be, they are always the same.

"For there is only one task that seems worth while to the modern man, and that is the making of money. Just why moneymaking is so important is a question that I cannot answer; but it must be important indeed, for everyone is involved in it, especially those who have more already than they know what to do with. Doubtless this is why modern civilization runs so smoothly, why the wheels turn so regularly in so many mills, the shafts are sunk so deeply in so many mines, the forests are cut so completely from so many mountainsides, and men continue to spread out and multiply despite battles, pestilences, labor wars, earthquakes, and explosions."

In the latter part of my address I had rather lost control of myself, saying things I had not intended, things I did not exactly mean. But my enthusiasm carried me along irresistibly, and not until I was launched into mid-channel did I pause for a glimpse of my audience, and observe the stares of amazement, the nods of incredulity and the frowns of repulsion that greeted my words.

But if I was on the wrong track, how find the right one? Unless I described our industrial and mechanical progress, what was there for me to boast about?

As I returned to Xanocles' side a strained silence filled the air; the shocked, hostile glances of the audience showed what harm I had done to the cause of Emergence.

But though I had failed, Xanocles was equal to the emergency. Springing to his feet, during the lull that followed my fiasco, he motioned to the chairwoman, and for the second time was granted permission to address the meeting.

"Fellow citizens," he began, "it grieves me deeply to hear of the deplorable state of the Upper World. No doubt our friend has unconsciously exaggerated, for it is incredible that, after all these thousands of years, the unsubmerged races should still be in a primitive stage. Yet we must accept the picture as he paints it; we must reluctantly admit that our earth fellows are groping in the semi-savagery of the Age of Smoke and Iron, from which we Atlanteans escaped three thousand years ago.

"But does this mean that we should ignore the Upper World? No, my friends! To forget our brothers in their need would be unworthy of the disciples of Agripides. Indeed, the very limitations of the Upper World make it necessary for us to emerge! Let us convert the earth-folk to the wisdom of Atlantis. Let us teach them that steel and gold are but frail things. Let us send our missionaries to bring them the creed of Agripides. Do you not realize, fellow citizens, what an opportunity this is? Not only may you rescue the Upper World from its barbarities and teach it culture, but you may show its people how to build glass walls; and how to submerge."

In this bold vein Xanocles rambled on and on, while his hearers followed him with enthusiasm that seemed gradually to mount to the point of conviction.

After all who desired had had their say, a vote was taken on Xanocles' emergence proposal. And, to our great joy, the motion carried—carried by the ratio of almost two to one!

However, before the measure could take effect, it had to be approved by a referendum of all the Atlanteans.

That referendum, according to the law, could not be held for thirty days, the interval being considered necessary for discussion. Hence an exciting month ensued for Xanocles and myself, as well as for all members of the parties of Emergence and Submergence. Not in three thousand years had so fundamental an issue been brought before the people. For the first time since the Good Destruction, the principles of Agripides were at stake!

Since there were no newspapers and no radios in Atlantis, at least two agencies of political excitement were lacking. But there were other agencies in abundance. Never—with the exception of those dreadful days following the discovery of the crack—had I seen the Atlanteans so agitated. In all the houses and meetings that I visited, the chief topic of conversation was the "Emergence Act"; everyone was anxious to deliver an opinion, and everyone, man, woman and child alike, seemed to have an opinion, which he was capable of expressing in pointed terms. But the desire for discussion was particularly evident at the great assemblies held daily at the Hall of Public Enlightenment; it was there that Xanocles and his fellow "Debating Delegates" of the Emergence Party made some eloquent pleas; while their rivals of the Submergence group were scarcely less fervid on behalf of the time honored policies. Such activities, I need hardly add, were not confined to one locality, but were participated in by all the eighteen cities of Atlantis.

Not the least eager among the fighters for Emergence were the thirty-nine members of the Upper World Club. While I myself was not ready to return to earth just now (being detained by thought of a certain blue-eyed woman), most of my comrades were passionately anxious to escape, since as time went by they found themselves increasingly out of place in this too-perfect land.

But if dissatisfied with the Sunken World and incapable of contributing to its culture, they proved both willing and competent when it came to helping the cause of Emergence. None of them was skilled enough in the language to speak in public, but they were all adept at private electioneering; they would stop every Atlantean they could inveigle into conversation, and plead the cause of Emergence. Sometimes, indeed, they did more harm than good. I remember that Stranahan repeated my error, and frightened away several prospective emergionists by boastfully describing the magnitude of wars in the Upper World; and once I overheard Rawson draw an involuntary cry of disgust from a hearer when he tactlessly pointed out the advantages of four-motored bombing planes. But, on the whole, the men were well coached by members of the Emergence Party, and knew enough to confine themselves to describing the beauty of the Upper World; and partly because of their aid, but chiefly by virtue of the vigorous campaign being conducted throughout Atlantis, we had hopes that the revolutionary measure was to become law.

CRUCIAL MOMENTS

AN ELECTION IN ATLANTIS WAS seldom accompanied by intense excitement. There was no registration, for all citizens were permanently enrolled with the population bureau; and on election day all men and women of voting age (which means all who had passed their High Initiation) appeared quietly at the designated polling places and cast a secret ballot. The election boards then slowly counted the votes, and the fate of the measure (for laws were the only things passed on by the voters of Atlantis) was disclosed at the Hall of Public Enlightenment.

But the Emergence proposal proved an exception to the rule. Flushed faces and trembling voices were eloquent of the agitation of the men and women thronging to the election chambers; and this agitation was heightened by the members of the Upper World Club, who used earthly political tactics by accosting the voters before they reached the polls and showering them with final pleas. It is doubtful whether these eleventh hour efforts had any effect; but, at the time, and during the days of suspense that followed, we remained buoyantly hopeful.

Then came the disillusioning blow. When, after three days, the results were announced, we learned that our party had polled more than two hundred thousand of nearly half a million votes cast, yet had failed by sixty thousand to equal the Submergence total.

Even so, we were not wholly discouraged. As Xanocles pointed out, the cause of Emergence had never before been able to attract one tenth as many voters; and we had reason to hope for an eventual majority. No sooner, therefore, had the news of our defeat reached us than we began to plan for further campaigns.

Yet in one respect I was already regretting my connection with the Emergence Party. My regrets, to be sure, were purely non-political; but they were none the less deep-rooted. To my surprise and chagrin, my activities were bringing me into disfavor with Aelios. As one of Agripides' staunch admirers and a devoted member of the Party of Submergence, she could not applaud my association with Xanocles and his kind; and during those little conferences which we were coming to have for the supposed purpose of discussing my "History of the Upper World," she would mildly reprove me and even suggest that my conduct savored of disloyalty.

Of course, I would plead my right as a citizen to espouse any political cause; but she would gravely nod in dissent. "Theoretically, you may have the right," she would remind me, "but don't you think you're showing remarkably bad taste? Remember, you came here uninvited, and have been received as one of us, and given citizenship and all the privileges of a native. And how do you show your appreciation? By taking sides with the party that would undermine our institutions."

To this I would reply that I had no intention of harming Atlantis; that I was trying to further its interests according to my own lights. And Aelios, while not convinced that my own lights were the right ones, would admit that my motives were sincere; and having reached this halfway point of agreement, we would turn to less provocative subjects.

Despite our conflicting Emergence views, she still gave me reason to feel encouraged. I saw her, while not as often as I wished, at least enough to be sure of her friendship; and now and then I had caught again in her eyes a tender, warm light, which made my heart beat fast with the hope that what she felt might be more than friendship.

In any case, we could not continue to see one another and yet retain a mere brother-and-sister attitude. How it was with her I do not know, but I was the son of a world whose passions burn gustily and strong. More than ever, I was becoming painfully obsessed with the thought of her; more than ever, I would be given to long fits of melancholy in her absence, while at times in her presence I would be tantalized by her passionless calm, and would feel the old sweet primitive prompting to slip my arms about her, and enfold her as one might enfold the Ultimate.

And yet, though secretly absorbed by her as by some exquisite perfume that provoked and allured, I recalled the chiding words she had spoken during one of my visits, and repressed my eagerness for months, awaiting that opportunity which in the end, I felt sure, time and circumstances must provide.

And in the end my patience was rewarded. It all happened after one of my rare and delightful afternoons with Aelios. We had been strolling together about the city, and had gone for a moment's rest into the "Temple of the Stars," that majestic edifice in which Rawson and I had once been trapped. Seated on a stone bench in the darkness, we gazed awe-stricken at the spectacle above us—the whole glittering panorama of the night-skies, almost as I had known them on earth. And as I peered up at the image of those heavens I could hardly hope to see again, a reminiscent mood came over me. I could fancy myself once more on earth, and was wistful for all that earth contained; I missed the friends I had known, the sparkle of the sunshine, the magnificence of white-throated mountains. I longed for the bluster and cannonade of tempests, the icy tingling of the snow, the splashing and foamy turbulence of the ocean. And Aelios, although she had never known these things and could scarcely imagine what they meant, was strangely responsive to my mood. She asked me gently about the world I had left, and how it felt to wander among the great cities of the earth, and how it felt to hear the purling of mountain brooks or to sit on a grassy knoll with the sun blazing in the blue above. And, re-living the days before my captivity in Atlantis, I described all that my life had been, and told of my adventures and wanderings, my happy childhood and youth and early manhood; and drew upon my imagination for gorgeous pictures of the Upper World, and painted the home I had lost as little less than Paradise...

"Ah, now I see why you've joined the Emergence Party..." Aelios remarked, her face glowing dimly in the near-starlight, and her eyes soft with a kindly luster. "Of course, you must sometimes wish yourself back amid all those wonderful scenes."

"Yes, sometimes," I admitted, in low tones. "Sometimes I almost wish to be again in my native land. But at other times I am glad, very glad to be here, and would not go back if I could—not if you offered me the whole world."

"And when is that?" asked Aelios. "When you are in the beautiful buildings here, or look at the exquisite statuary?"

"Yes, sometimes then. But not only then. There are other exquisite things that make me want to stay."

"Ah, I can understand," she declared, still apparently innocent of the trend of my remarks. "The paintings, for example, or the colonnades, or—"

"No, not only that," I interrupted. "There is something more personal, more human—something that—"

Here I hesitated, hardly able to proceed.

"You mean, you like the people?" she volunteered, still with perfect candor.

"Yes, indeed," I vowed, fervently. "And one person in particular..."

She remained silent, and the darkness concealed any blush that may have suffused her face.

"But don't you understand, Aelios?" I persisted. "Don't you know whom in particular I mean?"

Still she was silent.

"Why, Aelios," I continued, "whom should I have for my particular friend? Whom, but yourself?"

"Myself?" she repeated. "Myself?"

For a moment no word passed between us. But this time there could be no doubt about the blush that mounted to her face.

At length she turned to me with softly smoldering eyes; and the assurance of victory entered my heart and then receded as she murmured, bashfully, "I am pleased, very much pleased, to know that you feel that way. It is a great compliment, and I am very proud, for nothing in Atlantis is held more precious than friendship."

"Oh, but it's not only friendship!" I remonstrated, wondering if it were possible that she still misunderstood. "It's not only friendship, Aelios... It is love!"

"Love?" she echoed, in low tones. And another silence followed, while I waited eagerly for the syllables that did not come, and she averted her head so that not even the dimly glowing eyes were visible.

"Yes. Love!" I insisted. "Love! You do not know how you have been for me the light of this whole world. You do not know how you are with me day and night—a sweet haunting presence that will not leave, that will give me no peace. You do not know how I am happy only when you are near, and sad and ill at ease when you are away."

Again there was silence. I was aware, even amid the darkness, that her lips were quivering; that her whole form trembled.

"Who am I," she said at length, in a barely audible voice. "Who am I to make you feel so strangely?"

"You are life to me, Aelios," I rushed on, with rising emotion. "You are life—beauty—tenderness. Can you not understand how I felt when I arrived here—bewildered, despairing, a castaway from all known things? Then suddenly you danced across my sight… It was warmth where all had been cold and unkindly, the touch of a comforting hand where there had been no friendliness. Your beauty filled my mind, and put a halo around my days; the music of your voice and manners filled my heart. Life had meaning once more. It had meaning such as I had not imagined possible…"

I was conscious that she was listening, listening intently; I could hear her breath coming fast. But she uttered not a word.

As if by instinct, my hand reached out and caught and held hers. But for a moment yet I restrained the prompting—which I had felt so often, and never more powerfully than now—to let my arms find their way about her, and my lips cling to hers, and feel her lovely, palpitating form pressing against my own.

"So you see, Aelios…" I continued, after a momentary silence. "So you see, all my life is built about you. Without you, it is nothing—it can have meaning only where you are. Without you, it would be like a harp that lacks a player."

Still she was held in some spell of speechlessness. For several tense seconds—low-dragging seconds that seemed minutes long— I waited for her to break silence. Meanwhile, above us, the dim twinkling lights blinked and gleamed, as if to shed a blessing, as the stars had done so many times for lovers on earth.

"Anson—dear Anson," she at length said, almost in a whisper. "I have never heard anyone speak as you have done. Here in Atlantis—here in Atlantis we do not—"

She hesitated; the words would not come.

"Yes, here in Atlantis you keep your love more in discipline," I finished for her, on the surge of my emotion. "But why? Why? Can you not feel how my heart beats? How the blood in my veins flows fast for you? How every nerve is a-tingle, Aelios? Do you not feel the same? Tell me, do you not feel the same?"

Her hand had broken from my hold; vaguely, in the darkness, I saw that she had risen. At the same time, I sprang to my feet; my arms leapt out, and, before I quite knew how it happened, I felt her soft throbbing form in my clasp. I felt my lips on hers, and the world reeled in the ecstasy of our first embrace.

But after one divine second it was over. Somehow, she had slipped free, and stood dimly outlined before me in the shadows, herself no more than a shadow in this unreal world.

"Not yet, my lover, not yet," she forbade, in gentle tones that seemed vaguely wistful.

And again I seized her; and again, for one dizzying instant, knew the wonder of her lips and arms.

But, for the second time, she broke loose from me. "No, no— you must not..." she murmured. "Lovers in Atlantis— Lovers in Atlantis do not let themselves go out of control—"

"Ah, but they miss the best in life!" I swore. And though she answered only with a sigh, some sure inner sense told me that my lovemaking, impetuous and alien as it might seem, was not very much to her distaste.

"When shall the happy time be, Aelios?" I demanded, seeking to press my advantage. "When—when shall we get married?"

"Married?" she repeated. "Married? But I—it is not right to speak of marriage now. I do not know—I do not know just what I feel towards you, I cannot be sure—"

"But you think that some time—some time—" I gasped, borne on by a new wave of hope.

"Yes, perhaps some time. But not yet for a while, if ever," she decided. "We must wait—must wait until we are both quite certain."

"As for me—I could not be more certain in ten thousand years!"

There was a long pause; she had concealed herself somewhere amid the shadows. And when she spoke again, her voice came as if from a distance, and had a more controlled and casual tone.

"Besides, we must not think of ourselves only. Remember, you have a duty to perform—an all-important duty with which neither pleasure nor love must interfere."

"But what after I have performed my duty? What after my work is complete? Will you then—"

"I will then be ready to listen to you again. Come, let us go."

And she started for the door; and, once outside, began speaking of impersonal subjects. But in her eyes there was an unusual sparkle, and on her cheeks an unwonted glow; and after I had left her and she had gone tripping out of sight, I pursued my way thoughtfully homeward, my steps made buoyant by a hope I would once not have dared to entertain.

THE HISTORY OF THE UPPER WORLD

DAY AFTER DAY MY THOUGHTS continued to be so much occupied with Aelios that I often found myself neglecting my work. It was hard to concentrate upon a dry and somber subject such as "The History of the Upper World", when Atlantis contained the living and adorable reality of my beloved. Yet I persisted, and goaded myself on no matter how my fancy wandered; and finally, after I had been in Atlantis more than two years, I completed my task.

Considering the magnitude of the work, it surprises me to remember that I finished it so quickly. Though it was but a moderate-sized volume and though I had received much help from Aelios, as well as from Xanocles and other natives, I had been retarded by having to write in an adopted tongue and without references other than those of my own memory.

It was a proud day, and yet a day of many doubts, when I bore the manuscript to the office of the Literary Registrar. This official, assisted by a board of fifteen critics, passed upon all literary works submitted by the authors of Atlantis; and all books found worthy of perpetuation were published under his direction, while advice and criticism were given to promising aspirants. In the case of my own book, there could be no doubt as to publication, for I had been specifically directed to write it, and all Atlantis was eagerly awaiting the information it was expected to convey. None the less, it had to undergo the regular procedure of inspection by the Registrar; and as it happened, this was more than a fruitless formality. Before the manuscript was given to the press, a trained essayist was appointed to help me reconstruct the style; and thus my writing attained a dignity and polish I myself could not have supplied.

But when at last publication was ordered, I had cause to be gratified. An edition of fifty thousand was to be issued—an edition of phenomenal size considering the population of Atlantis.

Naturally one will ask the reason for this enormous printing; and the answer is to be found in the methods of book distribution in the Sunken World. Publication, like all other activities, was in the hands of the government; and copies of all the hundreds of books issued each year were sent as a matter of course to every library in the land. Furthermore, every citizen was permitted to choose fifty of the year's books; and men and women engaged in research work were allowed in excess of that number. In the case of my own book, public interest was at such a pitch that a large percentage of the people were certain to include it among those chosen fifty; and the first edition was therefore regarded as conservative in size.

Such, in fact, it proved to be. The book was hardly off the press when orders began to pour in so rapidly that a second edition of fifty thousand had to be prepared. For it was literally true that everyone was reading "The History of the Upper World"; and this does not mean one man in a hundred, as might be the case were I writing of a "best seller" on earth; it means that there was actually not a person of reading age who did not feel bound to acquaint himself with the contents of my book.

In consequence, my life began to take on a tinge of unwonted excitement. For it was with a start of surprise, a gasp of incredulity and a wail of horror that Atlantis read the news of the Upper World. Previously, when I had ventured a few hints as to life on earth, I had witnessed some queer reactions; but the people's former bewilderment and disgust seemed insignificant by comparison. It would be impossible to exaggerate their repugnance to earthly life as I portrayed it; it was almost as if they had learned that we had gone back on all fours, or had joined the orangutan or the gibbon in the trees. The dozens of letters I received, the dozens of visitors that poured in upon me, and the dozens of inquiries addressed to me at public meetings, all gave evidence of a single, but profound emotion.

Perhaps the general attitude was to be seen most clearly in the reviews of the book—reviews which, unlike most earthly criticisms, were not printed, but were delivered orally at the Hall of Public Enlightenment.

Let me quote from a typical address. The speaker was Carmanides, a well-known writer on social and philosophic questions; and his views were milder in many ways than those of his audience. Speaking before an assemblage of four or five hundred, he showed himself to be precise and thorough in his acquaintance with my book.

"Since we have no reason to believe that the author has deliberately exaggerated," he declared, after summarizing the contents, "we must accept the picture of Upper World life as he presents it. And what, therefore, must we conclude? That Agripides was wise, wonderfully wise. There can hardly be any more distressing subject than the history of the earth, even the most daring satirist—playing upon his imagination to expose the stupidity of the human race—could not offer a blacker picture of follies, crimes and insanities than Anson Harkness has painted for us in all seriousness. For what are the outstanding historical facts as he depicts them? Has the human race gone continuously forward, forgetting its savage instincts in perfecting a civilization at once beautiful and secure? Has man come to look on man otherwise than as beast looks on beast? No, my friends— unfortunately, no, if we would believe the volume before us. Slave raids and wars; rebellions and murders; conquest and persecution; treachery and rapine and exploitation; dynasties that crumble, and empires that decompose—these are the signposts of the past three thousand years; and evidently there has been no concerted effort to create less revolting landmarks.

"Yet though the darkness seems impenetrable, I can see one faint glimmer of hope. In the self-satisfied blindness of the Upper World, there reposes a possible solution. It is not a solution altogether pleasing to contemplate, but it is the sort of cleansing remedy that nature sometimes provides when a wound has festered beyond possibility of healing. For if no ordinary cure be obtainable, life may take the sword into her own hands, and with one blow wipe out all her old mistakes. It is that stroke which, it seems to me, is about to fall upon Upper World man, smiting his civilization, and turning upon his own throat the knife with which he thinks to stab his foe. And this is no doubt well, my friends, for after earthly man has committed suicide, the world will be ready for a population of less short-sighted and quarrelsome creatures, be they only beetles or ants!"

With a thankful gesture, as of one who lectures on the impending extinction of cannibalism, the speaker returned to his seat; while; much to my chagrin, I noted that his words had found high favor with the audience. One and all, the men and women that arose in the ensuing discussion were intensely narrow-minded. All seemed to interpret my book as a sort of horror tale instead of as a restrained and veracious history; and either they suggested that I had exaggerated hopelessly, or else agreed that the Upper World was ripe for a second "Good Destruction."

But while all Atlantis was reading the book and being provoked and shocked, I was surprised to observe one effect that I deplored even more than the gross misunderstanding of the Upper World. For the "History" had acted like a bombshell against the Party of Emergence! Deserters from our standards were now legion; in a few weeks, we had lost all that we had gained following the discovery of the crack in the wall. And at a test vote of an Emergence measure six weeks after the appearance of "The History of the Upper World," we were overwhelmed in the ratio of ten to one.

In my disappointment, I bitterly regretted that I had not written my book from a less realistic point of view. Nothing short of a catastrophe or a miracle could now open up the lanes back to earth.

A HAPPY CONSUMMATION

ONLY A MONTH OR two after the publication of "The History of the Upper World," there occurred a vastly more important event. At least, it was vastly more important to me—the most fortunate episode of all my life in Atlantis. Ever since that encouraging talk with Aelios in "The Temple of the Stars," I had been drawing gradually nearer to her. With the customary restraint of her people, she again checked my advance, and would not permit me to press her close, as on one never-to-be-forgotten occasion; but at times in her eyes I would catch a reassuring look; and in our increasingly frequent meetings her manner was tinged by something indefinably wistful, and indefinably gentle in a way that I had not previously observed.

The climax occurred, not unnaturally, upon one of my visits to her home, when we were alone together in a tapestried room of the pale blue lanterns. Nothing had suggested that our meeting today was to differ from previous interviews; but somehow the discussion turned into unexpected channels, and we found ourselves on the most provocative of subjects.

"What is the power, the law on which you Atlanteans' place the most hope and reliance?" I asked quite casually, in the course of the conversation. "What is it that you consider the ruling motive of the universe?"

And in low tones that startled me like a thunderclap, she declared, simply, "Love."

"Love?" I exclaimed.

"Yes, love—that great love which embraces all things. The love of the Maker of the Worlds for his tiniest creature. The love that covers all mankind, and all beings on earth. We believe that at the heart of creation there is a loving purpose."

"A consoling philosophy," I commented. "But what of more personal love? The love of a man for a woman? The love such as I feel for you?"

Her head was averted; her voice scarcely rose above a whisper as she replied, "That is all a part of the greater, the universal love."

"But no, Aelios," I dissented. "It is complete—complete in itself. It is too vast to be *part* of anything. It is itself a universe!"

"Itself a universe?" she echoed, and rose to her feet, and with downcast eyes moved slowly along the tapestried wall.

"Aelios, listen to me...*listen*," I pleaded, starting up and following her, while my emotions sprang to impetuous life. "I have been waiting long— I have been burnt by love for you— have been blest by it—have been tortured by waiting— To be always with you, to feel your hand in mine, your breast against my breast—that is what I have been hoping and praying for! Must I wait longer? Aelios, can you not take pity?"

Suddenly I was aware that her whole form was convulsed. Her shoulders heaved; the tears gushed down the beautiful pale cheeks. And, almost before I realized what was happening, she had turned and, with a quick spasmodic movement, had flung herself towards me.

Weeping, laughing, murmuring, babbling with mad incoherence, we clung together. "My beloved! O my beloved! At last…at last…" she cried. And no further words were needed to tell me that the consummation of my dreams was at hand…

"I was not sure before," she said, when the first sweet frenzy had died down. "But now, my beloved, I am certain. Let me not live anywhere except where you are. If it were in a cave—beneath the ground—if it were in the cold and the darkness—I could not find joy anywhere but with you. For already our hearts are wedded."

"Indeed they are," I concurred. "But we will not have to live in a cave beneath the ground—nor in the cold or darkness. Tell me, when shall the happy day be? When do you say?"

"When do you want me to say?" she returned, surprised. "If we are both sure, what need to delay?"

Previously, when I had dared to think of the possibility of marriage, I had been half reconciled to the prospect of a long engagement, and had assumed that an interval of months or even years might be considered proper. But now, in response to my question, Aelios assured me that long engagements were unknown in Atlantis. The natives, usually so slow-going, were hasty enough in this regard; once two people had decided upon marriage, it was not usual to allow more than the few days necessary for the preparations. It had always been so, Aelios explained, and she could not imagine how it could be otherwise.

And so I was bewildered at the same time as I was overjoyed at the unexpected nearness of our union. I was like a man, long blind, who suddenly sees a flash of light; it took me a while to adjust myself to the dazzling new vistas.

To begin with, I was not sure quite what was expected of me. Should I present Aelios with a ring or some similar trinket? Or was some more elaborate gift deemed necessary?

In my perplexity, I consulted Xanocles, who merely smiled at my doubts. "Marriage with us," he explained, "is not treated as a form of barter, nor as a bargain wherein precious articles must be given as surety. When two of our people are united, they would think it degrading to have to give anything beyond themselves."

Even after my doubts on this important subject had been relieved, there was still much that troubled me. Aelios had decided that the ceremony was to be held in eight days (this being about the usual time); and despite all my joyous anticipations, I trembled just a little at the thought of so quickly exchanging my known, if monotonous, bachelor life for an unknown career as Atlantean husband.

Perhaps it was fortunate that my hours were completely occupied. For one thing, I spent a great deal of time with Aelios; for another thing, I was much entertained by my friends, who were loudly congratulatory, and insisted upon putting me through long ordeals of questions, laughter, and amiably chaffing remarks. An entire meeting of the Upper World Club was given over to a celebration allegedly in my honor; and President Gavison, after unbending from his official sternness to wish me luck in terms that I thought just a little wistful and a little reminiscent of his own lost happiness, was followed in quick succession by the other club members, all of whom strove to express themselves with appropriate levity. Had there been such a thing as an intoxicant in Atlantis, we would have had a merry old time; but, for lack of the proper stimulus, the men had to be content with their questionable jests, with poking me in the ribs, with slapping me on the back, and with laughing and guffawing in a generally irresponsible and uproarious manner.

But as the few remaining days slid by, did I have no thought of her whom I had once loved on earth? Did I not think of Alma Huntley? Perhaps I should be ashamed, but I am not, to say that the memory of her scarcely entered my mind. She was no more than a shadow in a world that was growing more shadowy, in an existence that I had outlived and could not expect to re-enter; and if at times she would obtrude herself before me, it was but as a dim, melancholy presence without color or form.

About three days after reaching our decision, my betrothed and I, in pursuance of the custom of the land, visited the local housing bureau, which was to assign us our new lodgings. After we had duly placed our names side by side in a great venerable-looking ledger, we passed an exciting afternoon in the company of the chief housing representative, who showed us all the available dwellings with the same obliging courtesy as when I had selected my bachelor quarters. As on the former occasion, there were so many desirable locations that the choice was difficult; on passing each new threshold, Aelios would pause with a little cry of wonder or surprise, and point in admiration to some distinctive feature of arrangement or decoration. Needless to say, I too was dazzled and delighted; particularly since I had previously seen only apartments designed for single people, whereas now I was shown into houses detached like bungalows. None of these were very large; indeed, most of them had but three or four rooms in addition to the roof sleeping chambers and the almost invariable central court; but they were the most home-like little nooks you could imagine, with their tastefully-furnished rooms, and their surrounding lawns and flowering gardens.

Our choice was in favor of a little butterfly-shaped dwelling, with silvery walls inlaid with mother-of-pearl, and high arched windows surrounded by vivid bands of stained glass. "You may move in at any time after your names are registered in the Marriage Book," said the housing representative, when he had duly recorded our decision. "And if ever you should find this house unsatisfactory, you have but to enter your complaint, and we will try to provide another dwelling."

With these words, the housing representative bowed a gracious retreat, while Aelios and I were left to inspect the home so soon to be ours. Enthusiastic as children, we examined every nook and corner. Aelios was radiant; I had never seen her eyes sparkle more brightly, or her cheeks glow more vividly.

"Is it not the strangest whim of fate," she asked, "that you have come down here to me, my beloved? How easily I might have missed you. How easily we might each have gone through life not knowing the other existed…"

"So it has been with all lovers since the world began," I returned. "Even in Atlantis, love must always seem a miracle."

"Even in Atlantis, it always *is* a miracle," she amended. And she looked at me with a smile so luminous that I fervently swore that she was right.

The days that followed this delightful interview are a blur in my memory. Although every hour was slow-footed with suspense, it seemed to me that but a moment elapsed between our departure from our chosen home and our happy return...our happy return on that never-to-be-forgotten day when Aelios and I entered the office of the Local Adviser and were officially united.

The actual ceremony was insignificant—indeed, there was no ceremony at all. We had merely to record our names for a second time, writing them in the Marriage Book which the housing representative had mentioned—an enormously thick volume bound in blue and gold, with thousands of pages, one of which was devoted to the history of each marriage. There were no questions asked; there were no high-sounding formulas to be spoken by clockwork; there were no official representatives of saintliness; there were no vows to be taken, no promises to be made, no witnesses to gape or snicker, no pompous giving or receiving of the bride. We merely furnished the State with the record that it required, and did so without having to purchase a printed tag; and after we had entered our names in the book, we were not embarrassed by any attempt to sanctify proceedings with words of antique witchcraft.

Of course, if we desired to celebrate our nuptials with a festival of any sort, that was our privilege—and one which the State would recognize by providing an appropriate hall for the day. As it happened, most bridal couples availed themselves of this right, and we were no exception; when our marriage had been officially recorded, we repaired to a flower-decked chamber where a few of Aelios' friends and relatives were awaiting us. And after receiving their greetings and congratulations, we did not pass our time in feasting or drinking, nor in making merry, nor in riotous jests; but we danced a sedate dance timed to ethereal strains of music; and later we all sat quietly about the room, Aelios at my side and the others on mats and sofas opposite, while the lights were subdued and we listened to still more ethereal music, which rose and quavered in a voice of joy like the notes of melodious birds, then faintly trilled like a far-off elfin call or throbbed and sang in an organ-burst of ecstasy, until one was moved almost to tears by the revealed poignancy and beauty of life, and came to look upon love with a new reverence and a new wonder.

THE FLOODGATES OPEN

WHEN I LOOK BACK TODAY, my life in Atlantis seems to divide itself into two periods, of which the longer and by far the more tranquil dates from my union with Aelios. In the newfound contentment of our marriage (for ours was no exception to the rule that most marriages in Atlantis were harmonious), we seemed to lose track of time; the days, the months and the years began gliding by at a smooth, even pace that was most deceptive, though the period of our bliss was to be alas, all too fleeting.

Perhaps one secret of our happiness was that we were both amply occupied; that each had his own work. Aelios still tutored for several hours a day, and still led in the dances at public festivals; for in Atlantis no distinction was made between a married and a single woman, except in the event of motherhood; and even a mother, while released from prescribed duties, was expected to keep alive a broad interest in life by performing some optional services.

For my own part, I was as busy as Aelios. After completing my "History of the Upper World," I had again been summoned by the Committee on Selective Assignments, and had been directed to write a treatise on "Social Traditions and Institutions in the Upper World," wherein I might describe conditions above seas in greater detail than in my previous book. This task, while far from uncongenial, was proving both lengthy and laborious; and the further I proceeded the harder the work became, since the more I learned of Atlantis the more difficult it appeared to represent the earth in a flattering light.

I was now quite reconciled to passing my remaining days in Atlantis. Although Xanocles and his colleagues persisted with their agitation, the cause of Emergence was dwindling in my mind to an impossible dream; and, had it not been for the cataclysm that scourged us all to frenzied action, I might have been content to grow gray and wrinkled in the Sunken World. For now that Aelios was mine, I found life far richer than ever before; I found that all things shared the glow of a comradeship that put to shame my most dazzling previous visions. And not only was I surrounded by affection and steeped in pleasurable activity, but there was an almost charmed absence of strain and hurry—a leisure and a serenity that once would have seemed possible only in Nirvana.

It is true, of course, that I could not escape all the ordinary physical ills of life. Once, for example, when my awkwardness betrayed me in one of those athletic contests that were almost as common a means of recreation in Atlantis as on earth, I suffered a broken arm and was taken to a State hospital, where a State physician skillfully treated my injury. And once, when the incessant golden glare began to tell upon my eyes, I had to visit a State oculist, who relieved the strain by prescribing a pair of wide-rimmed, amber-tinged glasses.

My appearance was changing, also, in other ways than by my wearing of glasses. I had acquired a full beard, owing to the habits formed during my first days in Atlantis; and my complexion was taking on a curious greenish tint, due to some peculiar action of the Atlantean light—an action against which the natives had an inherited immunity. But I was not alone in my queer pistache complexion; there were thirty-eight others with the same distinctive pigmentation, which was so marked that, as the men sometimes declared, our origin was "written on our skins."

My fellow members of the Upper World Club, meanwhile, did not share my liking for Atlantis. With the exception of Gavison, who had written a brief, but, popular, "Comparison of Upper and Lower World Civilizations," not one of them was adapting himself to life in Atlantis or was not remiss in his obligations as a citizen. While they had all acquired at least a rudimentary knowledge of the language and were all successful enough in performing some prescribed mechanical task for two or three hours a day, yet none of them had accomplished anything in any of those artistic or intellectual pursuits that alone were considered worth while. How, indeed, conform to the standards of a world that had so little in common with their own? Apparently the natives did not even expect them to conform, and tolerated lapses that would have been considered disgraceful in born Atlanteans. But they themselves appeared to feel that they were somehow inferior, somehow out of place; and I could easily understand their restlessness, their longing to escape, their desire for a less ideal and a more familiar mode of life.

Considering the eagerness with which they would have exchanged the ease of Atlantis for the most strenuous labors and hardships of the earth, it seems ironic that the man ultimately chosen to emerge was he whose marriage to an Atlantean had resigned him to the Sunken World. My sole excuse is that the choice, when it fell upon me, was made wholly upon the suggestion of others, and occurred at a time of such acute peril that the happiness or fate of individuals was as nothing.

For the hour was to come—and to come with startling suddenness—when a fateful writing was to glare from the walls of Atlantis. I had been in the Sunken World five years when the menace burst forth, and was not there so much as a week after it appeared... But in the interval I was a witness to scenes of such horror, confusion and despair as I had never seen before and fervently hope I shall never see again.

It torments me now to recall that all that terror and all that irremediable loss might have been avoided. Had we but heeded the advice of Peliades. Peliades who insisted that the crack in the wall had not been healed...

But let me not anticipate, I must describe as dispassionately as I can those overwhelming events which descended like lightning to blast Atlantean life, and which are so disturbing even in memory that my pen trembles and my startled mind takes fresh alarm. Merely to try to record those distracting days and nights is to be obsessed as by an old madness. I can feel a palsying fear spreading once more through all my nerves. I can feel my brain turn numb, my eyes grow strained and distended, my arteries throb with delirious haste. And all the while confused visions swarm across my mind—visions of roaring vigils by lamp-lit walls of glass, visions of huddled faces, weeping or praying or with terror-stricken eyes, visions of thundering, waters, panicky flights, submerged temples and inundated plains. And it all seems like some nightmare I dreamt long ago, yet more vivid than any nightmare, for there are sobs and lamentations that echo even now in my memory, and pleading lips that shall never stir again, and agonized eyes that peer at me like phantoms which will not be exorcised.

Long before, in moments of aimless fancy, I had sought to picture to myself the end of a world—to imagine the consternation and horror of an earth threatened with impending doom. But I had never thought that I myself would be the spectator of a crumbling universe...

As in the case of the crack in the wall years before, the danger appeared with devastating suddenness. One moment, all was tranquil; the next moment, the Sunken World was in a frenzy. I remember that one afternoon Aelios and I had gone to the Agripides Amphitheater to witness a performance of some sort (its precise nature has slipped from my mind); and at the close of the first act the warning came. From the unexplained absence of the chorus that usually sang during intermissions, I might have suspected that something was wrong; but actually I was without misgivings until suddenly a great burnished silvery horn was lifted quietly on to the stage.

At this unexpected sight, a stab of alarm darted through me. Aelios seized my hand and held it as if for reassurance. The audience sat rigid and erect, like persons who behold a ghost. For an instant, we heard no sound save the quick breathing of our neighbors; then the strained silence was broken by an uncanny voice that issued sonorously as if from nowhere.

"A great misfortune has befallen," announced the unseen, in hollow and sepulchral tones. "The crack in the glass wall has reappeared, and this time it is of more serious proportions."

The voice faltered and halted, while murmurs of dismay, terror and unbelief shuddered through the audience.

In a more deliberate and even graver manner, the speaker continued. "Late last evening our navigators observed that the Salty River was higher than usual; and an investigating party sent out today by the High Chief Adviser has discovered that the wall has given way at one point, and that the water is pouring in through a fissure several feet across. There is as yet no cause for despair, for the surplus water can be expelled by the reserve capacity of our inter-atomic pumps, which are equipped to discharge fifty percent more than their usual volume. But there is danger that the break will expand before repairs can be made; and for this reason the High Chief Adviser requests that you try to meet the situation courageously, and freely enlist your brains and your services till the peril is overcome."

It would be hopeless to attempt to convey any idea of the commotion created by these words. The people did indeed follow the High Chief Adviser's advice to be courageous, and there was no more than a hint of panic. But there could be no further thought of the performance in the amphitheater. After an instant's chill silence, the audience rose as of one accord. Men's faces were blanched and women could be heard muttering in fear as the crowd began pushing towards the exits. In their excitement, the people had forgotten their usual courtesy; Aelios and I were shoved and jostled in a way that reminded me of the New York subways. It was all I could do not to lose track of her amid the mob; yet we wished nothing less than to be separated, particularly since the speechless eagerness of the throng, the sighs of women, the rapid breathing of men and our own fast-beating hearts, all served to fill us with forebodings.

Once out of the theatre, the people were driven as by a common instinct towards the river. All seemed fearful of even a second's delay, as though our haste might repair the fractured wall. In a long, swiftly moving column, constantly augmented as we advanced, we followed the winding avenue towards the waterfront. None of us spoke more than an occasional word; even Aelios was silent, though she clutched my arm with confiding firmness, and looked up at me with eyes wherein apprehension alternated with a reassuring courage.

But there was no prop for courage in the sight that greeted us at the riverbank. The stream, which ordinarily flowed five or six feet beneath the docks, was now but twenty inches below flood level.

Speechless, we watched the broad, greenish-gray torrent go swishing and gurgling past. But what was there that we could do? Nothing, except to stand helplessly gaping at that swift-flowing, swollen stream. Indeed, we seemed worse than helpless, for as I remained rooted there with Aelios amid that horror-faced crowd, I became conscious—as during that other crisis years before—that I was arousing a powerful repulsion. My neighbors were edging away from me visibly; some were pointing towards me, or uttering half-suppressed oaths; I thought I heard someone ruefully mumbling something about, "That foreigner...cause of all our troubles..."

I would quickly have withdrawn from that hostile throng had I not observed a slim gray form approaching from far upstream. With racing speed it drew near, and soon was recognizable as an inter-atomic boat, similar to the one I had boarded years before. Much to my relief, it came to a rapid halt, drew up at the dock, and let down its gangplanks. And as the crowd forced its way aboard, Aelios and I were not slow in finding seats for what was sure to be an exciting trip.

And exciting it was—far more so than we could have desired. When we had been under way a few minutes, the looks of the river began to change disquietingly. Except for the current, it lost the aspect of a river entirely, and took on the appearance of a long lake. On both sides, the water spread in a smooth-flowing sheet two or three miles broad; and above the surface stared clumps and clusters of vegetation, with here and there a miniature island; while several temples and colonnades stood with marble bases buried in the water, like the palaces of some aquatic goddess.

But the extent of the disaster was not evident until we had left the vessel and approached the glass wall. This time it did not require a searchlight to reveal the nature of the injury; our ears might have told us, if our eyes had not. As we strode along the little clay path towards the wall, we became aware of a broad gleaming, greenish expanse between—a sheet of water where all had been dry land. And into the sheet of water, with a continuous thunder equal to the floods from the river valve, a long white torrent spurted in a gracefully curving jet, shooting outwards.

Hundreds of yards from the glass bulwark, and descending with a splashing as of some gigantic fountain. It was impossible to estimate the volume; nor could we see the extent of the leak, since the intervening water forbade our close approach. But we observed how the overflow worked its way circuitously into the

Salty River in a sort of channel of its own choosing; and occasional swift-moving lights, which even from our distance we could see flashing beyond the glass, showed us the repair ships were busy trying to seal up the crack.

But, from the beginning; we knew how hopeless were their efforts; with their midget vessels and midget tools, they were like ants trying to stem the flow of Niagara. The utter helplessness of their plight—and of ours—became apparent when suddenly a great, elongated gray mass came flying in with a splash and a clatter in a battered heap projecting from the waters—a repair ship that had been hurled in through the gap in the wall—

SWOLLEN TORRENTS

IT WAS FIVE DAYS LATER THAT I received my summons from the High Chief Adviser and made ready for the climax of my adventures.

In the interval, all Atlantis was in a state verging upon madness. The commotion created by the original discovery of the crack was insignificant beside the terror that now dominated every inhabitant. To say that the country seemed palsy-stricken would be to underestimate; rather, it was driven to a dumb distraction, like some great beast that feels its foot in a trap. Only one thought was in anyone's mind, only one topic on anyone's lips; the people drifted hither and thither like phantoms, rushing back and forth between the cities and the spurting leak in the wall, sometimes engaged furtively in whispered discussions, on other occasions muttering half-audible prayers or withdrawing into themselves like men brought face to face with Fate. Some would hover near the offices of the High Chief Adviser, awaiting hopeful news that did not come; some would haunt the river banks, watching the swelling torrents go whirling past; some would huddle together in small family groups, as though mortally afraid to lose sight of their dear ones; some would merely go pacing around like rats in a cage, their white faces and harried eyes expressive of a dread they dared not mention.

But none—none who were not driven by the most stringent orders—were heeding their daily duties. For the first time in history, the cities were inadequately supplied with food; the official producers and distributors shared the general inertia, and the people had to clamor at the doors of the great municipal warehouses for their meager rations, until actual starvation seemed in sight.

Still more appalling to my mind—vastly more appalling, since it was like the overthrow of the very order of nature—was the laxity with regard to the golden orbs that ruled the Atlantean day. Owing to the negligence of the official in charge, the clockwork that controlled these artificial suns ran down on what should have been the third night, and the luminaries continued in full blaze long after the usual hour of darkness. But few seemed even to notice the change, and most remained frenziedly watching the waters; while hardly anyone snatched even a few hours of troubled sleep during the unintermittent daylight.

Meanwhile, the Salty River continued to rise. Slowly and insidiously, by inches and half inches, it crept up and up and up, until after two days not more than a hand's breadth separated it from the top of the embankment. And after three days it had not more than a finger's breadth to go, while on the fourth day we could see thin sparkling streams flowing down the more low-lying streets, not deep enough to make them quite impassable, but lending to the columned thoroughfares the aspect of some pathetic Venice. Simultaneously the news was brought that the small towns of Malgos and Dorion had been inundated and their inhabitants had fled for higher ground; that the larger cities of Atolis, Lerenon and Aedla were rearing embankments to keep out the waters; and that the farm lands of eastern Atlantis were flooded as far as the eye could see. But little that was even mildly hopeful was reported. It was stated that the repair ships were still trying to cope with the leak, though without success; that the inter-atomic pumps were disposing of most of the surplus water, but were being taxed to capacity; that in several places huge electric shovels were at work, digging out great hollows into which the floods might be drained; that efforts were being made to freeze vast masses of water, and force the ice against the wall, in the attempt to stem the torrents... But, all the while, the river continued to rise.

After five days, the water was flowing to a depth of many inches through half the streets of Archeon; and only the erection of earthworks had saved the other half. And it was after five nerve-racking days that—as I have stated—I received the summons from the High Chief Adviser.

The messenger—a wan-faced old man who seemed in a breathless hurry—was awaiting me when I returned home with Aelios after wandering aimlessly for hours through the unflooded portions of town. From the grave manner of his greeting I knew at once that he had come on no pleasant duty; yet he had no explicit information to offer. "Anson Harkness... The High Chief Adviser wishes to see you without delay!" was all he would report. And immediately he began edging away, as though he had urgent business elsewhere.

There being nothing else to do, I accompanied the messenger after hastily assuring Aelios that I would return as soon as possible.

As I might have anticipated, our walk turned out to be as disagreeable as could be. The old man had evidently been trained in diplomacy, for I could not induce him to speak, except non-committally and in monosyllables. All the way to the office of the Adviser I was left to my own conjectures while we skirted public squares that looked like lakes, or waded ankle-deep through the salty water.

Arriving at the many-domed edifice where the Atlantean government had its headquarters, my companion bade me wait in an anteroom, and went to notify his chief of my arrival. But it was as though my coming had been already noted, for the old man had hardly left when he reappeared and motioned me to follow him.

I have a vague remembrance of accompanying him through long arched galleries; but of these my mind retains no definite impression, and the next thing I clearly recall is that I stood in a little blue-walled room before an impressive-looking, elderly man whose picture I had often seen. His long, furrowed, sagacious features were those of a scholar, but there was a squareness to the jaw that marked him also as a man of action; while at the same time there was a patriarchal benignity about the sympathetic lines of the face. But one quality there was that dominated him now; and which none of the pictures had shown: an air of utter fatigue, of melancholy, of despair, all too plainly written in the hollows that underlined the weary gray eyes, in the pale cheeks drained of blood, and in the haggard expression as of one who has not slept for days.

To the right of the High Chief Adviser was seated one whom I recognized with surprise. It was Xanocles, also looking pallid and worn; and as he rose to greet me I began to conceive some faint idea why I had been summoned.

The Chief Adviser gravely motioned me to a seat at his left.

"I need hardly tell you," he commenced, without formality, "how serious is the present crisis. But perhaps no one—except those of us who are on the inside—realizes the actual acuteness of the danger. Frankly speaking, we are incapable of dealing with the emergency. The inter-atomic pumps have been working to capacity for five days, but, even so, the water is pouring in at the rate of several tons a second faster than we can drive it out. This in itself would be ominous enough; but this is not the worst. Our engineers tell us that the crack is extending to fresh portions of the wall, which may give way at any time. When this happens, it will be—the end."

The High Chief Adviser paused, grimly frowning. Then, with a piercing glance at me, as if to see whether I had anticipated his meaning, he continued. "It is apparent that Atlantis cannot save herself. We are facing a unique peril, and have not the weapons to combat it. If help comes, it must come from outside. That is why I have summoned you."

"But I don't exactly see—"

"Let me explain," the official continued, impatiently. "You yourself, of course, can do nothing. But you come from a people, who, to judge from your writings, have developed remarkable engineering skill. I am hopeful that their science can devise some means of saving us, and so am planning to send you above seas for help. What do you think of the idea?"

"Why, I—I think it might be worth trying," was all I was able to gasp.

"Your friend Xanocles also thinks it worth trying. Now I, personally, have always been against the Emergence policy; but it is imperative to try new measures; and at times of crisis, fortunately, the law empowers me to take action on my own initiative.

Therefore I sent for Xanocles today as one of the most prominent members of the Emergence Party, and when I asked whom he would advise me to appoint as special envoy to the Upper World he immediately mentioned you."

"But why me?"

"Well, to be sure, you were not the only one. He also recommended your countryman, Gavison, but we will hold him in reserve, and if you do not return in a few days we will send him out with a second submarine. Meanwhile, if you would care to accept—"

"Why, of course—of course I'll accept—if it is for the good of Atlantis. Just what would you expect of me?"

"One of our submersible vessels, with a crew of four, will be ready at the docks early tomorrow morning. You will board it, and it will bear you out through the eastern valve to any part of the Upper World that you may direct. But you must waste no time. Inform your fellows of the menace to Atlantis—they, too, have submersible vessels, as your arrival here proves—let them send some of their ships, with materials to repair the wall. But, above all things, remember not to delay, not to delay!"

"I will do my best," I promised. "But let me not hold out any false hopes. The Upper World may not be able to assist."

"At any rate, you can try," sighed the head of the Atlantean government. "It is a chance worth taking."

And then, fixing me with that powerful magnetic glance common to all Atlanteans, he demanded. "You will spare no effort?"

"I will spare no effort," I solemnly vowed.

"Then the fates be with you..."

The High Chief Adviser rose, and firmly took both my hands. A dimness came into his eyes as he fervently continued, "I need say no more. You know as well as I how much depends on this."

The next moment, accompanied by Xanocles, I was passing through the outer galleries. My last glimpse of the High Chief Adviser showed me the great head sagging, the lids wearily drooping over the melancholy gray eyes...

From the Adviser's office I hastened home, leaving Xanocles after being assured that he would come to me early in the morning.

I found Aelios impatiently awaiting my return. "You have been long," she murmured, although it seemed to me that I had come back very quickly. And the big blue eyes looked up at me inquiringly, and I had to explain at once the meaning of the Adviser's summons.

She followed my recital without a word. But heavy furrows appeared upon her brow when I told how serious was the plight of Atlantis; and a big limpid teardrop flowed unheeded down one cheek.

"You did right to accept the commission," she said, coming to me when I had finished the story, and resting one hand affectionately upon my shoulder. "I am glad the choice has fallen upon you. When do we start on our voyage?"

"We?" I repeated, staring at her in surprise.

"Yes, we. I shall go with you, of course."

"But, Aelios, that's impossible—" I dissented, springing up and drawing her close. "You know how much I'd like to have you with me. But you don't realize—you don't realize the peril."

"Peril?" She laughed disdainfully, as she withdrew from me. "Do you think I'd have you submit to a peril I wouldn't share in? Besides, is it not in the interest of my own country? Should I stay here doing nothing when I might help you save Atlantis?"

"But even so, would you be permitted—"

"Would I? Of course! The High Chief Adviser would be more than willing—only he wouldn't ask me to take the risk."

"Neither would I ask you—" I objected. But she cut me short by demanding, sharply, "Do you think it's any greater than the risk of staying here?" And, with the air of one whose mind is irrevocably made up, she counseled, "We'd better be getting ready…"

But there was not much to prepare, for the submarine would be well provisioned. Except for a few personal trinkets, we could think of little to take with us. However, it occurred to me to bring a copy of Homer's lost masterpiece, the "Telegonus," which might convince the Upper World of the truth of my reports about Atlantis. And it also occurred to me to pay a pilfering expedition to the museum, which was now untenanted even by the doormen; and when I returned my pockets were weighed down with several pieces of gold, and my arms were laden with a large amorphous bundle, whose contents might have been identified as an Ensign's uniform.

Of the night that followed I have only the most confused remembrance. I know that I did not sleep, except to drowse by brief, nightmare-haunted spells; and I also know that Aelios did not sleep, since her mind, like mine, was busy contemplating the adventure before us.

The moment the lights were flashed on again (their clockwork mechanism having been put back in operating order), we renounced all attempts at slumber; and we had hardly arisen and made ourselves presentable when we began to receive visitors. Not only did Xanocles arrive as he had promised, but the entire Upper World Club appeared in a group, since I had told Gavison of my prospective departure and expressed my desire to, see all the men before I left.

As our visitors insisted on seeing us off, it was a good-sized company that attended us when we bade farewell to, our beloved little butterfly-shaped dwelling, and set out through the streets of the stricken city towards the river. Yet our escort added only to our depression. The strain of the past few days was written upon us all, and the pale cheeks and weary looks of the men matched their listless manners and their silence. One or two, and among them the unquenchable Stranahan—did indeed attempt to be jocular; but their efforts were half-hearted and flat, and their laughter rang thin and hollow like mockery. And as we drew nearer our goal and saw the flood rippling through the streets ahead, we heard no more of their jests, but all of us plunged onward speechlessly with stern, set faces.

When we reached the inundated districts, I urged my companions to turn back. But they paid no heed, and pressed gravely on their way, first wading ankle-deep, then halfway to their knees, while advancing in a long line amid scattered houses that looked like lake dwellings. Here a marble edifice, there a colonnade, yonder a cluster of statues, projected above the deluge, whose green-gray current went swishing past from an inexhaustible source. Amid those fluid wastes, which had obliterated all familiar landmarks and gave to well-known things a new and terrible majesty, it was impossible to be, sure of our way; once one of the men slipped into a depression so deep that he had to swim to save himself, and more than once someone tripped over some buried obstacle, and went floundering full-length into the water. So great were the dangers that we had to move very slowly; but we also moved with grim regularity, and our progress was without sound other than the monotonous splash, splash of our advancing feet.

It was not only our own plight that made us sad. As we plodded through the flooded districts, we were not reassured by our glimpses of the inhabitants. Here, through an open window, we would catch sight of several agile figures straining to bind some huge shapeless mass into a bundle; there we would observe a man descending from his doorstep into the waters, his back bent under a pile of household articles, a wan-faced woman clinging nervously to him or turning back with moist eyes to the home they were leaving. And we passed not one or two such refugees, but scores. One would have a three-year-old perched on his shoulders, another would be trying to soothe a crying babe, or would lead by the hand a frightened lad of five; some would be bearing off great heaps of clothing, or cans and boxes that looked like food containers, and a few were puffing and panting to save their books, rugs and paintings.

Meanwhile, the eyes of all the people were baleful with a wild, unnatural light; their features had a furtive, hunted expression; their voices had lost their music, and had grown nervous and shrill. All were looking bloodless and bedraggled; portentous hollows had formed in their cheeks and beneath their eyes; their clothes were soiled and untended, their beards scraggly and untrimmed; and many had lost their normal restraint, and sobbed and sobbed regardless of our approach, or growled and gibbered insanely to themselves.

When finally we drew near our destination, the flood reached our knees, and our progress was more laborious than ever. I now began to fear that we would not be able to locate the riverbank—how tell where the water had originally ended? At length, however, I was relieved to observe a wide, unbroken flowing expanse seven hundred yards ahead, and to note that a long rope, stretched in the water between wooden supports, marked the river's former edge.

Then, just when we came in sight of our goal, an unexpected horror befell. Even to this day I can recapture the amazed alarm of that moment; the abruptness and terror of it all overwhelms me anew. Had the waters swelled and swept over us in a tidal wave, I would have been panic-stricken, and yet halfway prepared—but I could not have anticipated that the blow was to strike from above.

Suddenly—although this was only the beginning of the day—the golden lights of the glass dome began to waver and flicker, then paled to a twilight glow, then (in less time than it takes to state) snapped into blackness.

So startled were we that we stood as if paralyzed, scarcely an oath issued from our petrified lips. The darkness was absolute; we could not see our nearest neighbors; we seemed walled in by oblivion. For a moment there was silence; then came a light splashing to my left, and simultaneously dozens of voices broke forth in terror and dismay.

And when that first horrified outburst was dying down, there swept over us from a distance other cries—confused cries as of many voices sighing and wailing. And all those voices seemed to form into one, and to grieve and drone in a single long-drawn sob, with echoes reminding me of lost souls mourning in the dark.

But soon that melancholy tumult passed away; and we were aware only that we stood there knee-deep in the flood, in a silence unbroken except by the gurgling waters.

Then it was that the most quick-witted of us all came to his senses. A vivid yellow light stabbed the gloom to my left. By its glare I could make out the tall form of Xanocles.

In his hands was a pocket flashlight. "I was a little afraid this might happen," he declared, trying to be matter-of-fact and speaking loudly enough for us all to hear. And, to our surprise, he drew several more flashlights from the folds of his garments, and passed them to his neighbors.

"The High Chief Adviser warned me yesterday of this possibility," he explained.

And then, while we all stood gaping at him, with fear-numbed minds, he continued, soothingly. "There is really nothing to be alarmed about. The water must have got into the power generators—that is all. In a few hours, the lights will be shining again."

But his words carried no conviction. In his voice was a note of concern that he could not wholly exclude; and as we glanced nervously into the gloom—a gloom that was all-enveloping except for our flashlights and an occasional firefly flicker in the distance— we could not believe that the golden luminaries would soon beam again.

It was a solemn procession that started splashing once more towards the river. Guided by the uncanny illumination of the flashlights, we could barely find our course; step by step, with laborious slowness, we plodded through the flood. None of us had the heart to utter a word; but from time to time, among my shadowy attendants, I caught glimpses of lips rigidly compressed, and faces firmly set. All the while Aelios was at my side, hovering close as if for shelter; and, when I could, I helped her over the more difficult places, though she, too, was speechless.

Then, for an instant, hope came flashing back. A sudden radiance burst upon us from above; the great luminaries were once more touched with light, which fitfully expanded from a pale red glow almost to the normal golden—and then fitfully died into utter gloom.

And our cries of rejoicing were frozen on our lips, and the darkness that ensued seemed more intense than ever. And once more there was only the silence, the wavering flashlights and the whirling floods.

Groping and floundering and sometimes sinking almost to the hips in the icy water, we at last approached the rope at the river's verge. And by turning upstream towards a dim yellow light, we managed to locate the docks and the submarine, which we recognized by the rays filtering through the portholes.

Then, almost before I realized that the final moment had come, I found myself assisting Aelios up the half-submerged gangplank to the deck of the grim, low-lying, shadowy ship. The next that I remember is that I was back again in two feet of water and that a multitude of hands clasped mine, a multitude of voices were lifted simultaneously—first the voices of a mob attempting a cheer that died prematurely, then the voices of individuals, shouting advice and farewells, wishing me a safe voyage, entreating me to make haste for the good of Atlantis. I have a recollection of seeing the earnest, grave face of Gavison by the uncertain, shifting illumination of the flashlights; the elongated, intellectual face of Xanocles; the youthful, but sad-eyed and frightened face of Rawson, and Stranahan's droll countenance now furrowed into a tragic severity.

But in an instant all those faces—so familiar, and so well liked—had drifted out of view. I stood upon the gangplank, lightly waving, although my heart seemed dull and dead within me. Then I mounted to the deck, cast a last glance at the darkness that hid the marble temples of Atlantis, and waved for the last time to the dim, watching figures. And as the flashlights began slowly to retreat, I descended a narrow stairway, heard the iron door clatter to a close above me, felt a jolt and a shudder that were followed by a regular incessant quivering—and knew that I was on my way back to the earth.

THE RETURN

THE FACTS OF MY RETURN FROM ATLANTIS have been reported so widely that it would be futile for me to dwell upon them. It is generally known how, having crossed the ocean at the sixty-knot speed made possible by our inter-atomic propellers, the submarine found its way to the mouth of the Potomac and almost up to Washington; how, after it had anchored obscurely some distance below the city, I donned my old uniform and made my way out under cover of night; how I hastened the next day to the offices of the naval department, disclosed my identity, and met with ridicule not only at my incredible tale, but at my strange appearance, my full beard, my goggles and greenish skin.

Unfortunately, in the haste and confusion of my departure from the Sunken World, I had made one oversight, I had forgotten the copy of Homer's lost "Telegonus," which I had hoped to exhibit in verification of my story. Scattered lines of the poem, to be sure, did keep trailing through my mind with a wild, ringing majesty; but they were the merest fragments, and to recite them would have been to brand myself as a madman. Yet I had little other evidence to display. Aelios could not help me, for she could not speak English; and despite her exceptional beauty, there was nothing to prove that she had not been born above seas. As for the four members of the submarine, crew, they staunchly refused to leave the vessel; and, besides, they likewise could not speak English, and their fantastic garb would have marked them also as lunatics.

And so there was nothing to do but wait, wait for days that seemed never-ending, haunting the naval offices, making myself a laughing-stock and a nuisance, yet repeating my pleas until at last they had to be heeded. But meanwhile I was losing time, all-important time. Even now Atlantis might be in its death-throes—a few hours might bridge the gap between safety and disaster. Would the authorities not make haste? Every day, with tears in her eyes, Aelios would ask when the rescuers were to set out; and every day I would sigh, "Perhaps tomorrow." But tomorrow would bring little hope; and even when an investigation was finally undertaken, it was careless and dilatory and it was long before I could convince the inspectors that I was actually one of the company of the lost *X-111*.

It was long, indeed, before I could even find anyone to identify me. So strikingly had my appearance altered that former acquaintances could not recognize me; while old friends, beneath the pressure of wartime, had been widely dispersed. Even Alma Huntley failed to reply to my letters; and it was months before I learned that she had left with Don Alders to be married on the Pacific Coast.

But though my messages to Alma never reached their destination, a letter to my old friend Frank Everett survived several forwardings and found its goal; and not only did Everett hasten to me from New York, but he summoned several others of our former group, whose testimony combined with the evidence of fingerprints and handwriting to identify me beyond dispute.

Matters now began to move more quickly. Almost overnight my story was flashed from end to end of the land, and I found myself a public figure. Newspaper headlines flaunted my name, and the word Atlantis was on everyone's lips; interviewers swarmed to see me, scientists poured out their demands for information, the heads of lecture bureaus, radio chains and motion picture corporations showered me with offers. But all that I cared about were the proffers of assistance for the Sunken World. Several men of means became interested, and placed large sums at our disposal; half a dozen engineers volunteered to accompany me back to Atlantis, and with their aid we secured implements and chemicals capable of sealing wide breaches in a glass wall. But we could produce no vessel other than the one in which we had left Atlantis, for the naval submarines were not equipped for the deep waters of the Sunken World; and when finally the rescuing party, set off down the Potomac from Washington, its members numbered only six in addition to the original crew, Aelios and myself.

The small size of the expedition and its limited equipment would alone have made us doubtful of success; but we remembered with acute misgivings that almost two months had passed since we left Archeon, and that during all this time the waters must have been rising. We were particularly uneasy because of the failure of Gavison to arrive in a second submarine, as the High Chief Adviser had promised; and, brooding upon his absence, we would recall with a shudder our farewell moments in Atlantis, the confusion of the people, and the swelling torrents swishing through the darkness.

To make matters worse (if they could possibly be worse) our voyage was beset with unforeseen difficulties. Owing to the absence of definite charts and our uncertainty as to the latitude and longitude of the Sunken World, we were lost for several days amid the wildest wastes of the Atlantic. At times we would dive to the sea bottom, and would cruise for hours amid a black infinity, staring through the portholes at the luminous-eyed creatures that flitted ghost-like about us, or gaping horror-stricken at some contorted, but eloquent rusty iron mass. But of Atlantis there was no sign.

At length our expedition converted itself into little more than a random questing for what did not appear to exist. Should we ever again catch a glimpse of the green-golden walls of our lost universe? There were moments when I had curious doubts, and felt that Atlantis, once lost, could never be found again. But all the time, while we kept dashing at prodigious speed through the vacant waters, we were given to fits of hope that alternated with spells of despair—hope when we would descry a far-off light that would turn out to be merely some elusive fishy lantern—despair that our help, already too long delayed, was being retarded to the point of impotence.

The final discovery came with startling suddenness. One day, gliding slowly downwards at a considerable depth, we were stopped by a hard flat barrier that spread beneath us like the sea bottom. But as we began to drift horizontally, we observed that the surface was smooth and light reflecting—and with gasps of dismay we recognized the substance as glass...

The surprise and horror of that moment are still vivid in my memory.

"Turn the searchlights down, down..." muttered the leader of the crew, in a voice that trembled.

And as the great water-piercing streamers began to quiver and shake and then descend in long rambling curves, Aelios came rushing to my side like a child who fears to be alone, and clung to me while we both stared through the portholes with faces rigid and eager.

But at first we saw nothing. All was dark beneath us—not a gleam, not a flicker, broke the blackness of the Sunken World. Then, as the searchlights swayed and shifted and swept the depths directly below, we began to make out familiar objects. Dimly, strangely, as though draped in a fog, the outlines of great domes, arches and colonnades were emerging, interspersed by Titanic columns and statuesque temples that appeared to waver uncannily.

"See! See! It is still there!" Aelios cried, frantically, as she pressed more closely to me. And with the agony of despair in her voice, there was mingled just a tinge of hope.

I took her hand, and sought to console her. But even as I did so, her whole body began to shake spasmodically, and her sobbing throbbed from end to end of the ship.

For many minutes she seemed unable to speak. Yet even while the long-drawn, heartbreaking sobs panted forth, she commenced to point—to point distractedly downwards, with blind, quivering fingers, forcing me to peer again through the porthole.

With my arms still about her, I scanned the ghostly twilight. But for a moment I observed nothing alarming. Then, as my gaze became focused upon a gray dome, just below, I too, cried out in dread realization.

Those glass-covered depths were not without sign of life, as I had thought... But here and there a lantern-bearing object, with flapping finny body, went wavering through the windows and above the temple roofs.

THE END

ABOUT STANTON A. COBLENTZ

Stanton A. Coblentz…

…was an American born poet and author known primarily for his science fiction and fantasy writings. Born in 1896, he started his prolific writing career in the 1920's. Many of his most memorable works came in the 1930s and 1940s for classic pulp magazines like *Amazing Stories.* His works were often filled with science fiction adventure on a grand scale. He was also known for his satirical style of writing and wrote numerous other works, many outside the realm of science fiction and fantasy— some dealing with historical subjects and literary criticism.

We here at Armchair Fiction have had the undeniable pleasure of releasing two *great* Coblentz novels, the volume contained herein and "Into Plutonian Depths." And we have to say that we enjoyed every single sentence of both stories! ☺

Mr. Coblentz passed way in 1982.

If you've enjoyed this book, you will not want to miss these terrific titles...

ARMCHAIR SCI-FI, FANTASY, & HORROR DOUBLE NOVELS, $12.95 *each*

D-1   **THE GALAXY RAIDERS** by William P. McGivern
       SPACE STATION #1 by Frank Belknap Long

D-2   **THE PROGRAMMED PEOPLE** by Jack Sharkey
       SLAVES OF THE CRYSTAL BRAIN by William Carter Sawtelle

D-3   **YOU'RE ALL ALONE** by Fritz Leiber
       THE LIQUID MAN by Bernard C. Gilford

D-4   **CITADEL OF THE STAR LORDS** by Edmund Hamilton
       VOYAGE TO ETERNITY by Milton Lesser

D-5   **IRON MEN OF VENUS** by Don Wilcox
       THE MAN WITH ABSOLUTE MOTION by Noel Loomis

D-6   **WHO SOWS THE WIND...** by Rog Phillips
       THE PUZZLE PLANET by Robert A. W. Lowndes

D-7   **PLANET OF DREAD** by Murray Leinster
       TWICE UPON A TIME by Charles L. Fontenay

D-8   **THE TERROR OUT OF SPACE** by Dwight V. Swain
       QUEST OF THE GOLDEN APE by Ivar Jorgensen and Adam Chase

D-9   **SECRET OF MARRACOTT DEEP** by Henry Slesar
       PAWN OF THE BLACK FLEET by Mark Clifton.

D-10   **BEYOND THE RINGS OF SATURN** by Robert Moore Williams
       A MAN OBSESSED by Alan E. Nourse

ARMCHAIR SCIENCE FICTION CLASSICS, $12.95 each

C-1   **THE GREEN MAN**
       by Harold M. Sherman

C-2   **A TRACE OF MEMORY**
       By Keith Laumer

C-3   **INTO PLUTONIAN DEPTHS**
       by Stanton A. Coblentz

ARMCHAIR MASTERS OF SCIENCE FICTION SERIES, $16.95 each

M-1   **MASTERS OF SCIENCE FICTION, Vol. One**
       Bryce Walton—"Dark of the Moon" and other tales

M-2   **MASTERS OF SCIENCE FICTION, Vol. Two**
       Jerome Bixby: "One Way Street" and other tales

If you've enjoyed this book, you will not want to miss these terrific titles…

ARMCHAIR SCI-FI & HORROR DOUBLE NOVELS, $12.95 each

D-11 **PERIL OF THE STARMEN** by Kris Neville
THE STRANGE INVASION by Murray Leinster

D-12 **THE STAR LORD** by Boyd Ellanby
CAPTIVES OF THE FLAME by Samuel R. Delaney

D-13 **MEN OF THE MORNING STAR** by Edmund Hamilton
PLANET FOR PLUNDER by Hal Clement and Sam Merwin, Jr.

D-14 **ICE CITY OF THE GORGON** by Chester S. Geier and Richard Shaver
WHEN THE WORLD TOTTERED by Lester Del Rey

D-15 **WORLDS WITHOUT END** by Clifford D. Simak
THE LAVENDER VINE OF DEATH by Don Wilcox

D-16 **SHADOW ON THE MOON** by Joe Gibson
ARMAGEDDON EARTH by Geoff St. Reynard

D-17 **THE GIRL WHO LOVED DEATH** by Paul W. Fairman
SLAVE PLANET by Laurence M. Janifer

D-18 **SECOND CHANCE** by J. F. Bone
MISSION TO A DISTANT STAR by Frank Belknap Long

D-19 **THE SYNDIC** by C. M. Kornbluth
FLIGHT TO FOREVER by Poul Anderson

D-20 **SOMEWHERE I'LL FIND YOU** by Milton Lesser
THE TIME ARMADA by Fox B. Holden

ARMCHAIR SCIENCE FICTION CLASSICS, $12.95 each

C-4 **CORPUS EARTHLING**
by Louis Charbonneau

C-5 **THE TIME DISSOLVER**
by Jerry Sohl

C-6 **WEST OF THE SUN**
by Edgar Pangborn

ARMCHAIR SCIENCE FICTION & HORROR GEMS SERIES, $12.95 each

G-1 **SCIENCE FICTION GEMS, Vol. One**
Isaac Asimov and others

G-2 **HORROR GEMS, Vol. One**
Carl Jacobi and others

If you've enjoyed this book, you will not want to miss these terrific titles…

ARMCHAIR SCI-FI, FANTASY, & HORROR DOUBLE NOVELS, $12.95 each

D-21   **EMPIRE OF EVIL** by Robert Arnette
THE SIGN OF THE TIGER by Alan E. Nourse & J. A. Meyer

D-22   **OPERATION SQUARE PEG** by Frank Belknap Long
ENCHANTRESS OF VENUS by Leigh Brackett

D-23   **THE LIFE WATCH** by Lester Del Rey
CREATURES OF THE ABYSS by Murray Leinster

D-24   **LEGION OF LAZARUS** by Edmond Hamilton
STAR HUNTER by Andre Norton

D-25   **EMPIRE OF WOMEN** by John Fletcher
ONE OF OUR CITIES IS MISSING by Irving Cox

D-26   **THE WRONG SIDE OF PARADISE** by Raymond F. Jones
THE INVOLUNTARY IMMORTALS by Rog Phillips

D-27   **EARTH QUARTER** by Damon Knight
ENVOY TO NEW WORLDS by Keith Laumer

D-28   **SLAVES TO THE METAL HORDE** by Milton Lesser
HUNTERS OUT OF TIME by Joseph E. Kelleam

D-29   **RX JUPITER SAVE US** by Ward Moore
BEWARE THE USURPERS by Geoff St. Reynard

D-30   **SECRET OF THE SERPENT** by Don Wilcox
CRUSADE ACROSS THE VOID by Dwight V. Swain

ARMCHAIR SCIENCE FICTION CLASSICS, $12.95 each

C-7   **THE SHAVER MYSTERY, pt. 1**
by Richard S. Shaver

C-8   **THE SHAVER MYSTERY, pt. 2**
by Richard S. Shaver

C-9   **MURDER IN SPACE** by David V. Reed
by David V. Reed

ARMCHAIR MASTERS OF SCIENCE FICTION SERIES, $16.95 each

M-3   **MASTERS OF SCIENCE FICTION, Vol. Three**
Robert Sheckley, "The Perfect Woman" and other tales

M-4   **MASTERS OF SCIENCE FICTION, Vol. Four**
Mack Reynolds, "Stowaway" and other tales

If you've enjoyed this book, you will not want to miss these terrific titles...

ARMCHAIR SCI-FI & HORROR DOUBLE NOVELS, $12.95 each

D-31   **A HOAX IN TIME** by Keith Laumer
INSIDE EARTH by Poul Anderson

D-32   **TERROR STATION** by Dwight V. Swain
THE WEAPON FROM ETERNITY by Dwight V. Swain

D-33   **THE SHIP FROM INFINITY** by Edmond Hamilton
TAKEOFF by C. M. Kornbluth

D-34   **THE METAL DOOM** by David H. Keller
TWELVE TIMES ZERO by Howard Browne

D-35   **HUNTERS OUT OF SPACE** by Joseph Kelleam
INVASION FROM THE DEEP by Paul W. Fairman,

D-36   **THE BEES OF DEATH** by Robert Moore Williams
A PLAGUE OF PYTHONS by Frederick Pohl

D-37   **THE LORDS OF QUARMALL** by Fritz Leiber and Harry Fischer
BEACON TO ELSEWHERE by James H. Schmitz

D-38   **BEYOND PLUTO** by John S. Campbell
ARTERY OF FIRE by Thomas N. Scortia

D-39   **SPECIAL DELIVERY** by Kris Neville
NO TIME FOR TOFFEE by Charles F. Meyers

D-40   **RECALLED TO LIFE** by Robert Silverberg
JUNGLE IN THE SKY by Milton Lesser

ARMCHAIR SCIENCE FICTION CLASSICS, $12.95 each

C-10   **MARS IS MY DESTINATION**
by Frank Belknap Long

C-11   **SPACE PLAGUE**
by George O. Smith

C-12   **SO SHALL YE REAP**
by Rog Phillips

ARMCHAIR SCIENCE FICTION & HORROR GEMS SERIES, $12.95 each

G-3   **SCIENCE FICTION GEMS, Vol. Two**
James Blish and others

G-4   **HORROR GEMS, Vol. Two**
Joseph Payne Brennan and others

If you've enjoyed this book, you will not want to miss these terrific titles…

ARMCHAIR SCI-FI & HORROR DOUBLE NOVELS, $12.95 each

D-41 **FULL CYCLE** by Clifford D. Simak
IT WAS THE DAY OF THE ROBOT by Frank Belknap Long

D-42 **REIGN OF THE TELEPUPPETS** by Daniel Galouye
THIS CROWDED EARTH by Robert Bloch

D-43 **THE CRISPIN AFFAIR** by Jack Sharkey
THE RED HELL OF JUPITER by Paul Ernst

D-44 **PLANET OF DREAD** by Dwight V. Swain
WE THE MACHINE by Gerald Vance

D-45 **THE STAR HUNTER** by Edmond Hamilton
THE ALIEN by Raymond F. Jones

D-46 **WORLD OF IF** by Rog Phillips
SLAVE RAIDERS FROM MERCURY by Don Wilcox

D-47 **THE ULTIMATE PERIL** by Robert Abernathy
PLANET OF SHAME by Bruce Elliot

D-48 **THE FLYING EYES** by J. Hunter Holly
SOME FABULOUS YONDER by Phillip Jose Farmer

D-49 **THE COSMIC BUNGLARS** by Geoff St. Reynard
THE BUTTONED SKY by Geoff St. Reynard

D-50 **TYRANTS OF TIME** by Milton Lesser
PARIAH PLANET by Murray Leinster

ARMCHAIR SCIENCE FICTION CLASSICS, $12.95 each

C-13 **SUNKEN WORLD**
by Stanton A. Coblentz

C-14 **THE LAST VIAL**
by Sam McClatchie, M. D.

C-15 **WE WHO SURVIVED (THE FIFTH ICE AGE)**
by Sterling Noel

ARMCHAIR MASTERS OF SCIENCE FICTION SERIES, $16.95 each

MS-5 **MASTERS OF SCIENCE FICTION, Vol. Five**
Winston K. Marks—Test Colony and other classics

MS-6 **MASTERS OF SCIENCE FICTION, Vol. Six**
Fritz Leiber—Deadly Moon and other classics